I0597611

CAUGHT FROM BEHIND

SIERRA HOCKEY #2

ELISE FABER

CAUGHT FROM BEHIND
BY ELISE FABER

Newsletter sign-up
This is a work of fiction. Names, places, characters, and events are fictitious in every regard. Any similarities to actual events and persons, living or dead, are purely coincidental. Any trademarks, service marks, product names, or named features are assumed to be the property of their respective owners, and are used only for reference. There is no implied endorsement if any of these terms are used. Except for review purposes, the reproduction of this book in whole or part, electronically or mechanically, constitutes a copyright violation.

CAUGHT FROM BEHIND
Copyright © 2024 Elise Faber
Print ISBN-13: 978-1-63749-133-1
Ebook ISBN-13: 978-1-63749-132-4

SIERRA HOCKEY

Over the Line
Caught from Behind
The Big Skate
On the Fly

CHAPTER ONE

Daniela

"You're sexy as shit, you know that, right?"

All of my attention is focused on the big, burly hockey player sitting next to me, so I don't miss his hands tightening on the steering wheel.

Same as I don't miss how my words make his shoulders tense.

Or how his eyes—deep pools of melted chocolate—flick to mine and then away, back to the winding mountain road, tall pines crowding in on all sides, scattering patterns of shadows over the snow that catch the moonbeams overhead.

And I don't miss that Riggs doesn't reply.

I don't expect him to.

Not the big, burly, *taciturn* hockey player.

He doesn't say much to me. Not ever.

Not when we're hanging out with my best friend, Nova, and her boyfriend, Lake, who plays with him on the Sierra. Not when we're hanging with my brother, Knox, who's also his teammate.

Riggs watches me, though.

Lots.

Observing. Studying. *Assessing.*

And tonight, after a Christmas party that saw me drinking a plethora of Nova's honey rosemary mules (her twist on a Moscow mule that is herbal and sweet and, in a word, *delicious*), that assessment isn't exactly pleasant.

"You're drunk," he mutters, disdain heavy in those two words.

"No," I say. Am I buzzed? Definitely. Am I beyond the legal limits of driving? I sure am. But am I drunk? So drunk that I'll black out and won't know the consequences of my actions? Nope.

I've long moved beyond allowing myself to reach that state.

College life was free and loose and wild until…

I figured out the person I wanted to be—the life of the party, funny and witty and the best version of myself…and that didn't include drinking so much that I didn't know what I was doing, couldn't think through the consequences of my actions and put myself in danger.

It certainly didn't include puking on the boy I had a crush on.

So…low moments.

But also learning moments.

Learning my limits. Making alcohol my bitch.

Relaxed and comfortable and social…but not sloppy.

Now I just…

Use it to file away the sharp edges of real life.

Riggs's eyes flick back to mine, and it doesn't take a magnifying glass to see the disbelief in the dark brown depths. "You're *drunk*," he says again.

"Not drunk," I lean across the console, drop my hand onto his thigh, feeling the muscles flexing beneath my fingers and palm. Strong and thick, powerful enough to generate speed on the ice, to propel himself into other guys, finishing a check, slamming his body into theirs.

He can slam into something else.

Me.

Or rather, his cock can slam home deep inside me.

I shiver at the thought, at the fantasy I've had over and over again from the moment I met him and wonder if tonight is the night it will come true.

His hand covers mine—big and warm, his fingers and palm rough with callouses that I want to feel catching on my skin as he trails it over my thigh, my hips, my breasts, between my legs.

But he doesn't lace our fingers together.

Doesn't lift my hand and press it to his mouth, doesn't kiss my palm, or flick out his tongue, tasting my skin.

Instead, he drops my hand back on my own thigh and says, "You're drunk" again.

A kernel of something—maybe uncertainty or doubt or… *hurt*—settles heavy in my stomach like a single stone landing in a pond, sinking to the bottom seemingly unseen once the ripples have cleared, but still there, still on the sand-covered bottom.

Altering the water's flow, being covered with algae or used as shelter for a tiny creature.

There, even if it's unseen.

Causing change, no matter how small.

I don't want to feel that, don't want to think that—don't want life's sharp edges cutting me. Not now. Not ever again. So, I shove that feeling down, holding my breath until the surface of that imaginary pond calms.

It's a pebble, a tiny rock, barely larger than a grain of sand.

It's nothing.

Absolutely fucking *nothing.*

Which is why I reach back over the console, allowing my body to follow my hand this time, leaning toward Riggs, my palm dropping back onto his thigh. "I'm not drunk," I say, drifting closer, my breasts brushing his arm. "I had a couple of mules—"

"Six," he mutters. "You had *six* mules."

I freeze, start counting.

One. Two. Three. Four.

No, I only had—

Wait.

There was the time Nova refilled my copper mug with the extra mix.

So, five. Barely. That last one wasn't even a full drink.

"Six," he repeats, clearly registering that I'm counting. "Lake gave you his to finish off."

I still. Think. *Remember.*

And realize that he's right.

Which is…annoying.

But doesn't really change anything.

I'm not drunk. I'm buzzed and no, I wouldn't operate heavy machinery, but this pussy is primed, locked and loaded.

I know my own brain, my own mind, my own body.

And they're all ready for the orgasms—yes, *plural*—I know that this man can give me.

A hard body pressed close. A cock slipping home, stretching me so wide that it's almost uncomfortable. Rough strokes, fingers digging into my hips, lips and teeth and tongue—

I press my thighs together.

Yes, I'm ready for this man—quiet but always watching, thoughtful and protective and a hard worker, a good guy who wouldn't proposition his teammate's sister.

But Knox's and my relationship isn't a typical one. I'm not the weak little sister who needs to be looked after by the older, growly, cock-blocking brother. Knox has never interfered with my life because he knows I'm a grown woman who does what I want with my body, and that's that.

Easy as pie.

Riggs can't know that—it's not like the guys are having heart-to-hearts in the locker room.

From what I hear, they barely get along at all, the tenuous peace between the players holding only because Lake and Riggs and Knox have all but willed it to be that way.

So, Riggs might watch me with heat in his eyes, but he's not going to fuck things up with my brother.

So, obviously, it's up to me to make sure he knows this won't.

Just like it's up to me to make the first move.

No problem.

I got you, boo.

I squeeze that thick thigh, allow my breasts to brush more firmly against his arm. "Six," I agree. "But that doesn't mean I don't know that"—I slide my hand up, brush the head of his cock where it's growing against his leg, and, hell yes, the man is packing something I very much want to meet up close and personal—"I want you."

The car slides to a stop and I almost grin.

Right here?

Okay then. I'm down.

Or going to be *going* down. *Heh.*

Gentle fingers wrap around my wrist at the same time a hand settles in the middle of my chest, and he pushes me— *firmly*, albeit not roughly—back into my seat. "You're. Drunk," he growls. "Which isn't a surprise because you drink too much."

The kernel in my belly grows bigger, becomes harder to ignore, creating larger ripples beneath the surface of that imaginary pond.

"I know my limits."

Furious brown eyes on mine for a heartbeat, but I ignore that. I know how to make it better, know how to make us both feel good.

I slip my hand from his grip, drag my fingers along his

chest. "We'll both enjoy ourselves"—I slide my hand down, lower, *lower*, until I'm palming his cock, hard and hot and *huge* as it pulses beneath my fingers—"*immensely.*" I rise up, press my mouth to his.

For one second, the universe stops.

Then it bursts into a thousand shards of motion—his fingers plunge into my hair, tilting my head back. His tongue slips between my lips, and…

Riggs Ashford is giving me the hottest kiss of my life.

Deep and wet and a little rough.

Long enough that my lungs start to protest, that my body starts to melt, that…

I dip my fingers under the hem of his T-shirt, stroke them along taut, hot flesh, and—

Riggs breaks the kiss, snags my hand, and pulls it off him.

My lungs are heaving. My head is spinning. My body is so close to toppling into orgasm that I feel like I'm teetering on the edge a cliff. And all from just a kiss.

Okay, fine.

Not *just* anything.

The best, hottest, most perfect kiss of my life.

I reach for him again.

"No," he says.

"Riggs," I beg, knowing I'm whining but unable to stop it.

He pushes me back into my seat again—still firmly but gently—but his voice, when he says, "*No*" again, is rough.

Cold. Sharp.

Just *no.*

It slices right through the pulsing need in my belly, the need that's been poking at me from the moment I first laid eyes on this gorgeous, bearded man of few words.

No.

He doesn't want this.

Doesn't want *me.*

A bucket of icy water over my head, dousing need and confidence at once.

Of course he didn't—

Of course he couldn't—

Of course he wouldn't—

I'm an idiot.

A big, giant idiot.

Thank God he's turning away, reaching for the steering wheel.

Because it means he can't see my face.

And thank God he drops me in my driveway, not walking me up to the door—not tonight.

Because it means I don't have those cold brown eyes judging me when I go to the kitchen and snag the bottle of vodka from the freezer.

The fucking sharp edges of life have sliced deep tonight.

CHAPTER TWO

Riggs

"THAT'S NOT GOOD ENOUGH," my dad says, pacing across my hotel room. "You play like one of those morons who joins a team for *fun*."

Spoken like having fun while playing hockey is the cardinal sin itself.

And it *is* exactly that—at least according to my dad.

Sport is to be dominated, to be controlled. It should be *work* from the moment the season starts and all the way to the end of it—and work in the off-season too.

So, really, work…all year round.

No fun. Not ever.

Yup. My dad's a blast to be around. A grumpy, surly old bastard who is never satisfied.

Which is why I don't bother to reply to what he thinks is the worst insult he can give me.

What he doesn't understand—won't *ever* understand—is that there aren't any insults, any tough love, any criticisms as a form to further motivate me that will actually hit home. Maybe there was a time they affected me, that his sharp words cut deeply—

I bite back a sigh.

Or maybe there's a part of me that hopes for the days before this shit, before he changed.

When he was my *dad*.

When we'd get up early and head to the rink, grabbing Dunkin on the way, the sticky glaze from the donuts I downed like potato chips lingering on my fingertips all through practice. When we would hang out in hotels during tournaments and watch movies that I didn't understand because the plots were over my head. We'd stay up too late and then still get up early, stocking up on the free breakfast before I'd get to do my favorite thing in the world—

Play hockey.

Now, though…that's long gone.

The love of the sport is softened, changed. It's become a job that I enjoy, that I want to work hard and excel at. But it's a *job*, and nothing more, and it's certainly not the same sport that used to sing to my soul.

Still, it's those memories with my dad, the dumbass hope that things will be different…

That has me continuing to answer his calls.

And not kicking his ass out of my room.

It's why I'm propping up the door of my hotel room, watching him pace and listening to him be an asshole.

I don't know how he tracked down which one we're at—except that I do, I guess. We're playing my hometown team tomorrow and there aren't that many hotels in this city that can cater to the needs of a professional sports organization like this one can.

And my dad has the connections—not to mention, the bullying skills—to get that information.

But I'm tired.

All I want to do is to sleep. Pretend that we didn't lose the previous night, traveled for several hours, get bussed to the hotel, and then arrive in the lobby where my dad was waiting for me. I want to pretend this isn't happening. Pretend that I'll actually get a good night's sleep for the first time in a few days and not spend hours lying in bed thinking and dreaming about what it felt like to have Ella's hand wrapped around my cock.

Pretend it was easy to turn her down, to drive her home like I didn't want to stay parked on the side of the road and pull her into my lap, feeling the tight sheath of her cunt squeezing my dick.

She was drunk.

Again.

Christ.

"And, for fuck's sake," my dad snaps, jarring me back into the present, "how goddamned hard is it to break out the puck? You skate, you pass, you create an option, and you move your fucking feet!"

I grind my teeth together, resist the urge to glance up at the ceiling—because that will give my dad more fuel for his rant—as I debate my options.

If I stay silent, I'll have to keep listening to this shit.

If I tell him to leave, he'll make another fucking scene—a worse one that will likely prevent my teammates from getting the rest they need.

Maybe I muzzle him then drag him down to the lobby, shove his ass in a cab, and—

A knock behind my head.

My dad cuts off and I grind my teeth together as I open the door.

"Hey."

My spine goes stiff when I see Knox standing there, tablet in hand.

He holds it up in my direction. "Ready to watch that tape now?"

We have no plans to watch tape at nearly three in the morning.

But I'm not dumb enough to leave the lifeline he's tossed me floating in the waves, drifting away and out of reach.

I glance over my shoulder at my dad, thankful to see a sliver of approval in his eyes. He likes how hard Knox works, how my teammate and friend plays. He doesn't get that we have the same routine, that we're in the gym together often, that we usually tag team in those extra hours on and off the ice.

Knox is determined and focused.

I'm…never good enough.

It's fine. I came to terms many years ago with the fact that I'll never make my dad proud.

"I'll see you after the game tomorrow," my dad says, clapping me on the shoulder. "We'll break it down before you fly home to Tahoe."

Great.

Just what I want.

At least with the team's plane planning an imminent take-off, the verbal reaming won't last long.

"Sounds good," I mutter, stepping away from him so that Knox can come in.

I close the door, not bothering to say goodbye.

He's my dad, yeah, but he hasn't done anything to earn my respect—not in many years.

"You good?" Knox mutters, perching on the end of the bed.

I grunt and look through the peephole in case my dad's lurking there.

Thankfully, Knox doesn't bother to press me for more of an answer.

A good thing since I don't have anything else to say.

And anyway, he has plenty of words to fill in the blanks for me as he flops back on the bed and starts talking about what he's going to do with our off day when we get back home.

"Not skiing," he says, tossing the tablet to the side, "even though Ella will no doubt be out on the slopes now that the lifts are up and running." Because there was a Snowmaggedon not long before, dumping enough snow in the Sierra Nevadas that towns and roads were shut down and ski resorts had more of the white fluffy stuff than they knew how to deal with. "I'll stay in the lodge and pick up some ski bunnies, I guess, since I don't want Coach on my ass for doing something against my contract."

Because our bodies belong to the team.

Because we've agreed to live and breathe and bleed for hockey.

Tearing an MCL on a black diamond run with his sister wouldn't make the powers that be happy.

Same as Knox wouldn't be happy knowing that his sister was open to a fuck on the side of the road—and then a fuck or three back in my bed, because *I* wouldn't be happy with having her just once.

Making the horn go in repeat as I pumped up into her. Bending her over my kitchen counter. Fucking her on the stairs. Tossing her into my bed, kissing my way up her body, and—

"Hell," Knox grumbles. "Ella keeps *telling* me that she wants to ski, but I think she's more excited about hanging in the lodge, charming the bartender into free drinks, and finding some asshole to take her home for the night."

I scowl.

He sighs, tucks his hands behind his head. "I need to get her hooked up with someone who'll take care of her, not take advantage."

Like I could have on Christmas.

Something I don't say because I like my teeth where they are.

"What about you?" Knox says. "You're awfully monkish

for a single, relatively attractive"—I roll my eyes—"professional athlete."

"It's late," I mutter. "You should go to bed."

"And risk coming across your dad lurking in the hall?" he asks before glancing at his watch. "We have at least ten minutes to wait before I can slink my ass to my room."

He's not wrong.

"So?"

"So what?"

"Why are you"—he waves a hand—"all monk-like?"

I debate whether or not he'll let this go.

But I know Knox too well.

He's got the stubborn Adler gene.

I've got to give him something.

Give him enough so that he'll be satisfied.

And then I'll dream about fucking his sister.

"I'm not like you. I don't love whipping my dick out and dunking it into whatever pussy I can find." Sex means something to me. It's more than mutual pleasure, more than a drunk fuck on the side of the road—no matter how good that would have been.

I had my fair share of road pussy, of puck bunnies, until—

I shudder.

Until I learned that it doesn't mean anything unless feelings are involved.

For me, at least.

The rest of the world, including Knox and Ella, can do what they want.

Knox sputters out a laugh. "Gross, man," he mock grumbles, rolling over to face me. "You know it's not like that."

I just lift an eyebrow.

He shoves an elbow under himself, glares at me. "It's not."

I shrug, not biting on the argument, and reach for the door handle to encourage him out as I quote, *"We Adlers are free and loose with their lovin'."* Something he said the first time Ella left with a guy in front of us—*something* that had Lake and I out of our chairs, ready to pummel the asshole until he saw reason and left her alone.

Knox talked us down, let her go.

More than once.

I grind my teeth together, ignore the familiar rage that wants to well up inside me.

Not mine.

Knox sighs as he pushes off the bed and I freeze.

Because the sound is decidedly *not* free and loose.

"That was before," he says, walking toward me.

My fingers convulse on the handle, clenching the metal tightly enough I'm surprised it doesn't groan in protest. "Before what?" I ask, something like fear coiling in my belly.

"Before I realized that my sister needs handling before she fucks up her life."

"*Handling*?" I croak, knowing that Ella would blow a gasket if she heard that shit.

Knox's mouth curves. "Yup. *Handling*." He claps me on the shoulder as he strolls out into the hall, mischief in blue eyes that are identical to Ella's.

Hell, even the mischief itself is identical.

As is that impish smile.

"And you're just the man to do it."

CHAPTER THREE

Daniela

"I LOVE IT," my client says, beaming at her reflection and running her fingers through the curls I'd meticulously created.

Then brushed them out into soft, beachy waves.

Undoing most of my hard work.

But that's part of the process.

Hair is a living, breathing form of art. I can make it someone's best day if I'm on my game, and I can make it their worst day if I fuck up.

Today, thankfully, is a good day.

"You look gorgeous," I say, reaching for the back of the cape and giving it a light tug.

The buttons undo, and I pull it free, fixing a curl or two before we walk over to our receptionist, Kit. I give her a hug and leave her in his capable hands to take care of payment and escort her to the door…

He flicks the lock.

We exchange smiles…and relieved breaths.

The day's over.

It's closing time and we don't want someone sneaking in and demanding a service when all we want to do is go home.

It's after Christmas. The holiday parties are over. Things should be calming down.

Except…New Year's Eve is just around the corner and there are plenty of people who want their coiffure looking good or touched up to ring in the New Year—not to mention the influx we'll get with all of those shiny new resolutions that are soon to be made, kept for a few days or weeks, and then left behind forever.

"Done?" Kit asks as he rounds his desk and starts closing out the computer.

"*So* done," I tell him as I head back to my station, wincing as I roll out my shoulders. It's been a long day, but I need to do at least a basic cleanup so I don't hate myself in the morning. So, I gird my loins, pick up my hairdryer, and start wrapping the cord around the handle in a way I would advise my clients against (because it pulls on the delicate connection at the base of the motor), but doing it anyway because no one—least of all me—has time to do anything beyond a messy twist, especially since I've had eight clients today and my arms are positively Jell-O.

Right now it's about survival.

Kit sighs.

I immediately stop thinking about my biceps and how they're angry at me just for considering picking up the broom and glance over at my friend.

He's staring at his cell, his brows furrowed, and I can tell, just by the tense way he's holding his shoulders, that his boyfriend, Patton, is being an asshole.

Again.

Ignoring my pissed-off biceps, I snag the broom and start sweeping, mostly so I don't snatch the phone out of Kit's hands and launch it against the wall. Patton would still find a way to get his hooks into Kit again, to seduce him with his yummy body and perfect hair into ignoring no shortage of red flags.

I need to employ my sneaky matchmaking skills.

Or *un*matching in this case.

I sweep up the hair, use my foot to trigger the fancy vacuum that means we don't have to use dustpans, and then make my way over to Kit once he sets his phone aside.

"Spill," I order.

He looks up at me guiltily.

"Kit," I say softly.

"He doesn't mean it," my friend begins, "and this time it was my fault, I—"

I grind my teeth together, biting back the rejoinder that Kit always says it's his fault—for working too much, for wanting their apartment clean, for wanting to hang out with his friends, for needing to have a life that doesn't solely revolve around his relationship.

Patton wants Kit in a box, small and contained.

And I can't stand that.

Kit is sweet and kind and has a wicked sense of humor. The world deserves to see that.

"Do you want to talk about it?" I ask softly when he doesn't go on.

"No," he says, shoving his phone in his pocket. "I'll just hash it out with him when he gets home."

I do some more grinding, knowing Kit's an adult and can make his own decisions—

But they're bad decisions!

He needs to be with someone who can love him like he deserves to be loved.

"And if you two can't hash it out?" I can't help but ask.

I want him to say that they'll break up.

He doesn't.

He never does.

Instead, he just sighs and fiddles with a strand of his hair, pushing it off before releasing it and allowing it to fall forward over his forehead again. Then repeating the process and making my fingers itch to take over. "It'll be fine," he finally says. "We're always fine."

I want Kit to have more than *fine*.

But now's not the time.

So, I just bat his hands away, fix the strand of hair he's fussing with, and give him a hug, whispering, "You deserve the world, honey. I hope you know that."

"You're a good friend, Ells," he murmurs as he squeezes me back. Then he's breaking the hug and gathering up his stuff, logging off his computer, moving toward the front door, waving goodbye. But I don't miss that he doesn't agree with me.

"Damn," I whisper, locking the door behind him. "Just… damn."

I finish up the bare minimum of prep I need to do for the next day then grab my jacket and purse. It's thick, heavy enough that Knox likes to give me shit about it. But I haven't spent as much time in the mountains as my brother, so my blood isn't as thick. I need the extra layers—even if I look like a giant marshmallow.

Grinning, I'm just reaching the door when I hear the knock, see that my bestie is standing on the other side.

Frowning, I flick the lock, push the door open. "Nova, are you ok—?"

But I bite back the rest of my question when I see what she's wearing.

A Sierra jersey.

The game—the first home game after the team's short road trip.

The game I agreed to go to.

The same game that Lake and Knox fought about providing us tickets for—snarking back and forth about who could get us the best ones (and no surprise, captain Lake

Jordan and my friend's grumpy hockey beau won out on that particular battle with the on-the-glass seats).

The game…I don't want to go to.

No.

A scorching kiss I swear that I can still feel.

No.

The word as cold as Riggs's eyes.

No.

His hands pushing me back into my own seat.

No.

My embarrassment at his refusal slicing through me.

No—

Bile rises up in my throat because…God, no.

I can't face Riggs. Not right now.

"Are we getting food at the arena?" Nova asks, bustling inside. "Or in town?" She's excited, bouncing on her toes, her cheeks high with color. "I would prefer the arena because I brought my camera and want to get some shots of the guys during warm-ups."

Nova is a photographer, namely of nature and landscapes, but since she's decided to lay down roots in Tahoe, she's expanded her skills.

Expanded them all the way to sexy hockey players, apparently.

Thinking of exactly how sexy Riggs is, I bite back a groan and try to cobble together a response to get out of this. "I'm actually kind of—"

She takes my arm. "You're not going to flake on me, right?" Her fingers tighten. "You remember how many strings that Lake pulled for these tickets, right?"

Guilt boils up in my belly.

Still, I might have ignored it if not for her adding, "And I haven't seen enough of you lately. You've been working so much and I…" Her voice grows quiet, fading until it's barely audible. "I miss my friend."

Damn.

I know how hard it is for her to say that.

I know because she battled and pushed through her own demons that had once sent her flitting around the world like a migrating Monarch butterfly, too scared to be vulnerable in one place, too scared to ask for what she wanted.

And she's saying that she misses *me*.

She's *here* saying it. Not hiding out in Australia or Greenland or Zimbabwe.

Damn, my girl is all grown up.

It almost brings a tear to my eye—especially because it all started when I arranged for her to get away from her asshole ex and a supremely shitty situation and to do it while she stayed in Lake's house.

See? My matchmaking prowess is unparalleled.

She and Lake are now happily paired off and…

My friend is asking for what she needs.

Which is why I don't flake on her, don't flake on the game.

Instead, I finish my statement, albeit different than the one I'd first intended. "I'm *actually* kind of craving a soft pretzel and *all* the arena snacks"—her face relaxes—"so, would you mind if we eat at the game?"

A huge smile.

A tight hug.

My best friend happy.

And my torture imminent.

Because I'm about to see Riggs Ashford for the first time since he kissed me senseless…

Then so firmly turned me down.

CHAPTER FOUR

Riggs

"DID you think about what I said?" Knox asks.

I freeze just outside the door to our home arena. In a second, we'll walk through, the blast of cool air clinging to my skin. The smell of the Zamboni, the bite of the muscle cream our trainer, Samantha, uses on us, the scent of the showers as the guys clean up after their pregame workouts—helping them stay warm and loose—the hint of arena food in the air mingling with the faint funk of hockey equipment and sweaty dudes will override my senses.

The door is one of transition—from simple man to professional athlete.

We'll walk through and shove the outside world down, our focus on hockey and *solely* hockey. The rest of it—asshole fathers, subpar game play, exasperating women and brothers trying to play matchmaker…all the shit that sticks in my head and rolls through again and *again* on repeat in the dark hours of night—will be tucked away.

It all comes down to winning. To snagging those two points. To finding a way to triumph over each and every one of the small battles…and sometimes still losing the war in the end.

But knowing, throughout it all, that I've done my best—even if my dad doesn't think so.

My dad.

Christ.

I'm done thinking about him and his text messages, his angry words and heavy criticisms.

I'm done thinking about the past.

Post-game will come soon enough, and I know I'll get a fresh dose of this man I barely recognize as my father.

It's enough that his sharp voice had accompanied me on the bus to the airport and on the flight home. Enough that it had stayed by my side all through my day off yesterday.

Hockey.

Winning.

Not good enough—

Stop.

Stop thinking about my dad.

Stop thinking about the way Ella's hand felt wrapped tightly around my cock.

Stop—

A hand claps down onto my shoulder—albeit not the one I want touching me. "Riggs," Knox says, drawing me to a halt. "I asked if you thought about what I said?"

My temple pulses with pain—not an uncommon phenomenon to experience when it comes to the stubborn-as-shit Adlers.

"Dude," I mutter, shoving him off. "Please tell me you're not actually serious about this shit." I shake my head. "Telling me to go after your sister?"

"Not *go after*," he says. "I'm telling you to get a handle on her."

I snort. "Ella's the last woman on the planet who needs someone *handling* her."

"Look—" He steps in front of me, and it's his sister's eyes that are holding mine, deep pools of blue that I can get lost in —because I never know if they were going to flash with mischief or wicked humor or a deep sense of empathy.

Thankfully, I've only seen *Ella's* darken to navy, desire clinging to those irises.

"I'm just saying that Ella needs someone to look after her, and you already do that, man." He tilts his head toward the door.

I have no choice but to follow.

Because we literally have the same hockey game to play in.

"I'm not a complete idiot," he says, pausing to scan his badge and bumping his shoulder against mine. "I've seen you watch her. Seen you look at her like she's the fucking last slice of cheesecake."

His favorite.

"You and fucking cheesecake," I mutter, going for light, going for anything that will make this conversation end. "You just want a break from looking out for Ella because she's as much of a menace as you are"—I brush by him and reach for the handle—"but, news flash, asshole, your sister can take care of herself."

"I know that." Knox sighs. "I'm just..." The seriousness in his words has me halting next to him. "You're a good guy, yeah? And Ella's a great person. If you two wanted to...I don't know...figure your shit out and have something meaningful—"

I lift my brows because this is coming from the man who never takes anything serious.

"Hey," he says, probably reading that in my expression and holding up his hands, palms out. "Just because I'm not into commitment doesn't mean I don't want my sister to find something like what Nova and Lake have."

My heart spasms.

Because it may be sappy as shit, but seeing my captain and

his woman together fills me with such intense jealousy that sometimes it's hard to breathe around them.

Because they're intensely happy, two halves to the same soul.

Because I *want* that.

The person who has my back, who likes me for me, who doesn't see all of my failures each and every time they look at me.

My temple throbs again.

Fucking Adlers.

Making me think in circles.

"Enough, man," I mutter, "I need less conversations about commitment and cheesecake and your fucking sister, and more focus on hockey."

He purses his lips together then sighs and shakes his head. "Fine," he says, starting forward again, "we'll focus on hockey, but"—a knowing look in my direction, mischief in blue depths —"I'm just *saying*..."

I groan.

He chuckles, but thankfully—fucking *finally*—drops the subject to focus on our game tonight against the Oakland Eagles. "What do you think about Rome Dawson? With the strength and speed he's been bringing to his games we're going to have a hard time stopping him tonight."

"The kid just parks his ass in front of the net," I say, grasping onto that conversational shift like the lifeline it is, "and goes for the tip."

Rome smirks over at me, waggles his brows. "Good thing you're excellent at clearing the crease."

"Goddamn, asshole," I grumble, shoving him to the side and walking down the hall. "You can make anything sound dirty."

He pushes past *me*. "It's a gift."

"It's a goddamned curse," I mutter, but he doesn't hear.

Because he's moved into the locker room and officially switched into Hockey Mode.

And I've got no choice but to do the same.

———

HOCKEY MODE HAS no power against the Adlers.

Specifically, a certain female Adler who's currently sitting on the other side of the glass from me, surrounded by snacks and kids who are begging her to do their hair. And, even though I know she worked a full day—because she always works full days—she ensures that everyone who wants their hair braided or ponytailed and doused with glitter in the Sierra's colors gets their chance. And all the while, she and Nova are smiling and laughing, two beautiful souls highlighted in the bright lights of the arena.

Lake approaches his woman and they grin and wave at him, helping him distribute the pucks he tosses over the glass, making sure all the littles get a free souvenir.

Nova snaps a couple of pictures, mouths something to her man, and then Lake is skating away, disappearing down the hall, slipping back into Hockey Mode, prepping to beat the Eagles.

Knox wraps up a few more warm-up exercises before joining him.

And then I'm mostly alone on the ice—a couple of skaters from the Eagles playing straggler like I am.

"Enough," I mutter, turning for the bench, for the locker room.

I need to focus on the game, snap into that Hockey Mode my teammates have adopted.

But then I see the Sharpie.

And the pile of pucks.

And remember Lake tossing them over the glass to Ella and Nova.

And...fuck me sideways, but Knox's words slide through my brain.

Ella smiles again, mischief and brightness evident even from all the way across the ice.

A hand on my thigh, breasts brushing against my arm, the soft scent of woman in my nose.

My cock twitches in my cup—not comfortable in the least. But it's a reminder of what I've felt from the moment I saw this woman—need, desire, a thread linking me to her.

It's that thread that has me picking up the marker.

And a puck.

And skating across the ice.

CHAPTER FIVE

Daniela

Cool air kisses my cheeks.

The noise of the rapidly filling hockey arena echoes around the enclosed space, making my ears ring.

I so don't want to be here, but I plaster a smile on my face and sit in our fancy glass-front seats anyway. I'm with my best friend and it's fun watching Nova moon over Lake.

No. Not *fun*.

It's *incredible* that my friend who was so scared to form attachments has planted deep roots here, has reached for what makes her happy.

And it's all because of me.

I smother a grin, mentally buff my knuckles on my shoulder.

I should quit doing hair and go into full-time matchmaking —or open a matchmaking *and* hair salon. Get some low lights while also finding the love of your life.

Bam. Business plan made.

The *crack* of a stick on the ice has me tucking away business strategies and focusing back on the little girl standing in front of me, who's hair I'm braiding. I add a dash of glitter, tie on a colorful bow and then she's running back up to her parentals.

"I still don't know how you do that so fast," Nova says as I tuck my supplies away and lean back in my seat. "I'm so totally hopeless with braids."

"I got you, boo." I pull my glitter back out, threaten to sprinkle it over her. "Tahoe blue? Or pine tree green?"

"Oh, it's got to be the sparkly white snow," she says on a laugh, snagging the little container and threatening me right back.

Luckily, thanks to Knox making me practice with him so often growing up, I have quick hands. I snag it back, pocket the little canisters of craft store herpes. "Too slow," I tease, blowing her a kiss.

I love that she grins in reply. I love that she's happy.

She returns her focus to the ice, and I'm forced to face what I've been avoiding all night—

The teams warming up on the ice in front of me.

The man in particular who sends a bolt of shame through me.

Enough. Move on. Enjoy this experience. Enjoy the time with my bestie.

I close my eyes for a long moment, grasping on to that, and when I open them again, I'm more centered. I'm ready to have a good time.

And really, how can I not? These are *great* seats. For as many games as I've gone to, I've never been this close to the ice. Not in an NHL arena, anyway.

But, damn, I can see everything.

Everyone.

Including Riggs.

Or maybe…especially Riggs.

Ugh.

I deliberately turn my gaze away from the bearded big guy who I just want to watch all night—

Preferably naked. While he's fucking me senseless—

Only he doesn't want that, does he? He doesn't want me, and—

Seats. These are fantastic *seats*.

So comfy.

Clearly, Lake's won this round of spoiling Nova—and me by side benefit.

Though, I don't think Knox has quietly admitted defeat.

One of the perks of having a professional hockey-playing brother?

Free tickets to pretty much any home game I want.

Another?

Him having an uber-competitive streak that means his need to win this war with Lake will reap me further benefits. *Muahaha.*

I can see it now—goading them into giving Nova and I spa days and fancy dinners. Or a new pair of sparkly pumps—that I can't wear in the snow. Right. So, that's less than beneficial. Maybe an all-expenses-paid trip to somewhere that's not freezing cold. Or hell, I'll even take them not giving me noogies the moment I walk through the door.

My lips twitch.

Yup. Soon enough I'll be living the *life.*

No noogies.

A pair of impractical shoes.

And—

A puck *thunks* against the boards in front of me and I jump, glaring over at my brother. Of course, it's Knox tormenting me —noogies and teasing and scaring me when I least suspect it.

Big brothers. Swear to God.

I narrow my eyes. And fine. So it's likely that the noogies won't stop—even if I can somehow make that part of the pissing contest between him and Lake—but I can probably score a hot stone massage for my troubles.

And maybe that new blow dryer I've been eyeing.

Heh.

Just for good measure, I keep glaring at him until he skates away (and doing it smirking, the big lug). And…

Dammit.

I hate that my eyes are drawn from my brother back over to Riggs.

Who's warming up in a deliberate and fuckable fashion.

Then again, everything about him is fuckable.

I sigh softly, feeling the pulse of desire between my thighs.

He's tall and thick—as I became familiar with last week—with yummy, muscular thighs—something else I'd also gotten the pleasure to experience. *And* he has a great ass—that I, alas, haven't gotten my hands on. Not to mention that broody, taciturn personality.

My personal kiss of death when it comes to the opposite sex. Strong, big, handsome, and grumpy.

Unfortunately, he doesn't like me.

How have I come to this brilliant conclusion?

The car.

The kiss.

The invitation.

And the firm refusal.

No.

I shudder, throat growing tight, embarrassment eating away at my insides.

Dumb. I should have let sleeping dogs lie, but the mules and the snow, the mistletoe and the way I caught him looking at me over and over again, not just on Christmas but before and…

I was dumb.

Spending time with the friends who I consider my family, since Knox and I are the only two Adlers still alive.

I'd gotten romantic. Needy.

Dumb.

Nearly ruining all of the goodness I'd found with one scorching kiss and—

I need to tuck that away, focus on what's important, on what I *can* have, can do.

Helping the people I love.

Spending time with Nova, with Knox. And that's going to involve watching my brother play hockey, watching Lake, and…watching Riggs. It's going to involve sitting in this discomfort because it means that I get to spend time with my bestie while she moons over the love of her life.

Even if it's impossible to ignore the embarrassment churning in my belly.

Even if it makes me want to pick up the drink sitting in the cup holder at my feet, and down it.

But that's something else Riggs doesn't like about me.

He thinks I drink too much.

And maybe I do.

Maybe I drink so I don't have to think, to feel—

Tap. Tap. Tap.

I jerk and look up from the tempting cocktail, seeing that Lake is standing in front of the glass, smiling at Nova, who—swear to fuck—just seems to blossom under his gaze.

Bright and beautiful, showing the world the gorgeous person she is inside.

She lifts her camera and fires off a couple of shots, causing Lake to wink before he skates off to finish his warm-up.

My brother is now on the far side of the ice, stretching and stick handling, getting ready for the game with a sure-minded focus that he doesn't have in many other places. Minus giving me a hard time, they all involve hockey—off-ice training, studying tape, hitting the gym to be strong and explosive, never missing a practice, spending loads of extra time on the rink.

I'll get my goofy Knox back after the buzzer goes in the third.

Right now he has laser focus.

"I'm going to sneak up to the bathroom," Nova murmurs a few minutes later, after I've struggled to keep my eyes away from a certain bearded hottie.

"I'll hold the fort," I tell her, forcing my tone to be light, and getting a smile in return.

She squeezes my arm. "I know that you were tired and you've been working too much, but"—a kiss to the top of my head—"I appreciate you spending the night with me."

My heart squeezes and I drag her into a hug, holding her tight for a long moment then releasing her before the stinging in the backs of my eyes turns into something stupid and sappy. "I need peanut M&Ms," I tell her.

She grins, nudges my foot with hers. "Brat." But I know she'll come back with the medicinal chocolate.

Because she's my best friend.

I watch her making her way up the long concrete staircase.

Then my gaze goes back to Riggs.

Dammit.

I drag it away again. I want to reach for my drink—my mouth watering, my throat so freaking dry, my soul desperate for the way it'll dull all the sharp edges of my thoughts, will make the memories easier to suppress—

Tap. Tap. Tap.

I jerk my head up again, expecting it to be Lake wondering where his woman went.

Or Knox preparing to torment me again.

It's not either of them.

Riggs is standing on the other side of the glass—his brown eyes deep pools of chocolate, his beard just long enough to give a woman ideas about it being dragged along her inner thighs.

It's me. I'm the woman. It's me.

Tap. Tap. Tap.

I blink. Jesus, woman, get it together.

"What?" I mouth.

He holds up his gloved hand and I frown.

"I don't need a puck," I say, spotting the biscuit-shaped disc in his palm and shaking my head.

I grew up tripping over enough of those little bastards all through the house and yard and, hell, I know I have more than a few of them at my house even now that Knox has left behind like Hansel scattering his trail of breadcrumbs en route to the big bad witch.

Riggs can't possibly have heard my reply, but maybe he reads my lips because he just shakes his head, bangs his fist against the glass, and holds the puck up again.

I sigh, stand up, and hold out my hands.

Fine. Whatever.

I don't know a lot about Riggs, but I've seen his stubborn streak.

Experienced it firsthand.

So…might as well get this over with.

He nods, makes the toss…

And the puck lands with a *smack* in my open palms.

I force another smile, start to shove the puck into my purse—

Tap. Tap. Tap.

Freezing, I glance up.

He nods toward the puck and I drag my brows together.

"What?" I mouth again.

He looks at his hand, pretends to flip something over.

Brows dragging together, I frown, but I mirror his miming, glance down at my hand, and—

Flip the puck over.

My mouth drops open, my eyes go wide, my head jerks up—

He raises his brows in question.

I look from the puck to him, back down to the scrawled-out words on the black rubber.

Four numbers.

A pound sign.

And then four words that send my stomach into a tailspin.

My bed. Underwear optional.

"I—"

But I don't get further than that because he winks and skates off.

I stare down at the words, my belly heating because—

Holy shit, had quiet, strait-laced Riggs Ashford just written *that?*

CHAPTER SIX

Riggs

IF I SAID I took my time with my post-game routine, I'd be lying.

I sped through the media—which, thankfully, didn't take long because they'd learned a while ago that I'm not the guy for a good sound bite.

Knox is the one. Followed by Lake.

Even Leo or Bear are bound to come up with better one-liners.

I just spout off about skating harder and moving our feet and blocking shots.

Something I did a lot of tonight, considering the bruises that are blooming to life on my body.

Ignoring them, I yank on my sweats, pull my hoodie over my head, and shove my wallet and phone in my pocket.

And right on cue, my cell buzzes.

I know it's my dad, know it's going to piss me off and make me wish shit was different in equal measure.

Not going there right now.

Mostly because I didn't miss the look Ella tossed my way

after the buzzer went in the third period—our eyes connecting across the rink, the burst of heat, of energy, of *her* colliding with my chest, latching onto my heart, squeezing tight.

I hadn't heard the crowd cheering our victory over the Eagles.

Hadn't really felt the slaps on my back from my teammates, congratulating me for my final blocked shot—one that had prevented the tying goal, so we didn't have to go into overtime.

I wanted the win.

But selfishly, I wanted—*want*—the fuck more.

So, I ignore the texts I know will trigger me, shove on my jacket, grab my backpack, and grunt goodbye to the guys.

Luckily, that's not enough to trigger anyone's curiosity—though I don't miss that Knox is watching me expectantly. I'll have to deal with him, and likely do it soon, but tonight...

Tonight, I'm fucking doing this.

I want it. She does too. Her brother's not going to corner me and slice me to ribbons with the equipment manager's extra steel.

He *wants* me to do it—

Well, not to fuck his sister.

But...to have what Nova and Lake have.

And...

Maybe I *can* have that, have something that's unique to Ella and me but just as meaningful—

But I have to do it Ella's way.

Because Ella...well, she's not Nova.

And as much as she wants to pretend she's open to new experiences and free and loose and easygoing...

She's not. She keeps the world, keeps those around her at a careful distance.

So, I have to play this smart. I have to play it my way.

I have to play for keeps.

Which is why I gave her the code to my front door.

Why I all but dared her to show up naked in my bed.

I'm going to claim her, going to make her mine, and I'm going to do it in a way that she can't resist, can't use to keep any distance between us.

Ella Adler might think that she has all the answers figured out...

But I'm going to keep her guessing.

And pleasured.

Limp from so many orgasms she can't even begin to think about leaving.

Forever.

———

MY CELL BUZZES a few more times on the drive back to my place.

It's more centrally located to town than Lake's isolated cabin-that's-really-a-mansion, and on far less property. I have to manage it—have to shovel and weed and mow the tiny strip of grass that's more alpine weeds than actual grass.

I work hard.

I don't want to deal with acres of land, don't want to drive twenty minutes to get to a grocery store.

I want to get into my car, hit the road for fifteen minutes, pull into the heated—and thus, ice-free—driveway, and park in the garage.

With my woman waiting up in my bedroom.

My mouth hitches up when I hit the bottom of my stairs, see the light on in my bedroom, casting a fan of brightness on the carpet. Relief hits heavy and heady, mixing with pleasure, with need, with the memory of her fingers on my thigh, the sure way she'd cupped my dick.

Remembering that kiss, and the way she tasted, the soft pillows of her breasts pressing into my arm.

I'm going to see her naked, going to taste every inch of her, going to hear her moan out my name.

I'm going to give her so much pleasure that she's not going to think about leaving me.

Not fucking ever.

My dick twitches, and my heart is pounding, but I push through those thoughts, shove them down, focus. This a game I need to play to win.

I walk into the bedroom and the sight of her—

"Fuck," I growl softly.

It's everything I've dreamed of. *More.*

She's everything I've dreamed of.

Lush and curvy…and not wearing underwear.

I don't miss the flash of glistening pink when she spreads her legs, don't miss the flush that spreads over the tops of her breasts, drifting down toward the hardened tips of her nipples that I *need* to get my mouth on.

I don't miss…the bruise on her thigh.

Lightly trailing my fingers over it, I ask, "What happened?"

She looks down, frowns, as though she can't remember. "With Nova," she finally says. "She and Steve and I were having mules a few nights ago."

"You need to be careful," I murmur, leaning in to kiss the abused spot. "Need to take care of yourself."

Or let me do it.

But I don't say that, mostly because I'm inhaling the scent of her—flowers and woman and slick, hot desire. I flick out my tongue, tasting her, committing the earthy flavor of her to memory. I drag my tongue over her hip, along the indent of her waist, up her rib cage, brushing the side of her breast, trailing it in and up her throat, to her mouth, and—

Freezing.

The scent of alcohol is strong, burning into my senses.

I pull back, enough to see her eyes, to see the faint dullness clinging to the blue depths.

Fuck.

Her mouth curves up. "Teasing?" she asks coyly, wrapping a leg around my hip. "I figured after you told me that my panties were optional, you'd jump me and fuck me senseless." That sexy little smile grows. "Don't worry," she stage whispers, "I like being fucked within an inch of my life."

Orgasms. Driving her crazy. Addicting her to me.

That was the plan.

But she's drunk. *Again.*

She needs to drink to be here with me.

I can't just have Ella, can't have what Nova and Lake do.

She needs to hide, to dull her thoughts, to…down liquid courage to be with me.

Because I'm not enough.

I grind my teeth together, push that down, and shove myself off the bed.

Her brows draw into a deep vee. "Wh—?"

But I'm already moving into my closet, yanking out a pair of sweats and a hoodie, bringing them back to the bed.

"Riggs," she says softly.

"You're drunk," I manage to grind out.

"I'm not," she protests. "I just had a couple of cocktails at the arena and—"

"Don't bullshit me," I mutter. "I've seen it enough. I know the look in your eyes." I pull the hoodie over her head, yank up the sweats, covering the body I want almost more than my next breath. I search the room for her socks, her boots, see them tossed into the corner and retrieve them, shove them onto her feet. Her coat's crumpled at the edge of the bed and I snag it.

"Riggs," she says again.

I drag it onto her arms, straighten it over her torso, zip it up.

"Let's go," I mutter, taking her hand, pulling her up from the mattress, keeping her close as I guide her downstairs.

I'm not going to let her fall.

But I can't do this.

Not...*like this.*

Grinding my teeth together, disappointment and shame and frustration warring in my stomach, I draw her to my car.

I drive her home.

I make sure she gets safely inside.

And then I go back to my house…

And I open the text messages from my dad.

CHAPTER SEVEN

Ella

THE COLD BITES at my exposed cheeks. It's a rough, sharp kind of sensation, nothing like the cool kiss of the rink.

But that's fine.

I need the rough sharpness, need it to file away the edges of—

Last night.

Silence in the car.

A gentle hand at my back, urging me up the driveway, reaching over my shoulder and plugging in a code to the lock I didn't realize he knew—but I should have, considering that he's driven me home on many an occasion after mules with Nova or a night out at the local bar we prefer.

I was coaxed inside, the door closed behind me.

Putting the barrier between us.

Then he must have pushed another button because the lock *whirred* closed.

And I was alone.

In my dark house.

Again.

"Ella!"

I blink, force the thoughts away as I turn and plaster a smile on my face. One of my first clients I found when I moved up here, Donna, is five feet away from me and she's carrying a container.

Which means goodies.

Which *means* I don't need to think about a certain hockey player who offered his goodies but then took them away.

"Hi, honey," I say, pulling her into a quick squeeze before ushering her toward the front door of the salon and out of the cold. "Are we just doing your usual today?"

"Yes, ma'am." Donna comes in every week for something —a blowout, a trim, a root touch-up—and while my wallet loves it, my conscience hadn't at first.

I don't want people paying for services they don't need.

But then I understood it.

Donna lost her husband a decade ago and her kids don't live close and…she's lonely.

Her time in my chair is her chance to get out and chat, her social hour, bringing treats for all of us stylists, chatting about new grandbabies and kiddos and their afterschool activities. It's her way of staying connected to the outside world.

So, I block that time for her.

And, just saying, her hair is *fire.*

Not a split end or gray hair in sight. The pale blond color is perfect for her skin tone and her shadow root is…*chef's* kiss.

Not to mention, I can style this woman's hair to perfection.

"Brr," she says, stomping her feet on the mat as I help her out of her coat and hang it on the rack just inside the door. "I grew up here, but I'm still not used to the way it just seeps right through my layers and into my bones."

I squeeze her shoulder. "I'll get you a cup of coffee."

"Thanks, dear," she murmurs, patting me on the cheek. "That would be lovely." A nod toward our stations of mirrors, chairs, and sets of drawers. "My usual seat?"

Sometimes, if I'm juggling clients—something that's been common since the Christmas rush, putting color on one client then doing a haircut on someone else while it processes, or however I can cram people in so I can make that money—I'll commandeer an extra chair. But today will be quieter. No one's double stacked. "You may sit on your throne, my queen," I tease her. "It's all yours today."

She winks at me and then goes over to get settled.

I head to the coffee maker, but Kit is already there, adding cream and three spoons of sugar, just like Donna prefers it.

"Thanks, hun," I say when he passes it over.

"Of course."

But his tone is off and my stomach twists. "Kit," I begin.

His gaze flicks to mine and away, connecting for the barest second, but it's long enough for me to see that his eyes are reddened.

Like he's been up all night crying.

"Patton?" I ask.

His throat works. "Don't," he whispers. "I-I can't talk about it."

Seriously, Kit's boyfriend is a fucking asshole.

"Ella," he whispers, when I open my mouth anyway. "Please, just...don't."

Sighing, I nod and bite back the urge to start ranting. "Okay, honey," I whisper. "Just...okay." I let it go, but I don't return to Donna. Instead, I draw him into a one-armed hug, careful of the cup of coffee. "I love you."

He sniffs, hugs me back, then asks, "Donuts?"

I reach into my pocket, pass him a twenty. "Apple fritters all the way." I shove the cash into his hand. "And then whatever goodies Donna has in her box."

His lips twitch, and thank God, it's natural, not forced. "Apple fritters it is."

And then he's gone, disappearing out the front door of the salon and turning toward the bakery at the corner.

My mouth watering, I head back over to Donna. "What are the grandkids up to this week?"

She lights up, starts telling me about her youngest grandbaby, who's a crazy talented athlete and has been working really hard at soccer, along with the three other sports he participates in, and about how her daughter got a promotion at work. By then Kit's back with three apple fritters and we sit and nosh on them as her roots process. When she's washed and dried and styled, the goodies in her box are revealed to be the best chocolate chip cookies I've ever tasted.

So delicious, in fact, that I offer one to the older gentleman sitting in the next chair over.

A gentleman who's been eyeing her as intently as Riggs eyes me.

A blip in my stomach, but I shove it down, smiling as his expression lights up. "Good, right?"

He nods, nearly losing a strip of hair to the clippers my colleague, Tammy, is using. "They're delicious."

"Want me to ask her for the recipe so you can give it to your wife?" I ask.

"Oh." His face falls and I brace, because this is the dangerous part of matchmaking, tiptoeing through the trauma and baggage. "My wife passed about twenty years ago."

A widow who's a lovely person, enjoys cooking, is lonely, and likes to take care of people. And a widower who's just as lovely—and lonely—and loves to eat and adores his daughters —this being intel from Tammy, who nods to me when our gazes lock. She's barely holding back her smile. She's been on board with my matchmaking, even going so far as to reschedule Ernest's appointment so he'd show up right at the end of Donna's appointment for the dispensation of goodies.

Ding. Ding. Ding.

It's a match made in heaven.

I grin at Tammy.

And then…I let my magic work as they chat long after their appointments are finished.

Not to worry, though, I just commandeer another chair and keep pushing forward.

Because I cannot wait to hear all of the details of their date when Donna comes in next week.

CHAPTER EIGHT

Riggs

"Gotcha, bitches!"

Ella's triumphant as she settles the little plastic train down in the opening on the board, thus completing her win in the tournament of *Ticket to Ride*—and her overall board game—domination. I'm watching her—noting the deliberate way she's ignored me all night, barely a glimpse of those blue eyes on mine, while nursing a mule.

One. Mule.

Something inside me twists and then loosens.

It's anticipatory and it's fearful, and…it's a gnawing worry that I might have seriously fucked up.

I mean…no, I couldn't have fucked her, not like that.

But—

I'm not charming. I'm not smooth. I'm not a talker like Knox, who's blabbering next to me, and hasn't stopped since the moment we got in the car together after practice and headed to Lake's for a game night.

"…and *that's* when I flipped her over and—"

"Asked her to paddle your ass like the bad little boy you

are?" I say, switching into locker room banter without really thinking about it.

Conversation cuts out.

Knox gapes at me.

And…well, fuck, that just slipped out.

Ella's eyes are wide and she freezes, mid-sip of her honey-rosemary mule, and then she's choking.

And *then* I'm filing *that* away.

Is it the paddling? Or the dirty talk?

She'd certainly been ready when I told her that underwear was optional.

One drink. She's only had one and—

I pause, listen to my body, to the memories clinging to the edges of my brain always, and…

I can work with one drink.

"How'd you know?" Knox croons, battling his eyelashes up at me and leaning close.

I scowl at him.

Drunk idiot—something I don't *want* to work with.

"Those strong arms"—Knox strokes his hand down my biceps—"those rock-hard abs"—he waggles his brows at me then at Nova, Lake, Leo, and Jolie, soliciting a round of chuckles and giggles—"however am I going to control myself?" He sighs and flops against me, and I don't know if it's the same devil in me that had me writing on the puck, or just a need to wipe that smirk off Knox's face, but I wrap my arm around his chest, draw him tightly against me, and, fuck it, I press my lips to his.

He freezes.

Nova and Jolie cackle.

I pull back, shoving him into his own chair again.

"What the fuck?" he snaps.

I lift an eyebrow. "You play with the bull…"

Lake smirks.

Knox glares.

Leo collapses into a puddle of laughter.

"So, this is what you boys do on the road?" Nova teases.

Lake hauls her close, nips at her bottom lip. "Some of us."

I pick up my beer—my *one* beer I'll allow myself because I have to drive home, because I won't allow myself to get to the point that I can't control my actions, my thoughts, my words, my body—and salute him with it.

Ella chokes again.

"Don't worry," Knox says. "Riggs talks a big talk, but he likes to play monk on the road."

My eyes go to Ella's.

Her expression is…

Well, it has me lifting the bottle further, tipping the dredges of my beer into my mouth.

One beer.

Because I need to always be ready and on alert and—

Ready to leave in an instant.

Fuck.

The puck was a mistake.

This was a mistake.

Coming here tonight, searching for something, wanting… *more.*

I can't have what Nova and Lake do. Not what Jolie or Leo do either. I'm just…

Not good enough.

Gritting my teeth, I push up from my seat, head to the back door, staring out into the darkness, not able to see the snow I know is softly falling on the other side of the plate glass, not with the bright lights on inside and only the moon illuminating the expanse of Lake's back yard outside. Needing some fresh air, I reach for the handle, but just before I step onto the deck, bracing for the frigid planks to seep right in through my socks, I feel tiny claws pressing into my leg.

Steve, Nova's pug, snorts disapprovingly at me.

"You don't want to go out there," I tell him.

He grunts, spraying my jeans with snot. "Disgusting mutt," I grumble, but I scoop him up anyway, tucking him under my arm before I push outside.

His nose works in overtime (something I know because he snorts and snots and sniffs all over my bare skin beneath the sleeve of my tee), but I'm barely paying attention to it. Instead, I'm focused on the cold air sinking into my flesh, my T-shirt the barest bit of insulation. It bites into the soles of my feet, pricks at me through my jeans. In fact, the only part of me that's warm is my side, and that's only because Steve is pushed against it, his tiny body already shivering.

"Told you," I say on a sigh, turning and cracking the door, setting him down in the opening, and even though he likes to play the dum-dum, he proves that he's smart right then.

And that's because he zips off into the warmth, tearing across the hardwood floor and leaping—quite nimbly for the uncoordinated guy he is—into Nova's lap.

He starts licking her chin and she doesn't miss a beat in her conversation with Jolie, just cuddles her pup close and keeps chatting.

Smiling despite myself, I start to pull the door closed, but it doesn't shut.

Frowning, I glance up and see Ella standing in the opening, gripping the edge of the glass and wooden panel. Our eyes connect...hold.

Her throat works. Her teeth bite into her bottom lip.

Then she asks quietly, "Can I come out too?"

"No," I rasp.

Her face falls.

I straighten and step close, nudging the door further inward so that I can slip back inside. "It's cold," I say softly, "and you're not dressed for it."

Her eyes flick down then back up. "And you are?"

I shake my head. "The cold doesn't bother me."

"Who are you?" she teases and something in me eases.

Because the sparkle is back in her eyes. "Elsa? Let it gooo," she sings.

"Hilarious." I grunt then nudge her backward a little further so that I can close the door behind me.

She waggles her brows. "I can keep you warm."

I still, hold her gaze. "We tried that."

And she had to get drunk in order to crawl into my bed.

Her head tilts toward the big table that's littered with board game wreckage and empty glasses. "I only had one," she says. "I'm in complete control of my faculties." She stretches out an arm, bends it at the elbow, touching her finger to her nose like she's mid-sobriety test. "See?" Her lips twitch. "I can even recite the alphabet backwards or walk in a straight line." When I don't immediately respond, she hitches her thumb over her shoulder. "Want to see?"

I study her closely, throat suddenly tight.

She's sparkling, fucking beautiful in this light, and so damned full of life, but—

The words won't come free.

I just keep hearing all of the excuses I've held tight to from the first moment I met her.

This is wrong.

This can't be.

This…

"Okay," she adds softly, "maybe I *can't* walk in a straight line, but I'm not able to do that completely sober anyway." She winks and holds up her arm, showing me a bruise there. "See? The corner of the cabinet just jumped out to hurt me." A shrug. "So, don't hold the lack of coordination part against me."

Still, the words won't come.

Not as her smile flattens out.

Not when the teasing in her eyes fades and her arm drops back down to her side.

Not even when she takes a step away from me, embarrassment edging into her expression, and starts to turn away.

CHAPTER NINE

Ella

RIGHT.

This is enough.

Too much, really.

I'm not—

Well, I'm old enough and experienced enough to not keep tossing myself into the emotional blender. I was dumb to try again—fool me once and all that.

I start to turn away.

"Where'd you get that one?"

Before I can ask get what and where, soft fingers are capturing my elbow, turning me back toward him. He halts then with excruciating gentleness and lifts the sleeve of my T-shirt. Frowning, I glance down, see a bruise blooming on the outside of my arm.

"Where did you get"—he lightly brushes his thumb over the bruise—"*that* from?"

My frown deepens, thinking back, and not remembering hitting it on anything. Then again, I run into things often enough that I don't always pay attention to it…or the bruises that form in my clumsy wake. The universe only created one graceful Adler, and that's not me. "I don't know," I say with a shrug. "Probably at the salon today, same as I got the other one" I'm always bumping into the corners of our sets of drawers and doorframes and the rows of sinks at the salon. Not to mention burning myself on my curling iron and dropping color on my clothes and—

Well, like I said.

I'm not graceful.

He lifts my arm.

Higher. Higher. Up toward his face. Up toward his lips.

Until they press lightly against my skin. Over the bruise on my forearm…and the other on my bicep.

"You need to be careful," he murmurs.

I shiver—not because I'm cold, but because my nerves are alight—and my body drifts closer to his.

And maybe I'm a glutton for punishment, but I can't stand to walk away from him, can't stand the lost look in his eyes, the way they warm just at the edges when he doesn't realize I'm watching him watch me.

Plus, I can't resist celebrating his skill at shocking my brother.

First the quip then…

Riggs—quiet, grumpy, man-of-few-words *Riggs*—had kissed my brother to shut him up.

It didn't work for more than a few seconds, but…still.

Maybe I should be grossed out.

But all I could think when I'd watched it go down was… can I get some of that?

Except, longer and with open lips and lots of tongue and… well a *real* kiss to shut me up, like the one from his car, and not the smack he'd laid on Knox.

So, yeah, maybe I'm just that dumb or truly a glutton for punishment.

But I don't walk away.

I drift a little closer.

"*You* need to be careful," I say. "Taunting my brother like that."

One shoulder lifts, drops. "I can handle Knox."

"You sure about that?"

"Crystal."

The edges of my mouth tip up. "Well, I suppose we won't know if he wants to murder you or kiss you again until he follows through."

"On what?"

"On one of those two options—murder or locking lips."

A chuckle that coats my skin in dampened velvet. "He's not getting another kiss." That big shoulder lifts and drops again. "God knows I'm going to get enough shit in the locker room for that as it is."

"So why'd you do it?" I ask, curious.

His eyes come to mine. "I don't know."

Something occurs to me then and I cringe, embarrassment a sweeping wave.

"Is Knox who you—" I break off, unable to finish the words.

Fingers on my cheek. Reddened because I'm suddenly wondering…

Well, it's all twisted and confusing and—

His hand shifts, cupping my jaw, tilting my head up. "It was just to shut him up," he says softly. "And maybe I wanted to see if I could shock you as much as you're always shocking me."

I study him closely. "Well," I whisper, "you've certainly proved you have shock abilities—the puck, that comment to Knox, the kiss—"

I break off, not knowing for a second what kiss I'm talking about.

The one in the car?

Or the peck he'd laid on my brother?

I exhale, force myself to keep going. "—and I'm not admitting defeat, but I'm not sure my shock skills can keep up with yours."

"*I* think"—his thumb brushes over my cheek—"your shock skills are unparalleled."

We stand there like that for a moment, and although I'm aware of eyes on us, the conversation is dulled.

My focus is Riggs—and only Riggs.

"Why do you think I drink too much?" I blurt.

It's a dumb question, literally poking the bear.

I'm not an idiot. I love a drink, love the way it helps me feel loose and more like myself, love how it softens the day, the memories. Plus, I can't bring all of that shock value, the confidence, the always surprising everyone without it. I can't be myself, can't not give a fuck about what everyone else thinks —not without taking the edge off first.

Then it's easy to turn my attention to the outside world, to fix my clients' and friends' problems, to assist them over the bumps in the road. But focusing on myself? On my actions and laughter and the way I hold my hands and how my outfit looks on my body and if my weird cowlick in the back of my hair is showing and if one day, they'll all see through it and leave me, anyway?

That's utterly debilitating.

And the way Riggs is looking at me right now—with a complete and utter focus that burns into me, that threatens to see through my walls and tease out all of my secrets…makes me want to run.

"Never mind," I whisper, now utterly cognizant of the others in the room, playing another round of *Ticket to Ride* (a round I've been excluded from because I kick too much tiny, plastic train ass).

Riggs slants a glance over my shoulder, and for once, the two of us are in perfect harmony when he doesn't press me for answers.

"Are you tired?" he asks softly. "I can drive you home."

I'm his focus.

It's intense and unyielding and—

"Come on, *chérie*," he murmurs, taking my hand, making the decision for me.

The touch is a shock of sensation when his fingers wrap around mine, but not as much as the quiet way he's called me *chérie*.

Rough and with a hint of his French Canadian coming out.

I'd forgotten that the taciturn, grumpy man spoke French, and just the way that word rolls off his tongue has me melting a little, my body drifting closer to hers.

"I'm taking Ella home," he calls to the others.

I blink, look over to the game table, and don't miss that all of my friends are blatantly staring at me.

I half expect Knox to jump up and stop me...but that's a silly thought. We've never been like that, and I wouldn't appreciate him trying to control my life, not in this way. So, really, it's not a surprise that he just waves and calls in a singsongy voice, "Have fun, kids!" I narrow my eyes at him, clocking my brother's calculating gaze—which sends a blip of suspicion through me.

I also don't miss the curious glint in Nova's eyes as Riggs draws me over to the coatrack.

Nothing to be done about either of those things, not right now.

I'm leaving with Riggs and I don't want to mess it up, not this time.

Boots on, I spend a few seconds scratching Steve and murmuring sweet nothings into his goofy ears when he deigns to make his way to me to say goodbye, then I stand up and reach for my coat.

But Riggs is there already, slipping it onto my shoulders.

He bends and bestows his own scratches on Steve, who

huffs out a snotty breath and runs back to Nova, clearly dismissing us.

Smiling, I watch him go.

Then I hear the lock on the front door *click,* the quiet *whoosh* as it opens, and feel the cold bite of the winter air.

My eyes drift up to Riggs's.

He pulls the door wider.

"Let's go, *chérie.*"

CHAPTER TEN

Riggs

SHE'S QUIET, which is unlike her.

Staring out the window as the trees whip by.

So quiet that I find myself answering her question from before.

"It's not the drinking," I say softly.

Her head swivels, eyes catching mine, and then she's lifting her brows. "But you say I drink too much."

"You do," I blurt.

Fucking stupid.

Her brows pull together, those eyes clouding.

I turn back to the road, exhale sharply through my nose. "It's not the drinking," I say again. "It's that if you drink too much, if you're not in control...you're putting yourself at risk."

I feel her still next to me, the air in the car growing taut.

Reading between the lines.

Putting the pieces together.

"Riggs," she whispers, setting her hand on my thigh. "Did your girlfriend—?"

I go stiff and suck in a breath.

And I know she gets it then because she pauses…

It's long and sorrowful and—

Fuck, her face is full of pity when I glance over at her.

"You?" she whispers.

Yes, it happened to me.

I can't give voice to that. I fucking can't.

"Honey." Her fingers tense. "I'm so sorry that was done to you."

I don't know what I expected—maybe for her to pull back, to reject, to add to the shame I already felt. Not *this*. Not her sadness on my behalf and her continuing to touch me.

"It's not like you're thinking," I say quickly. "I wasn't raped or anything. I just…I used to drink a lot, drink too much really, and—"

The memory slams into me so abruptly that it steals my breath away, that it sends my mind into a tailspin. Suddenly, I can barely concentrate on the road.

Saying no.

Pushing her away.

My brain so damned fuzzy. My limbs so fucking heavy.

Saying no again. The word almost impossible to form on my tongue.

But I had. I KNOW I had said it. More than once.

"Riggs," Ella says sharply, those fingers squeezing on my leg, her palm coming to my cheek. But it's her scent—all flowers and woman—that pulls me back out, that grounds me.

I know her, even in the darkness.

Snapping back into reality, I realize that, somehow—thank fucking God, *somehow*—I've found a turnout and stopped the car.

"Breathe," she whispers.

I do just that for long minutes.

"We don't have to talk about it—"

"No." I clamp my eyes shut. "It's not like you think. I just woke up one morning after really indulging, after taking it too far, and there was a woman in my bed."

Her expression doesn't change and she doesn't retreat to her seat.

Just keeps touching me, grounding me.

"I told her no," I say. "I told her I didn't want it and—" My throat closes up but I push the words out, find myself saying the same thing aloud I've said a thousand times in my own head. "It's fine." I shrug. "I overindulged and everyone does stupid shit when they overindulge. But I drank so much that I didn't use a condom and she gave me an STI. After that, I promised myself I would never be that stupid again. Never get so sloppy drunk that I couldn't control my actions, control my body, my words and thoughts—" I grind my teeth together. "And where I put my dick."

Ella's a statue.

So fucking still that I don't think she's breathing.

Then she unsticks, her chest expanding on a huge breath.

Her fingers flex on my thigh, my face, and then she's abruptly pulling back, popping open the car door, stepping out onto the snow-covered turnout.

Leaving me.

Not good enough.

My stomach has a giant knot in it, but before I can process how truly shitty this feels, I hear—

"ARE YOU FUCKING KIDDING ME?!"

I jump, popping open my door in the next second, leaping out of the driver's seat and onto the road just in time to watch her march over to a tree and kick it.

"Are you fucking kidding me?" she shouts again. "Are. You. *Fucking*. Kidding. Me?" Punctuating each word with a kick against the thick trunk of the pine tree. She spins, shoving her hands into her hair, expression furious even from this distance.

When she realizes I've followed her from the car, she freezes, eyes going wide.

"Get back in the car, *chérie*," I say softly, walking slowly over to her like the cornered animal she is. Too fast and she'll snap again. Too fast and she'll bolt.

Probably too late for that.

Probably, I've already ruined it. Ruined this.

Ruined everything.

"It's too cold to do this right now," I say softly, reaching for her.

But she's already reaching for me, rising on tiptoe, hands on my cheeks, tilting my head down.

Her eyes spear into mine. "You told her no?"

Fear locks my spine in place and I want to tear free of her hold, want to be the one who's kicking the tree, kicking it so hard that it topples over, crushing everything in its shadows.

But I can't move, can't break her hold.

Not when she whispers, not in the form of a question this time. "You told her no."

Words stopper up in my throat, but I manage to nod.

"It wasn't an overindulgence," she says. "It wasn't that you did something stupid. It wasn't your fault. She *raped* you."

I start to shake my head.

But she tightens the hold on my face. "She did that to you. It's *her* fault. Not yours. Not *ever* yours." Then she releases me, takes my hand, and draws me to the car.

But not to the driver's seat.

I freeze, come back to myself. "I'll drive."

She studies my face, and I expect her to argue, but she doesn't, just keeps my hand in hers as she rounds the hood of my car, as she moves to the open passenger's side door. Her lips brush the back of my hand before she slips her fingers free and sits in the seat.

The loss of her touch leaves me wavering.

But only for a moment.

Because then the wind picks up, the frosty air biting at my exposed skin. Fucking freezing. And Ella's door is open.

She must be cold.

I lean into the opening, make sure that all of her limbs are safely tucked inside, and when I see that her seat belt isn't buckled, I do it up for her.

Her hand on my cheek. "Thanks, honey."

My lungs stall. Then inflate.

But I don't say anything as I maneuver out of the car, as I round the hood and get into the driver's seat, but before I can put the transmission into drive again, she covers my hand with hers, says again, "It wasn't your fault."

Christ.

The backs of my eyes burn like motherfuckers.

I nod at her then maneuver back onto the road.

Drive as carefully as I ever had all the way back to her house.

We're silent.

But her voice, her words ring through my mind.

It wasn't your fault.

I've never told anyone—because I thought it was. And wasn't it?

I told her no.

I *told* her no.

I close my eyes for a heartbeat, force that down, and park in front of Ella's place, opening my door and climbing out, making it around to her side as she puts her foot on the pavement and stands.

Her gaze comes to mine, unfathomable, but she doesn't say anything.

I still hear her voice sliding through my mind.

It wasn't your fault.

We walk up to the front door, side by side, shoulders brushing.

I wait next to her as she punches in the code, as the lock

whirs and retracts, as she turns the handle and pushes the wooden panel inward.

But when I start to turn away, to head back to my car, she grabs my arm.

"Stay," she whispers when I rotate to face her.

"Just…stay."

CHAPTER ELEVEN

HE TAKES a long time to fall asleep.

But I take longer, even though I force my body to go lax in his arms, to keep my breathing even and my eyes closed.

His face when I'd asked him to stay—disbelief and fear and…yes, panic.

But he'd locked it down, let me guide him inside and upstairs, though he'd stopped me so that he could double-check the lock to the front door, to the garage—something that filled my belly with butterflies.

Or maybe…well, maybe it was the fact that I was inviting a man to my bed.

To sleep.

Not to fuck.

Not to lose myself in the bliss of an orgasm.

But to…offer comfort.

I don't do that. I *can't* do that, can't get so attached. I just get down to business, make sure both of us are satisfied and feeling good. Sex is just mutual pleasure before going our separate ways.

Not fixing.

Not problem solving.

Except, those things are exactly what I do outside of horizontal naked time, aren't they?

The thought is the only thing that settles my pulse, that keeps me in Riggs's arms, that doesn't send me running from this moment in terror.

This is just a new thing to fix.

It doesn't mean I'll let him get close enough to hurt me when he leaves.

Calmed by that thought, I inhale, slow and steady, my exhale just as slow, just as steady.

And then…I allow the blackness to take me under.

But even in my dreams, I know Riggs is holding me closely.

———

AN ARM TIGHTENING around my middle wakes me.

Or maybe it's the alarm, I realize, my eyelids slowly peeling open.

I grunt against the bright sunshine pouring in through the windows, reach for the blanket and yank it over my head.

But the damn alarm won't shut up.

Buzz-buzz. Buzz-buzz. Buzz-buzz.

I can't stand loud beeps jerking me out of sleep—rest to utter wakefulness in a flash—but this is almost as bad.

Okay, anything waking me up is bad.

Because I love to sleep, and I hate to wake up, and—

The arm tightens for another second then loosens and I lose the heat of Riggs—because as grumpy as I am to wake up, there's absolutely no doubt to whom that strong, muscled arm belongs.

I scowl into my pillow, but that scowl smooths out when the buzzing stops.

And then Riggs is back, his arm returning around my

middle, his lips at my ear. "You need to get out of here very soon?"

I grunt.

A soft chuckle. "What?"

"Why are you talking so loud?" I hiss.

"I'm whispering."

I grunt again, yank the blanket closer.

And annoyingly, he just chuckles again.

"What?" I grumble.

"You're not a morning person," he whispers—because yes, he *is* whispering. "I didn't expect that."

I just grunt again, burrow into my pillows. "Shh."

To my grumpy relief, he doesn't keep talking.

But his hand begins moving over the blanket, slowly drifting over the side of my body, starting at my feet, tracing up to my calves, my knees and my hip, resting briefly in the indent of my waist that's engulfed in the tee he'd taken off the night before. The fabric still smells like him, spicy and male, and I remember how warm it had made me when I'd pulled it on in the bathroom, how my heart had skipped a beat at the sight of my reflection in the mirror.

It felt...*right.*

But not as right as him holding me, as him touching me now does.

His hand starts moving again, drifting up my rib cage, brushing lightly over the bottom curve of my breast.

I suck in a breath, but the touch is here again, gone tomorrow, his fingers continuing to move, sliding along the outside of my arm, moving in to stroke the curve of my neck.

A slight squeeze before his hand is moving higher, drifting over my blanket-covered head—

And gripping the edge of the material, yanking it down in one quick movement that leaves the sun blasting me in the face, the cool bite of the morning air on my exposed skin.

Gasping, I blink against the sudden rush of cold, the brightness scalding my eyes, and when my vision clears, I almost gasp again. Because Riggs's face is *right there.*

And he's so damned beautiful in the morning sunlight.

Even though it's sunlight…from the *morning.*

His hand rests on my cheek, grounding me in the moment, pulling me into the here and now…even as what he shared the night before threatens like storm clouds on the horizon.

My throat tightens and I know my emotions must show on my face because the teasing fades from his expression.

"I've never—" He shakes his head, but I don't rush him, don't break in and finish his sentence. Because his hand is still on my cheek and his body is still over mine, and he's…

Well, he's here.

And he eventually gets his thoughts together, his fingers flexing slightly as he whispers, "I've never told anyone that." His eyes close for a long moment. "So, I'd prefer that you didn't share—"

I can't keep silent any longer.

I drop my hand over his, holding it in place on my cheek. "It's your truth to tell." I will him to see that I'm on his side. "So, I will *never* breathe a word to anyone."

His eyes close again, but only for a second, and I want to tell him again that it's not his fault, want to fix how it's eating at him. But…I don't know how to do that. Don't know how to make it right, how to take his pain.

I just know…I can't.

I hate it—the guilt he's carrying, the fact that it happened at all, that I can't make everything better.

But before I can really sit in that, feel how truly vulnerable it makes me with him, his lids peel open, and the world shrinks down until it's just Riggs in front of me—not the man teasing me about my grumpy morning brain nor the one who took my hand and led me from Lake and Nova's house. Not even the man with the hurt buried deep in his soul.

It's *Riggs. My* Riggs.

Quiet. Watchful. Waiting. *Patient.*

With a heavy secret—the proverbial pea under the mattress, disturbing the pillowy top so he can't be at peace. Or maybe it's *his* pebble dropping beneath the surface of the water.

Settling on the bottom of the pool, unseen and yet…

Changing everything.

Even if the rest of the world hasn't noticed it yet.

I open my mouth to say something, to say *anything*—

Buzz-buzz! Buzz-buzz! Buzz-buzz!

He freezes.

Then he gives me something absolutely beautiful.

A gorgeous smile and dancing brown eyes.

His hand slides from beneath mine, moving away from my cheek as he braces himself on my pillow. He reaches over me for my cell phone again, silencing the alarm—one of many that work in tandem to get me up in the morning.

But, funny story, a sexy hockey player in my bed, smiling as he tugs the covers off my body and I don't seem to have a problem staying awake.

"You really *aren't* a morning person, are you?"

I scowl. "I get where I need to be *when* I need to be."

"And how many alarms does it take for you to wake up enough to get there?" he teases.

I feel my cheeks go hot—probably because the plethora of alarms I use in the morning is one of the few things that has Knox and Nova plotting murder when we spend the night in the same place.

"None of your business," I mutter, trying to snatch my cell so I can conceal the evidence.

But he beats me to it.

And proves that he knows me too fucking well because he promptly unlocks it and scrolls to the Clock App.

I start to sputter, but he doesn't miss a beat, just snags his phone from the other nightstand and tosses it onto my lap. "5-2-5-6," he tells me.

Stunned by the sudden turn of events—and the phone in my lap—I don't process that he's given me the code to unlock his cell, not until he nods at it and says, "Don't have anything to hide," he says. "Feel free to check out my own alarms…" A wink. "Or anything else."

"Or an-anything el-else?" I sputter, holding his phone like it's a bomb in my hand that's going to explode.

He's given me permission to snoop?

Just like that?

Who does that?

Riggs Ashford apparently.

I shake my head at myself, and then…

Well, *and then* I take advantage of the glimpse behind the curtain this man is giving me.

First, I look at the alarm app.

"Five AM?" I ask. "Jesus Christ, are you a glutton for punishment or what?"

He just holds up my phone screen in response…with all my alarms—each set ten minutes apart—showing on the screen. "I don't think you have room to talk, *chérie.*"

French Canadian coming out.

I shiver.

Yeah, I love the way it rolls over my skin, settles between my legs.

He grins, as though he knows precisely how that makes me melt.

I want to look through the rest of his cell—emails and social media, pictures and text messages…but I don't.

Partly because…privacy.

But mostly because he's snagging his phone from me before I can, tossing it aside—

And then he's turning off all of my alarms, tossing my cell in the direction of his.

"I—"

I don't finish that thought—not that I have any clue what it might have been.

Because he's climbing over me.

And *then* everything inside me realigns.

CHAPTER TWELVE

Riggs

For a second, she freezes and I half expect her to stop me from moving over her, halting to ask me if I'm okay, if I know what I'm doing when it comes to this.

But even as her lips part and I can practically see the question bubbling to the tip of her tongue, that plump mouth closes, curves up at the edges instead. "Is that five in the morning every day?"

"Not after a game," I say, attention wavering because now she's stroking a hand down my bare chest, drifting toward the button of the jeans I hadn't taken off the night before. "Or after a travel day, but—"

Silky fingertips sliding further south, slipping beneath the waistband of my jeans.

"Just every *other* day?" she asks when I don't go on, working her hand into my underwear.

Her fingers are barely an inch away from my cock now.

Still, I don't miss that she's watching me carefully.

I know it's because of last night.

But…I'm okay.

This isn't…well it isn't *that* night.

It's morning and we're both stone-cold sober. My head isn't spinning and her touch doesn't feel wrong and—

And the sun is shining through the windows.

And I spent all night with her in my arms.

And I just learned that she's not a morning person.

I lean down, brush my lips over her forehead, inhaling the scent of her shampoo.

And…she gave me a piece of *her*—one she doesn't show the rest of the world.

Bright, smart, sassy Ella gave me a tiny glimmer of the woman beneath the veneer.

Eight alarms to coax her out of bed. Super grumpy and doesn't want to chat while yanking the covers over her head and burrowing into her pillow—when the woman I've known has never met a conversation she doesn't like.

But…still Ella—or at least the Ella that I'm desperate to learn.

Her fingers wiggle, the tips teasing the head of my cock and sending it from morning wood to rock *fucking* hard— truthfully, not an uncommon state when I'm around this woman.

"Just every other day," I agree, my voice a rasp as I try not to thrust into her palm, try to focus on the conversation about alarms.

And now not interested in it in the least.

Because her hand—not the one that's so close to tightly holding my cock, but her other one—lifts, resting against my cheek, and that gentle touch steals every single thought from my brain, cock or alarm-related or otherwise. "You're exactly what I thought you were, Riggs Ashford."

My heart rolls over in my chest.

If it came from anyone else, I wouldn't take that as a compliment.

I'd be searching for something hidden and underhanded and cutting within those words, some insult I should deduce.

But…that's not Ella.

It's why I've been borderline obsessed with her from the first time Knox introduced us.

Beautiful. Bright. Guileless.

Everything that's been absent in my life over the last few years.

And I've been a fly to the proverbial honey ever since.

Ready and willing to be ensnared in the sweet, sticky substance of her.

I lift a shoulder, still desperate to focus. "I am who I am."

"No," she murmurs. "You're *more*."

My heart goes again, but before I can react, she does what she always does.

Keeps me on my toes.

Pivoting the conversation so quickly that my head spins—

"Am I going to finally get to see what you're packing?" she teases, one hand still on my jaw, her touch still gentle. But her other's moving now, swirling a fingertip in the damp bead of precum that's seeped from my dick, spreading it over the head of my cock, instantly arrowing in on and stroking the most sensitive spot, finding it like it's her superpower.

My dick convulses, pleasure exploding through me. I grind my teeth together so fiercely that a bolt of pain shoots through my jaw. *Christ.* I'm going to have to be careful, if only because this is going to go very fast unless I get myself under control.

"I'd rather become familiar with what *you're* packing," I murmur, reaching down and tugging her hand from my jeans, pressing a kiss to her palm and lifting it over her head.

"I'm not packing any—"

I drop my mouth to hers, taking advantage of her parted lips to kiss her exactly as I've wanted to since the moment I got my first taste of her in my car.

Deep and wet and with lots and lots of tongue.

I could keep kissing her for an eternity, and maybe I do, but eventually she plants a hand in the middle of my chest and shoves me back.

"Air," she gasps.

"Fuck that," I say, taking her mouth on another drugging kiss. "Fuck oxygen. I can survive on you."

Her cheeks are flushed, lips swollen, reddened from my beard. "Riggs," she moans softly.

Fuck. I want to kiss her all over, spread that flush along her body, piece by piece.

And I can.

She's here.

She wants me.

Another bolt of desire blasts through me, threatening to undo my control, but I focus enough to coax her fingers around one of the wooden slats of the headboard, repeating the same with her other hand, pressing down lightly so she understands, even if the words don't process. "Don't let go, *chérie.*"

She shivers, cheeks flushed, eyes half mast, upper body arched, those lush breasts of hers pushing against the tee she'd slept in.

My tee.

That she swept up and stole from the floor the night before, disappearing into the bathroom and coming out with it dwarfing her, the hem stopping at mid-thigh, leaving miles and miles of skin on display.

NOW IT'S RUCKED up around her waist, giving me a glimpse of even more bare skin, of a plump pussy that's barely covered by a strip of colorfully patterned cotton.

Right.

Kissing her all over.

All *fucking* over.

Still, I force myself to start slowly, pressing my lips to her forehead, to both cheeks, to the hinge of her jaw.

More shivers, her body shifting restlessly—something that increases when I nibble at her earlobe, when I kiss the sensitive spot just behind—

A hand lands on my back and I freeze, lifting my head.

God, she's pretty.

But I'm not sure what the touch means.

"Want to stop?" I ask quietly, holding her gaze, staring deep into the pools of vibrant blue, searching for any bit of hesitancy.

I don't see any.

But that's not a surprise.

Ella's not hesitant.

Not ever.

And, thank fuck, not now either.

Her nails bite lightly into my back. "No, but—"

I bend down, suck at the beaded nub of her nipple that's pressing against the fabric of my tee.

She gasps, both hands going to my hair, clutching tightly.

I let her have that, but only for a second, only because I want this shirt off her.

I break away from her breast, lift up enough to reach for the hem of my tee, yanking it up and over her head, tossing it to the side, and—

Christ.

She's beautiful.

So *fucking* beautiful.

She reaches for me again, but I capture her hands, drawing them up to the headboard again. "Keep them there."

"Riggs—"

I nip at her bottom lip. "Keep. Them. *There.*"

Her lips part, begging to be tasted again, pink growing in

her cheeks, but she continues holding on to the wood, back arching, breasts on perfect display for me.

I bend, kiss that pouty mouth, and then drag my lips down her throat, the rough hitch of her breaths tickling my ear.

Further.

Lower.

Slower.

I kiss my way along each collarbone, lave the soft indent at the base of her throat, then go further, tasting the rainbows adorning her skin from the sunshine streaming through the windows.

Red. Orange. Yellow. Green. Blue. Indigo. Vi—

"Oh God!" she cries as I suckle on her nipple, drawing the hardened tip deep, while I caress her other breast, rolling the peak between thumb and forefinger.

That hand hits my spine again, and I freeze, look up at her.

Eyes half-mast. Cheeks bright red. Mouth swollen. Whisker burn on her throat. Hair tangled and splayed out on her pillow. Delicate collarbones. Gorgeous breasts. The soft curve of her belly.

Narrow hips I need to hold on to as I fuck her hard and deep.

Strong legs—not a surprise considering she's on her feet all day—that I want wrapped around my waist, tightening with each of my thrusts.

In a word…she's a fucking goddess.

"*Chérie,*" I warn, the hot puff of the word on her breast making her shiver.

Those desire-filled eyes slowly focus on mine.

"Keep. Them. *There.*"

More desire. More proof that she likes my orders.

More blood flowing to my dick and eroding my control.

Especially when she reaches overhead, when she grips the headboard.

But, as usual, Ella takes me by surprise…

She wraps her legs around my waist, her hot pussy brushing my stomach, her lips coming to my ear, tongue flicking out, and—

The last of my control unravels.

CHAPTER THIRTEEN

Ella

I feel his body stiffen and for a moment, a blip of uncertainty hits me.

Is he—?

Did I—?

But then he groans, giving me his weight, his big, bulky body pinning me to the bed. His jeans are the sweetest abrasion, the hard ridge of his cock pressing against my stomach the worst kind of tease.

I want the layers gone.

I want it to be just him and me, our naked skin pressed together.

Especially when his groan is cut off by him sucking at my nipples again, his hand working my other breast with no quarter. Suction. Pressure. *Perfect.* Roughened fingertips and a sleek, wet tongue. A calloused palm and a mouth that is sin itself.

Just because I'm me, I reach for him again, this time brushing my fingers through the silky locks of his hair.

And am rewarded with a soft growl against my breast.

Grinning, I sneak one more touch then lift my hands again, holding on, grinding against him, and having the pleasure of him growling again—

"Behave," he snaps, kissing his way over to my other breast.

"Never," I say, though the declaration is softened by the fact that I'm panting, by the sweat that's breaking out on my skin, by my slick need soaking through the fabric of my underwear.

A nip to the underside of my breast as he dislodges my legs from around him. "Behave or I won't lick that pretty cunt of yours."

My throat dries up.

Not my pussy though.

That gushes with desire, convulses with need, empty and throbbing and—

Another nip. This time along my rib cage. Then my waist. My hip. Just below my belly button.

I suck in a breath.

Thankfully, he doesn't stop, just keeps slowly moving down my body, reaching for the waistband of my underwear, tugging it off my body, sending it in the direction of his T-shirt.

A hand on my knee, pushing my leg wide. "So pretty and pink and wet for me," he murmurs, tracing a finger through my pussy. He lifts that glistening finger to his lips and my body convulses when he draws it into his mouth.

Fuck.

I moan, reaching for him again, but one look at those molten brown eyes has me settling my hand back onto the headboard, has me clenching it tight.

One look to behave.

That should be insulting.

Instead, I'm perilously close to coming apart.

"Good girl," he murmurs, spreading my legs further, kneeling between them, mouth coming *oh so close.*

"Don't push it," I mutter.

A smirk…

Right before his mouth is on me.

"Oh God!" I gasp, thighs instinctively trying to close.

But those broad shoulders keep them open and then he's kissing me.

No.

He's *fucking* me with his lips and teeth and tongue, sending my already on-edge body hurtling on a collision course with a wall of pleasure that's so big and thick I actually experience a blip of fear.

But it's gone a heartbeat later, lost in the flurry of his movements, all of which are fucking incredible.

A sure tongue arrowing in on my clit, a thick finger sliding home. The barest flash of teeth and the soft cushion of his lips.

My whole body trembles—that wall already there, an inch from my nose.

"Riggs," I whisper.

Eyes coming to mine and the intensity in them…I feel the pleasure slamming into me, crashing down over me like a cascade of bricks.

Slam. Slam. Slam. Slam.

And then he slides another finger inside me.

I cry out, shattering into a million pieces under that tumult of bricks.

But he doesn't stop—his fingers keep pumping, his mouth continues working me, his shoulders keep my legs wide.

"I—"

A nip on my inner thigh has me jumping, nails scrabbling on the wood over my head.

And then he's slipping a third finger inside me, leaning back onto his knees, gaze shifting, watching as he finger fucks me slow and deep.

I'm practically shivering with need again, but he's not in any hurry.

The slick sounds of my desire tangle with the rasp of my pulse in my ears, with the rapid puffs of my breaths.

"Riggs," I say.

Or *beg*.

His eyes slowly lift to mine and I shiver again at the smile on his face. Cocky, confident…utterly in this moment with me.

"Please," I whisper.

I want him inside me. I *need* it.

I've been desperate for it for months now.

Something he seems to sense, or maybe it's that he's been in the same state as me—wanting me with greedy intent—because he reaches into his back pocket, pulls out his wallet, and retrieves a condom.

"Birth control is hot," I declare.

His eyes flick down to mine again and this time his smile is softer. This time it settles in me, *deep* inside me. "I've got you, baby," he murmurs.

There's that blip of fear again, of alarm and worry and panic tangling through my insides.

A crinkle.

The noise snaps me out of it, sending the twisted feelings away like smoke on the breeze as I watch him roll the condom down the length of his seriously impressive erection.

Then he's rising over me again.

He doesn't thrust home as I half expect—or maybe hope. Instead, he braces himself on one hand, reaches for where I'm still grabbing at the headboard and gently removes one of my hands and then the other.

"I don't have to *behave* any longer?" I tease.

That gorgeous mouth of his hitches up.

"Oh no, *chérie*," he says, drawing my arms around his neck. "You're not going to be thinking about behaving—" A press of his lips to mine. "Or *mis*behaving, rather." He notches the head of his cock at the entrance of my body, starts to press that wide, thick cock inside me. "You're not going to think about anything except for holding on."

And *then* he thrusts home.

And *then*…he's right.

I'm not thinking about teasing him.

I'm not thinking about the perfect burn of his cock stretching me wide, the hard thrusts of our bodies meeting, the hot, wet kiss he lays on me.

I'm not even thinking about the sun growing brighter through the windows as I moan obscenely loud—likely loud enough to wake the entire neighborhood.

And I'm not thinking about sprinting toward that wall of pleasure, not even remotely able to slow down, to stop myself from plowing into it.

Instead, I'm just…

Concentrating on holding on.

I clutch at his broad shoulders, revel in his groans, in the way he clamps a hand on my hip as he strokes into me. I dig my nails in as he fucks me hard and deep, as he whispers dirty words into the air—and even dirtier ones into my ear.

I love the filthy words, love when he tells me how much he loves the tight clasp of my cunt, the slick heat of my desire, the soft press of my tits, the way I'm clenching him tightly inside and out.

So, I let my body continue to plow forward.

Straight into that wall of desire, the wall that's threatening to send me to pieces again.

But I'm okay.

Because I'm still holding on to Riggs.

CHAPTER FOURTEEN

Riggs

Her cheeks are pink as she offers me a homemade muffin and I know it's not because they're flushed from the shower, or from us burning up the sheets.

She's giving me another side of her.

I touch that stretch of pink, stroke my finger over her silky skin, but don't otherwise comment on it before I take the proffered muffin.

She nibbles at her bottom lip, tears a paper towel from the roll on the counter and sets it in front of me, putting a second muffin on top of that before turning back to the coffeepot, fussing with the lid. I know she's avoiding eye contact, avoiding me, but I let her have that.

Plus, that means I can partake in my favorite activity.

Watching Ella.

Her hair is flowing down her back in a sea of perfect curls when not forty-five minutes ago it was a mess of tangles and wild twists.

Now it's beautifully styled—though I can't lie. I still prefer the just-been-fucked hair.

But it reminds me that for as many Sierra games she's been to—watching her brother, even though I like to pretend she's there for me—I've never seen her work.

Mostly because she only recently moved to town.

But also because—and I know this makes me an asshole—I didn't really find it interesting.

Hair's hair.

Slap some product in my hands, shove it through the strands to keep it out of my face, and call it good.

Only…watching her wash the strands in the shower, drying and styling her hair after—and doing it in a relaxed, confident way that told me she could do it in her sleep, the same way I know I can shoot a puck without really thinking about it—I knew there was so much more.

This is her art.

Her passion.

The things she's worked incredibly hard to master.

The coffee starts spitting out of the machine, filling her mug, and I don't miss that she still isn't looking at me. Nor that she's giving me lots of other insights into her like—

"Are you going to add the whole carton of milk to your coffee?"

She turns, cheeks still pink, but now her brows are dragged together, forming a perfect little vee between them that I want to kiss. "What?"

I push out of the chair, move toward her, carefully tugging the mug out of her hands, setting it on the counter to the side of us. "I asked"—I lean in, grasping the rounded edge of the counter, trapping her—"if you're going to add all of the carton of milk to your coffee."

She stills.

Shudders.

Probably because I've dropped my head, pressed my nose to her throat, inhaled the scent of her. Flowers and vanilla and *Ella.*

Then I realize it's not because I'm sniffing her like a dog.

But because I mentioned the milk.

"I—" Her throat works. "Did you want some milk?"

There's no missing the guilty tone in her question.

"I think there's still a little left in the carton." A breath, eyes flicking up to mine—and yup, guilty. "Or you can have my cup," she says in a rush. "I just thought I've heard you say that you like your coffee black, otherwise I would have—"

I kiss her, long and slow and deep. "I don't want milk, *chérie.*"

A blink. Then another. "But—"

My mouth tips up. "I was just teasing you, baby."

She exhales, shakes her head slightly, one of her curls catching on the cabinet pull behind her.

I reach up and untangle it, not missing when she leans slightly toward my hand, instinctively wanting me to touch her.

I like that.

I fucking *love* it.

Something she likely reads on my face considering her slightly befuddled expression fades and her eyes sharpen.

I don't want her sharp and focused and scheming.

I want her soft and melting and *mine.*

So, I slant my lips over hers, and I taste her.

Spice and cinnamon from those homemade muffins. The barest earthy note of coffee. Nails biting into my nape, a lush body pressed to mine. A hand on my chest, lightly pushing.

"Air," she gasps.

"No," I murmur, taking her mouth again, but just for a second, just for a quick taste, but as much as I want to lift Ella up onto the counter and kiss her thoroughly, to strip her naked, muss those curls, and fuck her senseless…

She has a client in a half hour.

And she loves what she does. I'm not going to fuck with that.

So I satisfy myself with that small taste, that caress of her tongue against mine.

Then I'm nudging her toward the table, into my chair. I tug the napkin with the muffin—the last one, I hadn't missed—in front of her. "Eat," I order softly, turning for the counter, snagging her mug, bringing it back over to her.

"I—"

I plunk the cup in front of her, order again, more firmly this time, "*Eat.*"

"Riggs."

"Christ," I mutter, leaning down and wrapping my arm around her middle. I lift her enough to drop my ass in the chair then tug her down into my lap. "Eat, *chérie*. I know that you have a long day ahead of you."

And *my* day is free, minus meeting up with Knox later today to do some off-ice.

Which sends my mind reeling forward, an idea forming... scheming maybe.

Taking a page out of Ella's book.

I grin, sweeping her curls aside and baring the slender curve of her neck. Bending, I press my lips to the soft skin there, inhaling the scent of her, loving that she trembles.

She likes that.

She's given me another piece of her.

And I've caught it. I'm holding it close.

Going to continue to catching those pieces until I have them all.

"How do you know I have a long day?" she asks a moment later.

I nudge the muffin closer, don't miss her sigh...nor the way she reaches for it a moment later, starts unpeeling the paper wrapper. "I know you have a long day," I say, "because Nova and Knox have both mentioned that you've been working nonstop."

And because I've driven by the salon late at night more times than I'll admit, have seen the lights on and only a couple of cars in the lot—hers being one of them.

Not that I tell her that.

Instead, I press my lips to the back of her neck. "Tell me about your clients today."

She stills. "Why?"

It's a quiet question, as though she can't fathom why I'd want to know what she has happening.

I snag her mug, lift it toward her mouth. "Is it a multiple cup of coffee day?"

She shifts in my lap, her eyes hitting mine before she greedily snags the mug and sips deeply. "It's *always* a multiple cup of coffee day."

I chuckle. "Isn't that the truth?"

"A hockey god such as yourself would dare to defile his body with something as terrible as caffeine?" she teases.

Lightly tugging a strand of her hair, I steal her muffin, take a bite of it. "Trouble."

"And proud of it," she says, setting the mug down and stealing it back.

But then she does something wonderful, something completely, totally *Ella.*

She breaks off a piece and feeds it to me, and then…

She tells me about her day.

"First I have a new client for a consult, then I have a full-head highlight, a root touch-up, and an all-over color—"

I see that I'm going to have to do some Googling.

Because I know those words belong to the English language but put together in that order and she may as well be speaking Greek.

"—and then I have a couple of other clients before Donna comes in for her weekly appointment to finish out my day."

"Who's Donna?"

Her face softens.
My heart starts to thud against my rib cage.
And then Ella gives me another piece of herself.
Because she tells me all about Donna.

CHAPTER FIFTEEN

Ella

"Try one of these, honey," Donna says, offering me a cookie. "George said they might even be better than my chocolate chip."

"Blasphemy," I tell her lightly, but I'm not the type of girl to turn down a cookie, and especially not one of Donna's, so I snag one from the container and take a big bite.

Flavor explodes on my tongue—salty and sweet, peanut butter and chocolate chip, sea salt and just a hint of caramel.

"Oh. My. *God*," I moan.

Her smile widens. "I see that George may be right."

"More than right," I tell her, shoving the rest of the delicious baked good in my mouth. "He's a genius."

Donna giggles. "I'll edit that so it doesn't go to his head."

I wink, steal another cookie, and salute her with it. "Wise woman. Now," I tell her, "I need to hear all about George and how he suddenly gets to have an opinion about your cookies."

Pink on Donna's cheeks, but it looks good on her. Especially when it's paired with a brightness in her eyes, and a joy to her words.

Grinning, my gaze goes to Tammy's, who's busy with her own client (who's also munching on one of Donna's yummy cookies), but we exchange a nod of job-well-done.

Matchmaking powers leveled up.

I make sure Donna's sleek bob is perfectly coiffed for her dinner with George tonight—why she came in late in the afternoon instead of her typical morning slot—and I'm so focused on the task at hand that I don't realize the bell over the door has rung, don't realize that Kit, who's manning the front desk like usual, has gone still and silent.

Eventually, though, I process that the blow dryer next to me has turned off, that the salon is almost silent.

Frowning, I turn around—

And Riggs is standing just inside the door.

Riggs.

The juxtaposition is almost comical.

Big, bearded hockey player meets the soft white, lavender, and gold of the salon.

Tattoos and sweatpants versus color-coded products and samples of hair extensions.

Both sights are beautiful in their own right…

But I only want to fuck one.

Okay, fine. I only want to fuck *Riggs.* Like maybe forever.

Which is a terrifying thought, but before panic can make me do something stupid, Kit jerks into motion, breaking the quiet that's fallen. "Can I…um…help you?"

The last comes out in a squeak.

A squeak that jars me into motion.

I set down my scissors, turn fully toward the front desk, eyes glued to Riggs as he moves forward, limbs loose, demeanor completely confident and relaxed. He plunks his elbows on the high counter. "I'm looking for a haircut," he tells Kit, eyes flicking to mine and holding for a heartbeat before returning to Kit's. "Can you help me with that?"

"I-uh—" Kit starts typing on the computer but doing it so frantically that he knocks the wireless keyboard to the floor.

Luckily, he has a rubber mat where he stands, so I don't think it's damaged as I walk over and put him out of his misery, sweeping it up, setting it back on the shelf. "I'll help Riggs, honey," I say softly, setting my hand on Kit's back.

He nods as he turns to me, not saying anything until he's fully facing me.

Then he mouths, "*This* is Riggs?"

And, yeah, I don't miss the sparkle in Kit's eyes…nor the determination—and I know that I'm going to be required to give a full report at the soonest opportunity.

"Yeah, yeah," I mutter under my breath before I nudge him to the side with my hip, tapping away at the keyboard and deliberately making my tone no-nonsense and business-like.

Even though, inside, I'm melting.

Riggs is here. *Here.*

"Hmm," I tell him, heart pounding so hard it feels like it's trying to claw up the back of my throat. "My schedule's pretty full." I begin tapping again, shaking my head before looking up at Riggs with a sad expression that I can barely keep in place because of the mirth gathering in my belly. "Maybe—" More tapping and then I sigh. "Nope." I tsk. "That won't work."

Kit is practically vibrating next to me, and I don't know if it's with laughter—because I haven't so much as bothered to bring up my schedule—or because my tapping on the keyboard means that I might mess something up in the intricate system he uses to run the salon.

I don't get the chance to find out.

Or to mess anything up.

Because Riggs leans across the counter, one big hand settling on mine.

My eyes fly up, lock with his, breath hitching.

"I'll pay double."

And I know that he doesn't mean with money.

My pussy clenches, knees wobbling, but I just lift my chin, not quite sure why I'm playing this game, but also loving it, loving that Riggs is playing along, loving the sensual retribution in his eyes.

Wanting him to knock the computer to the floor, to lift me up on the counter and fuck me senseless.

Wanting the salon to be empty so he *can* do that.

Wanting…

Him.

Just *him*.

"Here you go, honey," Donna says, coming up behind me and jarring me out of my sexual stupor. She passes me a couple of bills, and I mutely take them before she pats me on the cheek. "See you next week." Then turns to Riggs, her stare slow and assessing before her gaze flicks back to mine, her eyes sparkling. She lifts the container of cookies toward him. "Want a taste?"

Slowly, he smiles.

But he's not looking at Donna as he reaches forward and takes a cookie, and he's not directing his rasped-out words to her either.

Nope.

They're all for me.

"Yes, I want a taste."

My knees nearly buckle.

Then again when his lips slowly close around the cookie, as he chews and swallows, the strong cords of his throat working. As his tongue flicks out and captures an errant crumb clinging to his beard.

Fuck.

It's suddenly sweltering in here.

"Thank you," he tells Donna. "That's delicious."

Her eyes drift to mine again. Her smile grows.

"Enjoy." She plunks the container on the counter and I

distantly hear the bell ring as she walks out, as I try to come up with something to say, something witty and funny and—

"Ella has room for a haircut tonight!" Kit blurts.

Or not.

———

IT'S amazing how quickly a salon can empty out.

One second, Donna and Tammy and her client and Kit are all here, and the next I'm alone with Riggs, his deep brown eyes locked on mine in the mirror.

Somehow I've managed to get Riggs a cape, to sweep it out in front of his body and fasten it around his throat.

And now I'm standing behind him, staring at his handsome reflection, at those gorgeous eyes, that kissable mouth, the tattoos licking up the sides of his neck and…I'm just staring.

Focus, woman.

I exhale silently through my nose, focus on my job.

I'm so *not* giving this man a bad haircut.

Because if I do, I will never hear the end of it from Kit and Tammy, from Knox and Nova. Not to mention what Lake and the rest of the Sierra will say if I fuck up.

Plus…

I've been *dying* to get my hands on Riggs's hair.

Dying to even out the locks that kiss his nape, the shorter strands that always fall over his forehead, beckoning for my fingers to push them back into place.

This is my time.

So, I focus.

"What do you want done?" I ask softly, sinking my fingers into his hair, stroking through the locks that are like silk. His body goes stiff, a muscle in his jaw flexing, and I might have frozen, might have pulled back…

If not for the way his eyes blaze at me in the mirror.

My thighs tremble.

Gorgeous man.

"What would *you* do?" he asks quietly.

I sigh, continue to run my fingers through the strands for a moment as I study his face. "Pink highlights and keep the length."

For a second, my words don't seem to penetrate.

Then they do, his hand coming up to snag my wrist. "Always teasing me, aren't you, *chérie*?" He brushes his thumb lightly over my skin.

My heart is pitter-pattering in my chest, but I ignore it. "I'm serious," I say, choking back laughter when his fingers tighten and he scowls at me. "Some soft pink tones would look beautiful with your skin."

All olive and yummy and lickable—

"I think something else pink would look better *on* my skin."

I tremble.

And…

I come apart.

CHAPTER SIXTEEN

Riggs

HER THROAT BOBS, and I don't miss the shiver that wracks her body.

I want to fuck her, here and now.

But I also really want to see her do her thing. Which is why, instead of bending her over this chair and fucking her senseless, I lift her hand to my lips, press a kiss to the inside of her wrist. "Just do whatever you want, *chérie*."

She trembles again and I have to work really hard at the whole *not* fucking part.

It would be easy to plunk her on the desk, to knock the poor, abused keyboard to the ground in much more pleasurable fashion.

But this is where she *works*.

This is her art. Her love.

So, I bite back my groan, release her hand, smiling at her slightly befuddled reflection. Then I shrug. "Or pink highlights could work."

A blink.

Then another.

And then mischief enters the chat.

"Pink it is," she says, those pretty blue eyes sparkling as she turns away, heads for a room blocked off by a black curtain.

Oh shit.

This woman has enough balls that she might actually do it.

I'm out of my chair a heartbeat later, catching her just as she dips behind the black fabric, spying rows and rows of little boxes sitting on a wall of built-in shelves. A store room, I realize before I draw her back against me, the fucking fabric thing she snapped around my neck getting in my way.

"I need to get the pink dye," she says breathlessly.

"The fuck you do," I mutter, nipping at her jaw and turning us, pinning her between my body and the counter.

So fucking beautiful.

So fucking *mine.*

Not Nova and Lake. Not some shit I *thought* I wanted.

But *mine.*

Us.

I press my nose to her throat and inhale, taking in the scent of her, flowers and vanilla, mixed with a dozen other notes— soap and something sharp, like bleach, the fruity odor of someone's perfume, the chocolatey goodness of the cookies.

And Ella.

Mine.

"Mmm," I murmur, brushing my lips over her forehead, her cheek, her jaw, the column of her neck.

She shivers, hips moving against mine, even as her arm lifts over her head.

Okay, yeah, I like that. No, I fucking love it, love how it lifts her breasts, how it reminds me of this morning. If I could just have this woman holding on to something while I fuck her senseless for the rest of eternity, I'd be more than content.

I'd be fucking *perfect.*

"Got it," she says a little desperately, and I focus enough to read the label on the box in her hand.

Pink.

Christ. She is fucking incredible.

Still, the box reminds me why we're here.

So, I can see her work.

I slip the dye from her grip, toss it back onto the counter then take her hand and draw her from the room. "Come on, *chérie*," I say, releasing her as I settle into the chair. "Show me what you've got."

Blue eyes on mine in the mirror for a long moment. Then she exhales, her throat working, tone becoming no-nonsense. "Okay, mister," she declares. "If you don't want to end up with a lopsided buzz cut, you need to sit there and behave."

That's not going to happen—the behaving part.

But I will sit here and watch her in the mirror for the rest of all time.

Especially when she runs her fingers through my hair, nails sliding over my scalp and raising goose bumps on my arms. "You have great hair," she says softly, seeming more focused, as though touching the strands of my hair has centered her. She reaches by me, picks up a spray bottle, then opens a drawer and extracts a comb. "I'd recommend leaving most of the length on top but shortening the back and sides."

If it means she'll keep touching me, I'll agree to anything.

"Okay, *chérie*."

Her eyes lift from my hair to my eyes again. "Okay?" she asks. "Just like that?"

I lift a shoulder, drop it. "You're the expert."

"My men's haircuts are eighty-five dollars," she says, setting the comb and spray bottle aside, picking up the clippers and plugging them in.

My eyes bug out of my head. "*Eighty-five—*" But then I catch a glimmer in her eyes.

Mischief. Trouble.

Ella.

"How much will it be if I pay in orgasms?"

She doesn't miss a beat, just uses a plastic clip thing to tie my hair out of my face and away from where she's working. "Two hundred and five."

I flick my brows up. "Seriously?"

"I'm sorry what was that?" she asks, her smile wide as she clicks on the clippers, sending them buzzing and drowning out the sound of my reply.

It's for the best, anyway.

I didn't have anything witty or funny to say. Especially when all I want to do is continue to stare at her, to watch her as she shifts her focus back to my hair.

Her hands are steady as she lowers the clippers to my nape.

I feel the slight pull on my scalp as she guides the blade through my hair in one steady stroke.

Shorn strands fall, bouncing off my shoulders before they hit the floor.

And maybe it's the feel of her hands on me, or the soft silence that falls when she sets the clippers aside and begins using her scissors to cut the top of my hair—or maybe it's just that this woman with all of her brightness and mischief that brings out a little of the same in me.

God, I can hardly remember a time before Ella where I felt light enough to tease.

To joke.

It was just hockey and work and…living a half sort of life.

Things are different now.

"You know," I say as she lifts a strand of hair up, pulls it tight and begins doing some sort of fancy cutting with her scissors.

She pauses, lifts a brow.

"You know that I don't think I've slept that well in a long time."

Something soft in her eyes.

"Even if you are a bed hog."

Those eyes narrow.

"Well," she says tartly. "I don't normally let hockey players sleep in my bed."

I don't like that—not the plural of hockey players, nor the insinuation of other men in her bed, but I bite back my growl. "From what Knox has said, you don't normally let *anyone* stay the night in your bed." I meet her stare in the mirror again, can't resist adding, knowing my mouth is curved into a smirk, "Except me."

Her nose wrinkles, but she breaks our stare, focuses on my hair again. "Don't let it go to your head," she mutters.

"Which head?" I quip, earning another narrow-eyed look.

"Funny." A grumble.

"Tell me about your day," I say, instead of further antagonizing the woman with scissors next to my head.

"I told you about it this morning," she says.

"Before it happened," I point out. "Now the day's almost over. Did everything go smoothly?"

She lifts another section of my hair with her comb, does more scissor magic. "Yup. No problem clients—with the exception of Samantha, who showed up thirty minutes late." A sigh as she combs and cuts again. "I managed to accommodate her, but she wasn't happy that I could only do a few highlights and a cut."

"Instead of doing her whole head?" I ask, remembering our conversation from this morning and now also sort of knowing what I'm talking about, if only because of the power of the Google.

Her gaze comes to mine, blue eyes unfathomable. "Yeah," she says softly. "I rebooked her for sooner, though, and I'll get her what she wants." A shrug as she seems to finish with the scissors, setting them on the counter and going back for the clippers. She pauses with them near my head, asks, "How was *your* day?"

"Great," I tell her as she tilts my head down, begins cleaning up the cut on the back of my neck. "I started the day with a beautiful woman under me."

A soft inhale, the clippers going still.

"Then I hit the gym, caught up on some shit at my house, Googled some hairstylist terms—"

"Excuse me?" she asks.

I shrug, then still when she pulls the clippers away from me.

Right. Sharp objects near my head.

Sudden movements aren't recommended.

"It's your job," I explain. "The least I can do is know a little about it."

"Why?" she whispers. "Why is that the least you can do?"

"*Chérie*," I murmur, "look at me."

It takes a minute, but eventually she looks up and I hold her stare in the mirror again.

"Have I not made myself clear?" I ask softly.

She swallows, but eventually shakes her head, and something softens in my belly.

This bright, beautiful woman doesn't get it.

Doesn't understand that from the moment I picked up the Sharpie, wrote on that puck, and decided to toss it over the glass to her…

She belongs to me.

"I thought you were the prettiest fucking woman I'd ever seen the first time Knox introduced us."

She inhales sharply.

"And that hasn't changed, *chérie*. But that's not why I'm sitting in this chair right now." My mouth tips up. "And it's not because you give insanely expensive, but great haircuts either."

Because I haven't missed the great job she's done.

My hair looks top notch.

"S-so, why *are* you here?" she asks quietly.

"It's not because of how you look on the outside, as beautiful as you are."

Her throat works again, those clippers still buzzing away. "Then why?"

I could lie.

But I don't want to.

I love the befuddled expression on her face, love the wide eyes and pink cheeks. Love the wonder in her tone.

"I'm here because of what you look like on the inside, *chérie*."

A long pause before she returns the trimmer to my hair, even longer before she asks, "And what do I look like on the inside?"

"Like you're the woman I'm going to make mine."

And *that's* when the clippers slip.

CHAPTER SEVENTEEN

Ella

"Yo, Patches!" Lake calls when Riggs walks into the bar. "Bring us another round!"

My heart skips a beat.

I haven't seen him since this morning.

And he's just as yummy as always.

Even when he scowls—and I don't know if it's because of the order from his teammate, or if it's because of his new nickname. Shit talk amongst hockey players is relentless...and the strip of bald skin on the back of Riggs's head is an easy target.

Thus...Patches was born at practice today.

I know it's not my finest work, but I'm over my mess up.

Sort of.

I still can't believe it happened, and every time I see my handiwork I'm filled with a hysterical sort of amusement. But it should grow in quickly and, well...

Riggs didn't rage at me for fucking up his hair.

He could have.

Some might say he *should* have.

Instead, he was nice about it—taking my hand and snagging the clippers, turning them off and setting them on the counter. Then drawing me close and cupping my cheeks in his palms as I'd sputtered on and on with apologies.

"Oh my God. I'm so sorry. I can fix it. I promise. I can make it look okay—"

He kissed me gently, murmured in my ear, *"I don't give a fuck about my hair. It'll grow back, chérie. And look at the top"*—he positioned me in front of him, forced me to gaze into the mirror—*"it's the shit."*

While I was processing that, he ripped the cape off, tossed it on the chair, and had kissed me long enough that I forgot all about my fuck up.

Likely because he took me home, didn't wait for an invitation to come upstairs, then had fucked me senseless.

Then fucked me limp again when he woke me in the morning—at five fucking A.M.

The sun hadn't even been up.

But *he* sure as hell had been.

Heh.

I grin.

"So," Nova murmurs from next to me, deep into her third mule. I'm still sipping on my first for…reasons I'm pretending aren't affecting my reasoning but have everything to do with what Riggs shared and what I want to happen when I talk my way into testing out his mattress instead of mine tonight.

"So what?" I ask casually.

"When are you going to explain?"

"Explain what?" I slap on my most innocent expression—which has Knox snorting from his position next to Lake, even though most of his focus is on a gaggle of women at the next table over.

"I second that snort," Nova says, allowing Lake to draw her more firmly into his body. "Did you forget that we saw you two leave together the other night?"

"Nope," I say, popping the p and taking a dainty sip of my

mule when usually I would have drained the copper mug, if only to have an excuse to head up to the bar for a refill. "But I still don't know what you might possibly want me to explain."

Kit, who's joined us for the first time—likely for reconnaissance purposes—chokes on a laugh and I glare at him, but only for a second.

He is, after all, the one who got into the salon early this morning and swept up the evidence of my hairtastrophe then deleted the footage of Riggs's X-rated kiss—and the subsequent moments that led to it—from the security cameras positioned in the corners of the space.

Though, I do have a copy of it saved that he texted me.

It's as hot as I remember and—I mentally wince—it clearly shows off my poor clippering skills.

Luckily, I don't have to make up any more lies because then Riggs is there, a tray in his capable hands. He plunks down a beer in front of Knox and Lake, a mule in front of Kit and Nova and…me.

Stilling, I look up at him, eyes going wide.

Then wider when he tugs my chair back, lifts me from the pleather-covered cushion, sits and plunks me into his lap.

It happens in a manner of just a few seconds, but just like that, I'm surrounded by warm, hot Riggs.

His hand settles on my hip and I blink.

At him.

At Lake, who's smirking like the handsome, smug bastard he is.

At Knox, who's completely unfazed that his *sister* was just manhandled by his teammate and is currently occupying said teammate's lap. In fact, he just lifts his beer at Riggs in a salute that has me narrowing my eyes before he refocuses on the women nearby.

So, I return to blinking at Riggs.

Who's as quiet as usual in this public arena—and I haven't missed that he's positively chatty when he's alone with me, especially when he's discussing all of the body parts of mine that he likes and how he's planning on using them and—well, there's a lot of mention of slick heat and pretty pink and—

"Behave," he mutters, leaning in and nipping at the hinge of my jaw.

I realize that I've been rocking slightly on his lap, and that he's now hard beneath me.

Okay, so this sitting-on-his-lap stuff might have even better side effects than previously thought—and being surrounded in warm, strong Riggs, while his scent fills my nose and his voice rumbles against my back is pretty damned good.

But feeling the rigid length of his erection beneath my ass is…well, that's definitely a bonus.

A *big* bonus.

Heh.

"I'm just saying," I murmur, rocking back and not missing that his hand tightens on my hip, that a soft growl reverberates through his chest and into my back.

"You're not *saying* anything, *chérie*," he says when I don't go on, clamping that hand tighter, drawing me more firmly against him.

"Maybe not with words." I rock slightly, feel his cock twitch.

Okay, so *actually* this lap-sitting thing is pretty fucking great.

"And you're not using your words either," I go on, twisting so I can lift my lips to his ear, "especially with your caveman antics."

He leans in even closer, his voice damp puffs of air on my skin. "I think I made it clear that I intend to claim what's mine."

I shiver, heart rolling over in my chest.

If I was holding a pair of scissors…well, hair would have to watch out.

"Riggs," I whisper.

"I've got you," he says. "And I'm not going anywhere."

I still.

I want that.

God, how I want that.

But…I've heard it before—and then my mom passed and my dad got remarried and…well, we went from solid, from peaceful and happy and the place every one of our friends wanted to hang out to…alone.

To left behind.

So yeah, I've heard it before.

The only people in my life who've stuck are Nova and Knox.

But there's something about the way Riggs says it…

I *want* to believe it.

His hand strokes in, drifting up the inside of my thigh.

Gasping, I grab his wrist. "Did you forget that my brother's sitting at this table?" I tell him, even as I'm playing with fire, as I'm settling more firmly on the length of his cock.

He hisses, snags my hip and holds me still. "Your *brother* is the one who got my head out of my ass about you in the first place."

I blink at him, albeit in shock this time.

Then turn to Knox, who's still watching the group of women at the next table over. Though, I don't miss that half of his mouth is curved up.

"*I'm* the matchmaker."

That's *my* freaking job.

"It's in the Adler DNA." He lifts one shoulder, drops it. "Plus, I think Riggs is one of the few men who can handle you."

The PDA, the caveman antics that I can't deny I love, my brother fixing me up to be *handled.*

That's one step too far.

I lean back, narrowing my eyes at my brother. "Excuse me?"

He tosses back the rest of his beer, stands. "Time to go."

And then he's off, moving to the women, schmoozing like only my brother can.

"I'm going to fucking kill him," I snap, jumping to my feet.

"Shit," Riggs mutters, dragging me back down. "Don't be pissed. I've had a thing for you from the beginning"—he leans around me, snags my gaze—"remember? From the first moment I met you."

The hot looks from afar?

The ones that gave me many a nocturnal—and otherwise—orgasm in response to the memories of that scorching gaze?

Yeah, I remember.

Still, I don't soften my glare. "And?"

His mouth ticks up. "*And* I wouldn't have allowed myself to get this far," he says softly. "For *reasons*." His throat works as guilt slices through me. He's gone soft beneath me, and his hand loosens on my hip. "Not without Knox giving me the green light."

Damn. I had to ruin this moment by opening my big mouth. "Riggs," I begin, shoving the mule he'd brought over away when I nearly take it out with my elbow.

His eyes flick to the copper mug then back to mine, and he reaches forward, brings it closer. "Drink it, *chérie*. I'm not going to control what you do."

No, he'd just find a way to grin and bear it—or grind his teeth together and bury it. "*Riggs.*"

"Baby," he murmurs. "Drink the fucking cocktail. It's different. I see you—"

"And I see *you*," I say, shoving it away again. The pain he'd bared. Pain I won't ignore. I can soothe life's rough edges with orgasms and empty calories from more apple fritters.

I'll be fine.

"*Chérie*—"

"No," I snap.

"I'll drink it!" Nova says, scooping up the mug and sipping

at it triumphantly. "I'm certainly not going to allow my rosemary simple syrup to go to waste," she tells Lake, curling into his side.

The big man smiles at her before tucking a strand of hair behind her ear. "Of course not, butterfly."

And my heart rolls over in my chest, yearning heavy in my blood.

And panic.

There's a healthy dose of panic as well.

Because…

Turning down drinks. Sitting in his lap. Yearning for him when he isn't with me.

We've barely begun and I'm already in fucking deep.

I jump up again, but this time I must have taken Riggs by surprise because he doesn't yank me back down, and by the time he reaches for me, I'm skittering out of range.

"*Chérie.*"

"I'll be right back."

And then I'm pushing through the crowd, turning down the hall, and bursting out onto the bar's deserted back patio.

No one uses it in the winter, so it's not cleared of snow and I skid on the icy planks, nearly go down, but manage to stay on my feet, just barely.

Cold air hits my skin in a rush, but I barely feel it.

My head is spinning and my lungs are tight and—

"Breathe, *chérie.*"

My lungs decide to start working again, and I suck in a breath, release it slowly.

"I won't hurt you," I whisper.

Not like I've been hurt.

I can't. I *can't*—

"You're not going to hurt me," he says, cupping my cheek and stepping close.

How can he know that? How can he? It's like his promise

to be here, to stay here. We might have the best intentions, but—

"Ella," he says, wrapping his arms around me. "You have the biggest heart I've ever seen. You care about people and you pay attention—"

"I've already hurt you."

He goes still for a heartbeat then. "And when you found out you stopped doing it, but I don't need you to change for me, baby. I like *you* as you are. And I know you like this—hanging with your friends and tying one on—"

My lungs expand in a rush this time, oxygen hitting my blood so quickly that black spots gather at the edges of my vision.

"—so eat, drink, and be merry. It might take me a bit to be comfortable with how we end our night after all those mules, but we'll find a way."

Get *comfortable.*

Jesus.

My stomach twists all over again.

"Riggs," I say softly. "I don't want you to have to *get comfortable.*"

His expression gentles. "And *I* don't want *you* to make yourself smaller for some bullshit that doesn't really matter."

It matters.

It fucking *matters,* but before I can push that—even though this isn't the time or place—he keeps talking, his lips brushing my earlobe and making me shiver, making me forget why this argument is so damned important.

"And *we* might need to thank your brother because I wouldn't have touched you—here or anywhere—without Knox giving me the push." He brushes his knuckles over my cheek. "As beautiful and tempting as you are."

My heart feels like fluffy cotton candy—soft and sweet and so light it can float—but at risk of dissolving with the barest bit of liquid.

And below it?

That's what frightens me.

Which is why I revert to joking. "I would have worn you down."

His mouth curves, and it's almost a normal smile, but he doesn't tease me back, just kisses the tip of my nose. "Likely."

I start to say something else, to tease him until that smile is absent of the tinge of the past, but before the words can dance off the tip of my tongue, the door slams open, crashing into the wall of the patio.

We both jump.

And see a woman stumble out.

I start to turn back to Riggs to tell him we should go back to the table.

But then I process the woman's state.

Her dress is torn, her makeup is running from tears streaming down her face, and—

A man is crowding in behind her.

And Riggs…

Well, Riggs falls apart.

CHAPTER EIGHTEEN

Riggs

ONE SECOND, I'm enjoying the feel of Ella's lush body pressed to mine, knowing that she's slowly letting me in, letting me beyond the Ella she gives the rest of the world.

The next, I'm seeing the woman burst out of the bar, slipping on the icy wood of the patio.

She stumbles then regains her balance and Ella and I both take a step toward her.

But even as I'm processing the fear on her face, the torn dress, the tears dripping down her cheeks…

A man follows her out.

"No!" she cries, cringing back, feet slipping out from beneath her then, hitting the wooden planks hard enough that she cries out in pain again.

Scared. Hurt. *Cornered.*

The man steps closer.

"No!" she says again.

But the man doesn't stop reaching for her.

And…I snap.

I'm on him in a second, gripping the back of his shirt and

ripping him away from the woman, all but tossing him across the patio.

He hits a stack of chairs with a grunt, sending them crashing to the ground.

I flick a look behind me, see that Ella's with the woman, carefully helping her to her feet.

I turn my attention back to the bastard in front of me.

He's slowly climbing to his feet. "What the fuck!" he shouts, getting in my face, the alcohol on his breath—

No. NO!

I shudder and push the memory down, shoving him back. "You don't touch women like that."

"And who the fuck are you to even begin thinking about telling me what to do?"

"I'm fucking *no one*," I growl. "But you're still going to listen to me."

"Fuck you!" And then he punches me.

Or tries to.

I catch his arm, land a hard blow to his side. "Don't," I snap when he tries to knee me in the balls, gripping his throat and shoving him back against the railing.

"Fuck *you*." He grabs at my wrist, pushes at my chest. "Let me go."

Distantly, I hear Lake curse, and then he's next to me. "Easy, Riggs."

"He was hurting her," I grit out as the fucker in front of me begins to choke.

"I know," he says, setting a hand on my back. "Let him go. I'll make sure he's gone."

He's turning red, sputtering and coughing, digging his fingers into my arm.

It would be so easy to keep squeezing.

"Fuck," I grit out, releasing him and turning away, stalking to the opposite railing so I don't beat the fucker to a pulp. I look out to the darkness, trying to breathe easy and slow, clenching the snow-covered wood until I begin to feel the cold biting into my skin, until my temper begins to cool.

"Riggs?" Ella whispers, coming next to me, setting a tentative hand on my back.

"I'm fine."

"She's okay too," she whispers. "She's in the office with Nova, Lake and Leo have the asshole contained, and the cops are on their way."

I nod jerkily.

"She was saying no."

I sigh. "I'm fine."

"Honey." It's soft, but I hear it in her voice.

She expects me to shut her down, to push her away, to fuck up and drive her from me. To *leave*, even if it's just emotionally. And, I can't lie. I want to retreat. I don't want to talk about this shit—I fucking *don't*.

But I want her more.

So, just as she lifts her hand, as she starts to back away, I turn, snag her hand and draw her to me, burying my face in her throat, inhaling slow and steady until the scent of her is in my very soul. "I'm fine," I rasp. "I promise."

"You're not fine."

I grind my teeth together. "No," I admit. "I'm not."

"It's okay to not be…well, okay."

I laugh and it's broken. "You sure about that?"

She sighs, running her fingers over my head, through the strands on top, and along the shorn strip of hair at the back. "No," she eventually says. "But if it's not okay to not be okay…then what's the point of it all?"

"What do you mean?"

"Why have the good *and* the bad?" Her voice drops, her words almost contemplative, as though she's realizing this for herself for the first time too. "Why have the moments of joy and the deep, deep darkness that sometimes follows? Why not just exist, just plow forward day by day by fucking day without really living if we're going to make ourselves numb to all the rest of it?"

My heart starts pounding. "*Chérie.*"

"Why do it at all if we're going to bury everything and exist in…nothingness?"

I don't have an answer to that.

Because that's been my life.

Until her.

"I don't," I murmur. "I just know that when I'm with you, I feel *everything.*"

She inhales and her arms come tightly around me. "Honey," she whispers.

"I know."

I lift my head from her throat, stare out at the wide expanse of Lake Tahoe in front of us. The water is mostly black and navy, only a narrow strip illuminated by the bright, round moon overhead. But I can hear the waves hitting the shore repeatedly, the soft hoot of the owls in the nearby trees, the distant music from inside the bar.

And it settles me.

Settles me enough to realize that Ella's shivering next to me.

Shit.

I wrap an arm around her waist, draw her against my body. "We should go inside," I tell her.

A shake of her head. "I like it out here."

Something unlocks in my chest—or maybe it twists. Hard.

Because she's taking care of me.

Well, I'm going to do it right back.

"Come on, *chérie,*" I say, taking her hand, trying to draw her inside.

But she drags her feet, plants her palm in the center of my chest. "I *said,* I like it out here." Her smile is soft, beautiful—

Stubborn.

Mine.

Giving in for the moment, I draw her closer and say, "Tell me something no one else knows."

She stills, head tilting to the side, moonlight clinging to the ends of her lashes. "What do you mean?" she asks quietly.

"I mean," I say, smoothing back her hair, "I know the Ella who gives Knox a run for his money, and I know the Ella who's fiercely protective of the people she loves"—her body stiffens—"and I know the Ella who takes forty-two alarms to wake up in the morning unless I'm between your legs and tongue-fucking that gorgeous pussy of yours—"

She clamps a hand over my mouth, expression scandalized. *"Riggs!"*

I nip at her palm, peel her fingers free. "So, tell me something no one else knows."

I expect her to remain scandalized…

But as always, she surprises me—

"I've masturbated to the sound of your voice more times than I can count."

All the blood in my body rushes to my dick, and as much as I like that—fucking *love* it—that's not the answer I want.

"No, *chérie*," I murmur, drawing her even closer. "Tell me something that's not going to have me bending you over this railing and fucking you senseless."

A hand down my chest, mischief in her smile, her eyes. "That's not a deterrent, honey."

My dick is so fucking hard it's a miracle that I'm still upright, but I ignore the need burning through me. Something deep inside is telling me that I need to keep moving forward, need to own every part of her.

But I can see she's scared.

So…I can give her mine first.

"I have the first teddy bear my mom bought for me."

She freezes, and then she gives me a fucking gift. She smiles, her hand lifting to cup my cheek. "That's beautiful, honey." A beat. "What was she like?"

"I don't..." I sigh. "I don't remember. She died when I was young." I shake my head. "Sometimes I think I have flashes of her face, of her scent, but...I'm not sure. I don't know if it's my mind filling in the blanks, creating false memories, or if they're real."

Her expression gentles. "I hate skiing," she murmurs. "Even though I pretend to love it."

I grin. "I kind of got that when Knox said you'd rather hang in the lodge."

"The stink," she grumbles. "Giving away my secrets, trying to steal my matchmaking crown."

"He'll never win."

"Damn right, he won't."

Laughing, I kiss the top of her head, feeling her body tremble. We should go in, but I can't bring myself to end this moment.

"I have the cilantro tastes like soap gene," she whispers. "And I love Snickers bars."

More pieces of her.

More gifts.

I tuck them close, alongside the other precious pieces she's bestowed on me—they're a small part of the puzzle of Ella, hardly anything, but this woman is so fucking good at presenting the notion of being an open book while keeping everything important close to her chest that it feels like slamming home a game-winning goal in double overtime.

"What else?" I ask, even though I know I need to bring her inside, get her warm, let her spend time with her best friend and take her home before it gets too late.

"I used to want to be an astronaut."

That has me rocking back slightly on my heels in surprise. "Really?"

She shrugs, her cheeks a little pink and I know it's not from the cold. "It was before I realized I'd actually *have* to go to space, of course."

"Naturally."

"When Knox clued me in to that small detail, I realized I could appreciate the sky a lot better from down here." She glances up, studying the darkness overhead for a moment, and then points. "See there? That bright dot that looks like a big star near the horizon?"

"Yes," I murmur, running my fingers through the ends of her hair.

"That's Venus."

"Really?"

"And over there?" She points a bit to the side.

I nod. "That's…" She names a constellation I've never heard up. Then doesn't stop naming, guiding my eyes towards various spots in the sky, pointing out secrets I've never bothered to notice.

It's intoxicating listening to her talk, hearing the same excitement in her voice as when she talked about her clients the other morning.

Passion.

Joy.

Ella.

I'm so caught up in listening to her, in gathering the little secret pieces of her, that it takes me a long time to realize that she's shaking so hard her body is practically vibrating against mine, that her teeth are chattering and her hands are like ice when I capture them.

So, as much as I want to hear her go on, I call an end to this and nudge her toward the door. "Time to go inside, chérie."

She sighs but doesn't fight me.

Still, I don't miss that she hesitates as she reaches for the handle.

"What?" I ask quietly.

Long moments of silence.

Then she shakes her head and whispers, "Nothing."

I study her face. There's real fear there. Like she's content to share her childhood dreams…

But too scared to ask for what she really needs now.

That's okay.

I don't intend to make her ask.

"The night isn't going to end here, *chérie*," I say and then, because that makes her fear increase, I brush my lips over hers and add, "But I do need to get us inside because this patch on the back of my head is cold as shit."

She's motionless for one more second.

And then she's laughing, loud and bright and beautiful.

And I hold that close too.

Like the gift I know it is.

CHAPTER NINETEEN

Ella

I sit at my kitchen counter, staring at my phone and nibbling on my bottom lip. The Sierra have consistently been at the top of the league for the last few seasons—grinding out wins, making it to the playoffs (and often several rounds into the post-season), excelling as the team every other team hates to play against.

What they're *not* known for is getting blown out.

And the loss tonight was a blowout of epic proportions.

Losing eight to one against the Grizzlies—the newest expansion team in the league—is embarrassing.

At least that's what Knox said when I checked on him after the bench-clearing brawl that ended the game.

And ended with half of the guys bleeding.

Riggs had punched the guy that hit Knox but had taken a cheap shot to the back of the head for his trouble, one that sent him to his knees and the head trainer out onto the ice.

Knox says he's fine.

But Riggs hasn't replied to my texts…

And…fuck, is he okay?

Hence, the texting and the nibbling at my bottom lip and the drinking of a honey rosemary mule I had to make myself.

My phone buzzes and I lunge for it.

Then huff out a breath in disappointment when I see it's Nova texting.

> Lake's in a mood. Word of warning when dealing with a grumpy hockey player— enough hits to the head and they eventually come around.

I grin.

Mostly because Nova is pretty much the nicest person I've ever met—only Kit might be nicer—and I know she's never laid a hand on her hot, grumpy hockey hunk to hurt him.

Not to make him see reason.

Though, maybe the nail marks on his back might count.

Reasoning him right into an orgasm.

> Thanks for the advice, kid.

My phone buzzes almost immediately.

> Rude. Especially because you've been keeping mum about you and Riggs.

This isn't a lie.

I haven't meant to, exactly, and it's not like she didn't know I was into him. I just…well, I didn't share how much things have changed.

A blip of guilt blooms in my belly.

Because I know that I would be upset if the roles were reversed—I'd be pumping my best friend for information, not offering advice and a gentle reminder that friends share the important shit that goes on in their lives.

> Girls' night at my place tomorrow. You bring the stuff for mules and I'll cook you my world-famous lasagna.

> World famous because it comes from the freezer section and can be shoved straight into the oven, thus leaving plenty of time for us to gossip?

The guilt settles.

She's not mad, not my sweet friend who spent a lifetime holding things close to her chest.

> Damn right.

We exchange goodbyes, and I send her a plethora of bright red hearts because she's my bestie and I love her, and I *have* been keeping things too close to my chest. But if Riggs can be as strong as he is and share what he had…

I think I can share some of me too.

My phone buzzes again, and I expect it to be a series of increasingly more ridiculous emojis from Nova, but instead, my heart starts galloping in my chest.

Because the message is from Riggs.

> I'm fine, chérie.

I frown.

Just…*I'm fine?*

I wait for the "…" to appear, for him to elaborate on the fact that he was bleeding and motionless on the ice for far too fucking long before being escorted to the locker room by a trainer pressing a towel to his face, and all I get is he's *fine?*

Bullshit.

I jab at my phone screen, skipping straight over a phone call and diving right into FaceTime.

We haven't done this before.

But I know that I'm not going to rest easy, not until I see his face.

It rings that distinctive ring.

Once. Twice. And I half expect for him to let it go unanswered.

But just as I'm plotting my next move on how to ensure that the man is truly *fine* (even if it requires calling in my big brother), Riggs picks up.

"Oh, my glorious penis," I murmur.

"I was about to take a shower, *chérie*," he murmurs.

"This I know," I say. "Or *see*." My eyes slowly take in every inch—and there are a lot of them—that I can see of this man. I start with the hair that's fallen over his forehead, calling for my fingertips even through the screen. Then I'm moving my gaze over his sharp cheekbones, his proud nose. There's a cut beneath his right eye that has a butterfly bandage over it, presumably keeping it closed, that sends my pulse skittering. I don't like seeing him hurt. But I force myself to move past it, drifting my focus to the thick beard I want to run my fingers through, his lush mouth that brings so few words but so much pleasure.

The cords in his neck stand out sharply in relief, but he stays still as I study him through my phone screen.

Broad shoulders, cut arms, big hands. Pecs that are squeezable, abs that are flat and defined and totally lickable. Thighs—

God, his thighs.

They're powerful.

Like him. Like the draw he has over me.

Like the thick cock at half-mast between his legs.

"What'd you need, *chérie*?" he murmurs.

It takes me a second to tear my gaze from his ever-growing cock, I'm not even going to lie. "I wanted—"

He fists his cock, strokes once, twice, and I choke.

"Yeah, *chérie*?" he asks, his voice a rumble. "What did you want?"

To suck his cock deep, to feel the hot jets of him coming down my throat.

"*Ella.*"

I blink.

Focus.

"I was worried about you," I whisper. "You were hurt during the game and—"

He stills the hand that's wrapped tightly around his cock. "*Chérie.*"

Another blink, but this time, I manage to meet his deep brown eyes. "Yeah?"

"Thank you."

My heart rolls over in my chest. "Riggs—"

"Shh," he says. "Don't try to make this Queen Ella saves the day with her interference and giant heart. Just...let me enjoy the fact that you clearly give a shit about me instead of—"

My heart squeezes as I wait to hear the rest of that sentence.

"Instead of what?" I ask quietly when he doesn't finish it.

"Nothing," he says, moving toward the camera, picking it up from where he must have propped it, taking away my glorious view.

"Riggs—" I begin.

"What'd you do today?"

I study his face, debate pushing him for answers.

But...I don't think he's ready. So, I can be the one to share this time, even if it's only about something as innocuous as my day. "I worked. Watched the game." I lift my copper mug. "Had a mule while cursing the Grizzlies. Admired a penis I want to suck deep and then ride like I'm a cowgirl trying to tame a stallion."

"I'll get you the hat," he murmurs, leaning back against the wall, the shower running behind him, steam filling the room, blurring the edges of him on my screen.

I wink. "I think I'd look good in it."

"You look good in anything." A beat. "Or better yet, nothing at all."

I smile then sigh softly. "Will you tell me?"

"About the game?"

"I watched the game, honey," I say. "Though I'll listen if you want to break it down. I can even throw in a hockey term or a hundred if need be thanks to Knox's training." His expression gentles and I go for it. "I mean whatever happened between when you left a couple days ago and now to bring those shadows back out in your eyes."

CHAPTER TWENTY

Riggs

"I'M FINE," I say—

Or *start* to say, anyway, because her snort is loud enough to reach my ears even over the shower running in the background.

My skin is sticky from the steam, but I ignore it in lieu of talking with Ella.

One look from her and the dirty feeling leftover from the phone call, the one that had me wanting to stand under the stream of water and wash it all off—the failure, the frustration, the fear—is gone.

I would so much rather get lost in this woman than talk about the game.

About what came after.

"Riggs," she says, albeit gently. "I know that's bullshit, honey."

Unfortunately, she's too smart for her own good.

I prop my phone up again, ignore the words jabbing at my brain, and smile at her. "Maybe so," I admit. "But I've got my beautiful Ella's hungry eyes on me"—I wrap my hand around

my dick and it hardens further at the tiny hitch in her breath—
"and she wants to suck my cock."

Her flash of a wicked grin is like a gorgeous storm, like a fucking siren calling me to shore.

It would be terrifying if I hadn't already dived overboard, strong, sure strokes taking me right toward the rocks.

"I do want to suck your cock," she murmurs. "But, unfortunately, we need to be in the same room for that."

"Or you could get naked and we can get creative over video call," I proposition.

Her eyes sparkle, but she slowly shakes her head. "Baby," she says.

Just *baby*.

That's it.

But I hear the undertones in those four letters.

She's not going to let this go.

Dammit.

I open my mouth, but she beats me to the punch again. Only this time, it's in typical Ella form—surprising the shit out of me with the next words that come out of her mouth.

"I'm terrified."

"What's wrong?" I ask in a rush, heart clenching as I squint behind her, trying to see beyond the bright kitchen lights and into the darkness beyond. "Is someone there—"

"Not like that," she says softly, but evenly enough that the momentary panic fades and I'm able to focus on what she's saying and not some invisible threat behind her. "I...well, honey..." She winces. "Frankly, I thought this was going to be just hot sex for a few days, maybe for a few months, and then we'd go our separate ways."

The rebuttal rises up into the back of my throat—*mine*—but I don't let it escape.

And, thankfully, she keeps talking.

"But I think that was delusion speaking because it could

never just be that with you," she whispers. "With you, it's always been something more."

I pick up my phone again, trying to study her face on the tiny screen. "Why do you say that like it's a bad thing?"

"It's not," she murmurs, eyes sliding closed for a long moment. "It's just..."

I brace, holding perfectly still, knowing she's about to give me another precious piece of herself, another gift that is so fucking valuable, it's priceless.

"I never wanted that," she whispers.

I absorb the blow—and it's a fucking *blow*—trying desperately to figure out what that means and what I should do and what—

"Because part of me is scared that if I let you close...you'll leave."

The air that hits my bloodstream is heady, powerful, making me realize I was holding my breath for long enough for black to curl around the edges of my vision. "Why do you think that, *chérie*?"

A long pause, long enough for me to turn and wrench the handle of the shower off, to snag my boxer briefs from the floor and pull them on. I sink down onto the closed lid of the toilet and wait, watching her eyes close and open, her bottom lip tremble.

Hating that I'm here and not there.

Hating that I can't hold her.

Hating that she's in pain I can't take away.

"Because they always leave."

"Who?"

A delicate shrug. "Men." A shake of her head when I go to speak. "I've deliberately kept things casual, kept my distance, kept a careful wall between my heart and the men I date to make sure no one can get close enough to hurt me." A beat. "Because I can't risk it. Not again."

Dammit.

Her eyes are damp.

"*Chérie—*"

"But—" A breath. Her words steady because she's Ella fucking Adler and she's bright and brave and always keeps me on my toes. "But you've never just been another guy to me, Riggs. It's why…"

"Why it hurt you when I turned you down."

A nod.

Fuck.

Regret pools in my belly. "I didn't want to, *chérie*. I—"

"I know," she says. "I know now why—" A breath. "Same as I know there's something eating at you, something that's going to cling to my brain as I try to sleep, make me worry until you're home and I can hug you—"

"My dad." It just slips out.

Lie.

It's impossible to hold anything back from this woman.

She goes very, very still. Then her expression softens. "What happened?"

"He wasn't pleased about the loss and I didn't want to hear his bullshit tonight. We got into a fight and so shit was said on both sides that we can't take back and—" A throb starts in my temple just thinking about it. "And I'm so done with his bullshit."

Not good enough.

Not tonight, certainly.

Not ever.

"I shouldn't have answered," I tell her, moving out of the bathroom and climbing into bed, glad when she follows my unspoken lead, walking to her front door, checking the lock, and then heading upstairs and into her bedroom, perching on the side of her mattress. "It's not going to change. He's always going to be…"

"Your dad."

"Yeah. He's always going to be my dad, and despite it all, I love the old bastard." I sigh, scrub my hand over my face. "It was a shit game. And we got reamed from coach after the game for playing like shit. And there was that shit phone call." I shake my head. "It was just…a shit day all around."

"Until a gorgeous woman called, admired your penis, and reminded you how sexy you are." She waggles her brows.

"I think the first two happened," I say on a laugh. That she's on the phone with me, checking in on me, trying to make things better, that she gave me a little more of herself…

More fucking gifts.

I tuck them away, hold them close.

And make the deliberate choice to turn away from the heavy.

"Though, I'm not sure how sexy you'd find me if you knew that I had to huff the smelling salts tonight so I didn't pass out." I shake my head. "Hockey is fucking exhausting."

Her laugh is loud and bright.

"Now," I order. "Tell me about Donna's date with George."

Ella fist-pumps as she leans back against her pillows, gets cozy under the blankets. "I am the greatest matchmaker of them all. Even better than Knox," she adds before describing the moonlit trip on the gondola up the mountainside, the romantic dinner complete with candles and soft music that George had arranged. She sighs, clamps a hand to her chest. "If I wasn't afraid of heights, it would be pretty much perfect."

"My brave Ella wouldn't be felled by a gondola."

"You're right," she agrees on a yawn. "I would just shove that fear down and pretend to love it, just fake it until I make it, like I do every time I go skiing, and then reward myself with a drink at the top of the mountain to dull the adrenaline letdown."

The words are so light that they seem unimportant.

But I grasp them tight, commit them to memory.

Because they're a trifecta of puzzle pieces snapping into place—like I've found the final parts that form the edges of the picture and now the outline has shaped up and the rest of the inside will fill right in.

I turn them over in my head as she relates more about George and Donna's romantic date, as she relays her worries about Kit and his boyfriend, as we talk about everything and nothing and all the things in between.

But after her tenth or so yawn, I know I need to let her go. "Time for bed, *chérie*," I murmur.

Her heavy-lidded eyes fix on mine. "You'll call me if you can't sleep?"

I should be thinking *fuck no, I won't disturb your sleep*, but she'll see that, and she'll call me on it, and she won't let me off this call until I agree.

So, instead of lying…I give in.

A common occurrence with this woman.

But not something that bothers me.

Because…*mine.*

"I'll call if I need to," I say, "so long as you promise to do the same."

Her mouth quirks before her smile is broken up by yet another yawn. "Deal, honey."

And then I watch as she burrows beneath the covers and blows me a kiss before she disconnects.

CHAPTER TWENTY-ONE

Ella

COFFEE IS no match for waking up in a hot hockey player's arms.

Unfortunately, this morning I had to rely on my eight alarms, pure dint of character, and a gallon of caffeinated black brew in order to coax myself out of bed.

The game. The fight. His dad.

Damn.

I woke up a dozen times through the night, memories raking their claws through my mind. I hate that I understand what he's feeling, hate that we both have dads who can't be what we need.

And, even though I'd promised Riggs to call him if I couldn't sleep, I hadn't reached out and dialed during the fitful night. He needed the rest, needed the quiet, didn't need to talk me down from the countless dreams turned nightmares that had chased me through the night.

The pain on my mom's face. The screams. My fingers fumbling to call 9-1-1.

Knox at my side, both of us holding her hands.

The red and white flashing lights.

The feeling of her fingers slipping from mine as the paramedics loaded her on the gurney and into the back of the ambulance.

The stillness in her body when we'd finally been allowed to see her the next morning.

The empty kitchen. The empty master bedroom. The empty nursery. The empty house.

After…

Everything had been so damned empty.

I clench my teeth together and exhale sharply, deliberately pushing those memories away as I start to unlock the salon door.

Then freeze.

Because it's already unlocked.

Frowning, I turn the handle, seeing the lights are on and Kit is standing at the front desk with red-rimmed eyes. "Honey," I say, memories immediately the last thing on my mind. "What's wrong?"

He shakes his head, starts typing frantically at the keyboard. "Nothing," he says quickly. "I just wanted to come in early and get ahead of my stuff. Lyra is supposed to teach me how to do payroll today."

I lift my brows. "Is she giving you the pay raise that goes along with doing things like learning how to issue payroll?"

The salon doesn't have many direct employees—the stylists rent their stations—but we do have Kit and a few girls who take care of stocking supplies, cleaning, collecting dirty towels, and doing washes and blow dries as needed.

And Lyra.

Our absentee owner who loves to offload as much work as possible onto Kit who, as previously established, is a recovering people pleaser.

Recovering is a loose term.

Because, really, he should be the person with the sign: *X amount of days since people pleasing.*

Where X always equals zero.

Case in point?

He winces at my question and deliberately avoids giving an answer. "By the way," he says, "your nine o'clock called and canceled overnight. I ran the nonrefundable deposit and asked if your next client wanted to come in early."

This news doesn't make me happy.

Not what Kit did—he handled it perfectly.

But I could have slept in.

Or not slept, as it was.

I sigh, don't bite on the fact that Kit will go to bat for *me* when it comes to getting paid—but apparently not for himself, even when he does extra work—and I circle back to what drew me to the counter in the first place—

Those red-rimmed eyes.

"What did Patton do this time?" I ask quietly.

He freezes, his fingers poised above the keyboard. Then starts moving again, quickly and jerkily, belying his next words. "Nothing. Patton did nothing."

"Liar," I say, albeit gently.

"Ells—"

I touch his shoulder, strive for patience. "You don't have to talk to me about it, but I am really worried about you. You've been miserable more often than not lately." I sigh. "And nearly every time I see you lately, you two have been fighting."

He drops his chin to his chest, exhales shakily.

"We don't have to talk about it, but—" I hug him tightly, drop my voice to a whisper. "I'll be here when you're ready. And my couch is always open if you need a place to get away for a few days."

Another exhale, and then he turns in my arms, hugging me tightly in return. "You're a good friend."

"I love you, Kitty Kat."

"I love you too, Ellie Belly."

I grin then pull back, hitching my head for the door. "Since my nine o'clock flaked, how do you feel about eating our body weight in apple fritters?"

His mouth tips up. "I feel like this is a good plan."

———

SNORT!

"Ew!" I mutter, jumping back, my jeans now covered in Steve snot. I glare down at the tiny demon dog. "Thanks, butthead."

Nova's dog just pants up at me happily, having assumed a fully splat position on the concrete outside the cafe.

I'm on dog duty while Nova runs in for our lunch.

It's a beautiful day, albeit on the cold side. Then again, it's always on the cold side. Even in the summer, this high in the mountains is much more comfortable than the Bay Area where Knox and I used to live.

Plus, if it gets hot, we can just jump in snow-melt-filled lake.

Brisk is the right word.

"Woof!"

I glance down, wipe the snot off my pants, and shake my head at him. "I already gave you my last cookie, little terror. Don't even try the puppy dog eyes on me—" I grind my teeth together, trying to withstand the aforementioned puppy dog eyes...and failing. "All right," I grumble, reaching into my purse and pulling out my emergency Steve cookies. "Just *one* more. Nova says that the vet told her you're getting F-A-T."

He turns up the puppy dog eyes and whines.

I pass over a cookie. "Well, *I* didn't say it."

"Say what?"

I turn guiltily as Nova walks back over to me, a tray in her hands. "Nothing," I tell her, covering the innocent puglet's ears. "Just something a certain meanie head vet said."

My friend grins, passes me my sandwich and drink then leans back in her chair. "Okay, dish," she says.

"About what?" I ask, feigning innocence.

She swats at me.

"Shower Riggs is hot," I announce.

She grins. "I bet." She shakes her head, leaning back in the chair, expression sobering. "But, honey…"

"What?"

"This—dating, chatting on the phone, worrying about getting a man to confide in you, presumably confiding in him in return…"

My heart skips a beat. "I know."

"It's a big step for you."

"It is," I agree. "But…"

"He's different," she says.

"Yes."

"Different like what I have with Lake?"

Worry grips my insides—because he might leave me, because he says he won't, but…he still might, and—

I've let the man in far deeper than I've *ever* let in anyone, aside from Nova and Knox.

I haven't been vulnerable like this since—

That worry turns to terror, but I'm not a fucking weakling. I shove it down. I'm an Adler. I can handle this. I can handle anything. "Yes," I agree. "Like what you have with Lake."

Her face gentles and she takes my hand. "Then trust in that."

I close my eyes, exhale sharply, and open them again. "I'm trying to."

Her fingers squeeze mine. "And remember that it's okay to want something more than you think you deserve."

My heart rolls over in my chest as she gives me the words I once gave her. "Novs—"

"We can leave it there," she murmurs, slipping her hand from mine. "Just…don't forget the wise words of my best friend, okay? She's pretty damn smart."

"I think I rather agree—"

But I don't get to finish that thought because I catch a flash of movement behind Nova's shoulder…

And my world tips on its axis.

CHAPTER TWENTY-TWO

Riggs

THANKFULLY, our game against the Gold went better than the one against the Grizzlies—meaning that we managed to squeak out a win in a shootout instead of getting obliterated in regular time.

I jab at the button for my floor, waiting for the elevator's steel doors to slide closed, and ride the car up to the sixth story, where all of the team's rooms are located for tonight.

Tomorrow, we have one more game against the Southern California Vipers and then we'll be heading back up into the mountains.

Clear air instead of smog. Winding roads instead of multi-lane highways.

Ella instead of…a busty puck bunny one of my teammates is escorting down the hallway, disappearing into a room in the distance.

Shaking my head—because some things never change—I turn the other way, moving toward my own room, rounding the corner and—

Halting.

Because...

Some things *never* change.

"What the fuck are you idiots doing?" I ask, moving to where Lake is propped up against the wall, watching the shenanigans take place.

"Rookies," he says by way of explanation, and I get it then.

Get what Knox is spearheading.

"Storm," I mutter, spotting a familiar duffle bag on the end of the bed my idiot teammates have somehow moved out into the hallway.

The queen-sized bed. A pair of nightstands with lamps. The TV stand and television itself. An arm chair, floor lamp, and ottoman.

Jesus Christ, they've even brought a vase of flowers and the fucking bath mat.

"Yup," Lake says on a sigh as Bear carefully positions the floor lamp based on Knox's very specific instructions: "A little more to the left. A little more. No, a little *more*—"

Bear growls.

"Perfect," he announces wisely, spinning slowly as he takes stock of the hallway that now looks like one of the generic hotel rooms we're all staying in threw up in it. "Just perfect."

"This is why Leo offered to buy Storm and me a drink?" I ask Lake.

I knew that something was up—and that something was likely shenanigans—but I didn't expect *this*.

That a hotel room exploded in the hotel hallway.

Lake's mouth tips up slightly at the edges. "Gotta give the rookies their due."

"So long as my room isn't in the hallway," I mutter, "I fully support Knox's nonsense."

"Knox's Nonsense," my idiotic teammate in charge of this shit says, coming up and leaning against the wall on my other side, surveying his handiwork. "That should be the name of my prank show."

"Punked already existed a lifetime ago," Lake says.

"So, maybe I'll throw it out there on YouTube."

Lake lifts one shoulder, drops it. "People make a shit-ton of money on there."

"And none of *that* is telling me my shit isn't in the hall-way," I say, pinning him in place with a narrow-eyed stare.

Knox clamps his on my shoulder. "Your room is untouched," he says. "And only because you've gotten your head out of your ass about my sister."

I groan quietly, but Lake beats me to replying.

"You're the only motherfucker on the planet I know who's actively encouraging someone to fuck your sister."

Knox stiffens then exhales, shakes his head, waggling his finger at us. "Nice try, asshole," he mutters. "My sister is a virginal—" A smirk. "Or rather, Riggs here is the virgin—*ow!*" He clamps a hand to his arm, rubbing the spot I punched.

"Jesus," I mutter, shaking out my fist. "Fucker is a ball of muscle."

Lake shrugs again. "So much time in the gym, so little time to be an actual human being."

"Rude," Knox says. "Well, not about the muscles." He flexes, waggling his brows. "And your nonsense isn't true because I also spend a lot of time in the bedroom. *So* much time."

Lake groans, reaches over me to shove at his shoulder then pushes off the wall, turns for his room. "I've gotta get the fuck out of here." He brushes a finger over the shorn patch on the back of my head as the guys have begun to do—like I'm a fucking Buddha statue or a lucky rabbit's foot.

I smack him away. "Asshole."

"Night, Patches."

I narrow my eyes as he walks down the hall.

Knox sighs, drawing my focus. "My point was—"

"Oh, there's an actual point in all your rambling?"

"Shut the fuck up." He clamps a hand on my shoulder,

voice growing serious. "I know you"—his fingers tight—"and I know you'll treat my sister well."

There's the hint of a threat in his words.

Which I respect.

I have no plans to hurt Ella, but if it was *my* hypothetical sister that a teammate was sniffing around…

Yeah, threats would be made.

Even if I was responsible for them getting together in the first place.

"It's true," I say, knocking his hand from my shoulder. "Same as it's true that I care about your sister a whole fucking lot. So fucking much that you'll get to take credit for playing matchmaker for the rest of our lives." I push off the wall, turn in the direction of my room. "You can even give the wedding speech."

I look back, grin at his wide eyes.

God, there's nothing better than taking an Adler by surprise.

"I don't fuck around." I chuckle. "Not with women and meaningless sex." I lift my brows, hoping he might take a fucking hint and get his own bedroom in order. "And not when I've found someone I want to keep forever."

Those eyes are still wide.

Then he fist-pumps. "I fucking told you!" he says, practically bouncing on his toes in excitement. "Adler matchmaking at its finest."

He's not wrong.

Which is even worse.

Because I know I won't hear the end of it.

But I can't summon an ounce of outrage.

Ella's—

Mine.

Enough said.

The elevator dings from behind me and I glance over my shoulder in time to see Storm walk around the corner.

And skid to a halt in an almost comical fashion. "What the actual fuck?"

The guys start busting up.

Knox comes up behind me, slinging an arm around my shoulder, tilting his head down the hall for me to follow him to his room.

As Adlers are wont to do, I'm surprised.

There's food and beer and a video game console set up.

But I'm also not surprised.

Because Knox takes my phone—which has been buzzing with displeased texts and phone calls for the last couple of hours.

I haven't talked to my dad since our fight.

And he's made his displeasure very clear.

I was going to deal with it—with him—once I was alone in my room.

"Best of five," he mutters, tossing me a controller. "And then you're going to call my sister and tell her about the wedding plans—"

I snort as I recline back on the bed. "—you said you want me to look after your sister, right?"

Knox underhands me a beer and plunks down next to me. "She needs a handler."

"Well," I say, popping the top, "then don't do anything to fuck up that careful handling, yeah?"

He frowns.

I elaborate. "Your sister makes it hard enough to get close to her—"

Knox's gaze flies to mine.

"Yeah," he says softly. "She's really good at that."

"Well, I'm going to change that."

His mouth ticks up. "Never doubted it for a moment."

I smirk at him, but I'm still ready to change the subject.

Especially with my phone still buzzing on the dresser.

We play our best of five—Knox, the competitive fucker

taking three rounds of the first-person shooter game to my two —before I head out to check on my woman.

I call, expecting to hear her sexy voice pick up.

But it just rings and rings until it goes to voicemail.

Maybe she's still with Nova.

I shoot her a text.

> You awake, chérie? I was hoping to talk.

I wait five minutes. Ten. And I do it scrolling through my dad's messages, deleting the voicemails, less than thankful for the transcription feature to give me the context of them without hearing his sharp words.

…played like garbage.

Need to pull your weight before…

I hit the button to video call her.

Still no answer.

She's probably sleeping it off at Lake's place, her and Nova having indulged in one too many mules.

I'll catch her in the morning.

Sighing, I set my phone aside, push out of bed.

And then I go out into the hallway to help Storm move his shit back into his room.

CHAPTER TWENTY-THREE

Ella

Nova stares at me, brow furrowed in concern and I try to force my expression into an approximation of a smile.

This is fine.

Everything is fine.

The world is just…falling the fuck apart while I'm casually nibbling on a sandwich and trying to ignore the pug snot on my jeans.

While my dad is standing there with his replacement family.

A little girl on his shoulders, a boy clinging to his leg, a wife at his side.

It's Knox and me and my parents—only it's reflected in a morbidly wrong mirror.

Because my mom is gone. Because the man in that cruel likeness is long excised from my life.

Because the kids aren't Knox and me.

"Oh my God," Nova hisses, her wide eyes coming to mine. "Is that your *dad?*" Her aghast question channels the whirlwind of feelings in my belly.

I nod tightly, rasp, "Yeah."

Steve growls.

So does Nova. "Is he here to see you?"

"I-I don't think so." I haven't heard from him in…well, since his generic response to the birthday text I sent him last year—the same response as the previous year.

And the year before that.

And…the year before *that*.

> Happy Birthday, Dad. Hope you have a great day.

> Thanks, Daniela.

And that's it.

I close my eyes for a heartbeat, do my best to disappear into my chair—because it's either that or go over to my dad and his new wife and his happy family…and I can't even pretend that I'd survive that.

Not tough, impermeable Ella who's never met a problem she can't best.

And certainly not traumatized teenage Ella who's desperate for her dad, for any semblance of the way things were before.

"Breathe," Nova murmurs, her hand on mine again, fingers lacing tightly through mine. Her voice is quiet and even, reaching my ears even despite the noise of conversations and kids and traffic in the background. "In, two, three, four…out, two, three, four," she counts slowly.

I hang on to her words like the lifeline they are, desperate for any anchor in the sea of memories that are slamming through my brain like the relentless tide pounding against the shore.

"Daniela?"

My fingers clench on Nova's as my eyes shoot open and I see him standing there, surprise written into the lines of his face. He looks different now—somehow younger even though he's older, like creating this new family that doesn't include Knox and me has helped him shed the heavy weight of his trauma.

He dumped several hundred pounds of it, I suppose.

The little girl has blonde hair and blue eyes and she tilts her head as she studies me, a wide grin on her face. She's fucking cute and energetic, lifting her hand and waving it enthusiastically. "Hi," she says, entire body vibrating with exuberance, and—Jesus fucking Christ—but she has Knox's smile. "I'm Sophia."

"I'm Luke!" the boy, who appears to be a year or two older, says.

Steve snorts at my side, drawing Sophie's attention.

"It's a pug!" she shrieks, trying to climb down from my dad's shoulders.

Steve, no stranger to all manner of children fawning over him, promptly flops to his side, legs up, body primed for copious belly rubs. His tongue lolls out of his mouth, his little curled-up nub starts wagging.

"What do you say, sweetheart?" My dad's voice is gentle and laced with a parental indulgence that slices right through me.

"Can I pet your doggy?" she asks me, and God, her blue eyes are so much like my own.

Even if I could have spoken—which I can't because there's a knife currently lodged in my belly, slowly tearing upward—Steve isn't my dog.

I don't have the power to grant permission for belly rubs.

Thankfully, Nova, good friend that she is, recognizes I'm frozen. She squeezes my fingers one more time before slipping her hand from mine, pushing back her chair, and rounding the table, crouching down in front of Sophia and Luke. "Steve loves belly rubs," she says softly, showing them how to pet him gently. "Yup. Just like that. Nice job." She helps guide their little hands, supervising because I'm in no fucking shape to do so.

My gaze is on my dad.

My. *Dad*.

Who can't look at me—or can't be bothered to do so.

He's staring adoringly at his new kids…when a child—well, a child of his who's an adult, but still, his fucking *kid*—is sitting in front of him, desperate for the barest modicum of fucking acknowledgment.

"How are you, Daniela?"

I blink, tear my gaze from my dad, from him crouching next to Nova and asking *her* how she's doing, how work is treating *her*, what *she's* doing up in Tahoe.

Questions he should be asking *me*.

Answers he should already know.

I swallow hard and focus on Anne. On my dad's second wife.

That knife slices further.

"I'm fine," I say quietly.

I want to scream at Anne, want to ask her why she's made a whole other family with a man who abandoned his first one, but…Sophia and Luke.

They're innocent kids having a nice day.

I won't ruin that, even if the petty in me doesn't return the question, doesn't acknowledge her further, doesn't dive into a conversation about how Luke's elementary school teacher is or what Sophia might be learning in preschool. I don't ask if they're here for a weekend jaunt on the slopes or just getting away from the city for a couple of days.

I just…

Pick up my sandwich and start eating.

"No," Nova says, slanting a glance toward me, her pretty green eyes filled with concern, "I moved up here a few months back so I can be close to Ella and Knox and my boyfriend, Lake."

"Knox is here?"

I grind my teeth together.

His son is a professional hockey player—a fucking professional hockey player! It's a tiny sliver of the world's population who've been able to make it that far and he doesn't even know what team he's playing for?

"Yes," I grind out. "He plays for the Sierra and just signed an eight-year contract because he's one of their most consistent and highly productive players."

My dad's gaze comes to mine, but only for a heartbeat.

Then he looks back to Nova. "Right," he says softly and stands, glancing down at the kids. "Well, we have a reservation we need to get to."

That knife yanks upward, rending flesh, tearing through me, spilling all of my vulnerable insides.

"Bye, Steve!" Sophia says, scratching him one more time before my dad lifts her up and settles her on his shoulders again. "Bye!" she calls to me.

I wave, force a smile, then jerk slightly when I feel a little hand on my knee.

"Bye," Luke says.

I exhale, eyes stinging. "Bye, buddy."

Anne nods at me then takes Luke's hand and I can't help but watch as they walk away.

Not my life.

Not any longer.

"Ella—"

I stand so quickly that my chair almost tips over.

Luckily, I catch it before I can commit pugicide, righting it and grabbing my things. "I-uh—" A breath, voice steadying as I force myself to meet Nova's gaze. "I need to get back to the salon," I say. "I can't be late for Donna."

A lie because Donna isn't coming in today.

But Nova, nice person she is, doesn't call me on it. She just wraps up my sandwich and passes it over to me. "At least try to eat something when you feel up to it."

I nod, take the sandwich, but the moment I'm out of sight of her, I chuck it in a trash can.

And then I get in my car and I drive to the salon.

I make it through my appointments because I need the distraction, because Kit would know something is up if I canceled them and hid, and…

Because I know Nova will drive by the salon and look for my car, just to be sure I made it this far.

But the moment my last client leaves, I gather my things…

And I do my best to forget the shit show that's my life.

CHAPTER TWENTY-FOUR

Riggs

I PULL INTO HER DRIVEWAY, torn between worry and fury.

I've called. I've texted.

And I haven't received a single reply.

Only Kit answering the phone at the salon and telling me that she was alive and fine and up to her elbows in bleach kept me sane—or mostly sane, anyway.

Because my spidey sense is tingling and I know this isn't right and add in Nova texting me earlier, asking if I was going to Ella's place after the plane landed...

I'm defying the laws of physics to get here, speeding around corners, cutting through side streets, avoiding black ice like it's my fucking superpower.

Are you going to Ella's place?

I frowned, worry eating away at my insides.

Yes, why?

A pause long enough that I nearly ground my teeth down to nubs.

> I just think she could use someone to talk to —whether or not she actually agrees with that.

> WTF Nova. Tell me what happened.

> She's my best friend, Riggs. I love her and I'm worried about her, but unless she shares with you, I won't betray her confidence.

> You're playing with fire.

> Maybe. But as much as I love her, as much as I respect her privacy, I won't let her drown like so many other people in her life have.

> What the fuck does that mean?

But Nova stopped replying.

And now I'm rushing up Ella's driveway, heart pounding a million fucking miles per hour, trying desperately to stay calm as I wait for her to answer the doorbell I'm ringing repeatedly.

"Christ, *chérie*" I mutter, jabbing at it again. "What the fuck are you doing—?"

I don't get to finish the question because the door is swinging inward and my entire body is flooded with relief when I see her standing there in the entryway. She's wearing my T-shirt and it engulfs her body, hanging over lush curves, stopping just above her knees.

"Baby," I say, stepping toward her, plunking a hand on her belly and nudging her back enough for me to move inside, to close and lock the door. "What the fuck have you been playing at?"

Her brows furrows. "What do you mean?"

I frown, trying to pinpoint why that sounds wrong, why it *feels* wrong. "You haven't been answering my calls or texts."

A shrug before she whirls around, heads for the kitchen and my frown deepens when she pauses at the counter, lifts a bottle of vodka, and—

Pours.

That's what's off.

The hint of alcohol in the air. The slight waver in her gait. The glassiness in her eyes.

This isn't slightly tipsy Ella, hanging with Nova and having one too many mules. This is the sloppy Ella who tried to blow me in my car and propositioned me for one night—and one night only.

This is the Ella who made my skin crawl, who forcibly yanked those memories into the forefront of my mind.

Who's yanking them forward again now.

I grind my teeth together, push that down.

This isn't the Ella I've grown to know, the Ella I've grown to *love*.

This is wrong.

Something is *seriously* wrong.

So, I close my eyes, take a beat, and breathe. When I open them again and see her downing vodka from a coffee mug that says *Fresh out of fucks*, bile burns the back of my throat.

I move to her, snag the mug, and set it on the counter. "What are you doing, *chérie*?"

A shrug, her hand darting out to grab the cup.

I push it further away, draw her back against my chest. "What happened, baby?"

Her back arches, hips moving, ass rubbing against my crotch. I go hard in a second, even though some part of me feels sick at the thought of being turned on when she's like this, when this is all twisted and fucked up and tarnished.

I'm not ready.

And this isn't just tipsy.

This is *drowning*.

I clamp down the desire, the disgust, and focus on what's important.

"Nothing happened," she slurs, running a hand down my chest, my stomach, slipping fingers into the waistband of my sweats. "Nothing important anyway."

The alcohol on her breath burns my nose.

I catch her hand, even though part of me wants to let it continue moving south, wants to feel her fingers wrap around my dick, wants to fuck that hot, slick mouth, then that tight, wet cunt.

The rest of me…

Can't.

Especially when I say, "No, *chérie*," and she fights against my hold, fights to keep touching me.

To keep taking what I don't want to give.

Then it's not desire and need warring with conscience and worry.

It's keeping the past tucked away while dealing with the shit show of the present.

"No," I say again, tightening my hold. "Ella," I warn when she jerks her hand free, when she steps close and presses her body flush against mine.

It's fucking perfect—soft and warm and beautiful.

And it's fucking awful—drunk and not my Ella and laced with pain.

Mine *and* hers.

"Let's go to bed, baby," she says, lithe body undulating against mine, her hands tensing on my shoulders before one trails south again, nails biting into my chest, raking over my stomach. Her other slides up, scoring over my scalp.

I can fight her.

Or…I can let her win.

"Okay, *chérie*," I murmur.

Her smile is beautiful…and wrong. Especially, when she

snatches the mug before I can dump it out, draining it in a quick swallow.

"Jesus, Ella," I say, drawing her close again when she stumbles.

"You're sexy," she slurs.

"Yup." I scoop her up, hold her against my chest as I turn and carry her up the stairs. "Why are you drinking, *chérie*? What happened?"

She stills in my arms, and for one second her eyes clear. "I don't want to talk about it," she whispers. "It hurts."

Damn.

"Okay, baby," I tell her. "We don't have to talk about it right now."

She exhales and the glassiness returns, along with her wandering hands. "Good. Because I don't want to talk. I just want to fuck."

That's not happening.

But I'm trying to let her win—or at least *think* she's won.

"I want that too." Not a lie.

I just don't want it right now.

"But I've been traveling all day, *chérie*," I tell her. "I need to use the bathroom and then we can fuck, okay?"

"I have a bruise that needs to be kissed."

"Where?"

She lifts up the shirt, points between her legs.

Christ.

I tug her shirt down. "Later."

She pouts as I stop by the bed, as I lower her to the mattress.

"Just crawl under the blankets," I tell her, "and I'll be right back."

Her bottom lip pops out.

I can see the argument brewing on the tip of her tongue.

So, I do what I have to. I ignore the scent of booze, the way it shivers down my spine, and I kiss her, slow and deep and wet, kiss her until her eyes close and she melts back against the mattress.

Kiss her until she lets me draw the blankets up and over her.

Kiss her until her eyes droop…

And she falls soundly asleep.

Only *then* do I go get my bag from my car, clean up the kitchen, do my business in the bathroom.

I crawl into bed next to her, haul her back against my chest.

And, no closer to the truth, I let sleep take me under.

We can talk in the morning.

We *will* talk in the morning.

CHAPTER TWENTY-FIVE

Ella

"Thanks for siccing Riggs on me," I snap, shoving open the door and making Kit jump from where he's standing behind his desk at the salon.

Nova, arms crossed as she leans against the edge of the counter, scowls. "First of all, Miss Set-Me-Up-With-My-Brother's-Teammate-Without-Telling-Your-Best-Friend-About-Your-Machinations—"

"That's an absurdly long last name," I say, trying to distract her.

News flash—it doesn't work.

"Ha," she mutters, letting me know my attempt at a lame joke did nothing to veer her off course. "*I'm* your best friend. You saved me from drowning in a small, pathetic life and helped me find my place, my happiness. If you think I'm not going to do the same, with or without a side of stubborn, hot hockey player, you've lost your fucking mind."

"I'm fine," I lie. "I have a good thing going here. A good life." A beat. "Without Riggs."

He's too close.

They're *all* too close.

I need to retreat, need to build up my walls.

"You do have a good thing going," she agrees. "With us. With Riggs."

"I was wrong." I shrug. "He's nothing special."

"And you're a fucking liar."

"Nova," I begin.

She lifts her chin and marches to me, shoving a bag of apple fritters into my hand. I can smell the grease, the soft scent of the fruit, the spice of cinnamon, but for once, the vodka didn't sit right in my stomach and the idea of eating anything—even my favorite apple fritters—has bile burning in the back of my throat. Especially, when Nova's tone hardens and she says, "I never took you for a coward."

"Fuck you," I snap. "You know it's not that simple."

"Except it is, honey," she says, voice softening. "You want to be with him, you let him in. You let him *help*."

Yeah, and then what happens when he leaves?

I thought for a bit there that things might be different, but the fucking universe smacked me right back into reality.

He'll leave.

And one day—maybe even today because I fucked up so badly—he'll look at me like my dad does.

And…I can't take that.

It's why I slipped out of bed this morning before he woke up.

I had to go—*have* to go.

Before he does.

That burns through me and it takes everything for me to not turn and walk right out of this salon.

To *run* out.

But I'm an Adler. I'm stubborn as fuck. I'll make the tough call, take the damage, and I'll keep going.

Even if I'm about to cry, dammit.

"I have a client," I say, blinking rapidly as I turn for the break room, intending to stow away my purse and coat. "I need to get ready." Need to shore up some walls so that I don't feel like I'm going to fall apart, going to shatter into a million pieces with the wrong gust of wind.

Nova curses softly then blows out a breath. "Ella, honey, I'm not trying to be a pushy jerk—"

No. That's *my* job.

I start walking.

"It's just that you've spent the last couple of days shutting me out and I'm seriously worried about you."

"I'm fine."

She huffs out an unamused laugh as she draws up next to me. "Sure you are. That's why you've turned up here looking like you do."

Okay, now that's just rude.

"So I didn't have time to style my hair," I mutter.

Or do my makeup.

I *think*—strong emphasis on *think*—I brushed my teeth when I managed to peel myself out of bed sans eight million alarms because I didn't want to wake Riggs.

Didn't want to deal with knowing that I hurt him.

My eyes burn again, the nausea in my belly a hundred times worse as guilt eats away at my insides.

He opened up to me, made an effort to move beyond what happened to him, and…

I blew beyond all those boundaries.

Fucking pissed on them.

Because of my dad.

My heart squeezes.

No. Because of *me*.

I drank a bottle of vodka to numb my feelings then trod all over Riggs's.

"It's not your hair, sweets," Nova says quietly, moving closer, reaching for my cheek.

I skitter back and she freezes.

"It's *that*." She exhales. "Did you…did you at least talk to Riggs about it?"

"Like I said," I mutter, starting for the back room again. "I'm fine."

She sighs, shakes her head, and I have to appreciate her tenacity—even though I'm the one currently putting up with it—when she says, "Kit squeezed me in for a blow dry just before your lunch break. I'll bring grilled cheese and soup, you can give me a trim, and then I can help—"

Emotions are roiling in my belly and I can barely think straight. "I'm fine."

"It's done," she says on a shrug.

"Make it undone," I manage to grit out even though my head is spinning and I feel ready to collapse.

"No." She reaches for my arm, grips it tight.

"Stop, Nova."

Her fingers tighten and she steps closer. "Kit took the payment already and—"

Something in me snaps.

"*Kit* is an idiotic puppy who doesn't know how to say no and has no spine to speak of."

Crash.

I spin, breaking her hold, turning from her aghast expression and seeing Kit—my sweet, lovely *Kit*—standing just a couple of feet away, his pale face telling me that he heard me, heard the bullshit I was spewing that I clearly don't mean.

My anger fades.

My guilt boils over.

He heard the vitriol that proves I'm a shitty person.

That I'm—

"I need to go," he whispers, crouching and picking up the bottle of shampoo that exploded when he dropped it. "I'll get a towel and clean this up and then I need to go."

Fuck. Fuck. *Fuck!*

"Kit," I say, moving toward him, bending to help him clean

up the mess. "I'm sorry. I didn't mean it. I just…I'm really in a messed up place, and—"

He shifts away from me. "I need to go."

Fuck.

I reach for his hand, not surprised when he jerks it out of reach, when he slides back so I can't touch him.

I deserve that.

I deserve so much more than that.

"I'm sorry," I whisper. "I'm really, *really* sorry."

"I need to go," he says again.

Tears are flooding my vision as guilt slices through my middle over and over again. One burst of pain after another until I'm ready to beg the universe to intervene again, if only to help me feel nothing at all.

"Go," I tell him softly. "I'll clean this up. Just…do what you need to do."

He doesn't look at me when he nods, but I don't miss the tear sliding down his cheek, don't miss the way his shoulders have curled in on themselves, don't miss the ravaged expression when Nova takes his arm and guides him toward the door. "I'll drive you home," she murmurs, pausing on the threshold and looking over at me. "I'll be back," she says quietly.

I nod, but I'm already on my feet and heading for the storeroom.

Grabbing a towel and quickly disposing of the mess.

I ring up the bottle and pay for it, and then I spend the next fifteen minutes canceling and rebooking my clients, and somehow doing it with an even tone and plenty of apologies.

I manage to do all of that before Nova returns.

Which means that I'm able to make a clean getaway when I turn off my phone and leave the salon.

CHAPTER TWENTY-SIX

Riggs

THE LAST THING I want to be doing is stripping naked with a bunch of dudes.

If I had a nickel for as much dick as I've seen in my life—mine excluded—my retirement account would floweth over.

But that's the job, spending far too much time with other dudes, bonding over stupid shit, pulling stupid pranks, and then going to bed alone.

Or going to bed with someone but then *waking up* alone.

I went to the salon earlier, found it empty—no sign of Kit or Nova, though one of the stylists working had been nice enough to tell me she didn't have any clients booked for the day.

Something that would have been enough to make me worry even if I already hadn't been near panic because of last night's little shit show.

We were supposed to talk this morning.

But instead, I woke up with the sun flowing through the windows, my alarm suspiciously turned off, and the space beside me empty.

Then I spent the morning trying to track down a certain brown-haired beauty who was running from something.

From me?

From her past?

From something shitty that happened when I was gone?

I don't fucking know and that's killing me.

But she's not picking up my calls, not returning my texts. And she's not at her house or the salon or Lake and Nova's. She's not at the bar or on the patio, nor at the bakery or sandwich shop. She's not shopping at the base of the gondola—or not that I could see amongst the crush of people still enjoying the ski runs made possible by the Snowmaggedon a few months ago.

And then I had to pause my search.

Because of a bunch of dicks—literally and figuratively.

"My legs are fucking shot," Knox grumbles from next to me, towel knotted around his middle but split up this thigh, giving me a glimpse of his balls before I jerk my gaze away, grinding my teeth together.

See? Dicks.

I grunt.

Because my quads and hammies *are* on fire. Because Knox and I hit the gym after we crawled our asses off the ice.

We have a new offensive coach, which means working on implementing a new system. It's not game ready, yet, but Coach Joey—short for Josephine—is a perfectionist.

I'm excited.

She brings fresh blood and an enthusiasm for the game I haven't seen in years.

But our locker room isn't all camaraderie and sword fighting, crossing streams in the shower and pulling pranks on the rookies.

We have two main groups—Lake, Knox, me, Leo, Bear, Storm, and a few others form one. And the other...I look across the room, see them clapping shoulders and punching each other and generally acting like unfocused idiots—same as they behave on the ice.

We're winning—for the most part—so it hasn't created too much of a problem.

But…it's not great.

It's getting sloppy.

And I'm worried that we're going to get worse.

Plus, we haven't won a Cup, and we won't until they get their shit together.

Or maybe everything's fine and I'm in my own head because everything's fucked up with Ella.

I exhale, focus on Knox, who's still complaining about his legs.

"This was your workout," I remind him, pulling my underwear and pants on—see? Now I'm helping solve my dick problem.

"You got me there," Knox says, dropping the towel.

Jesus.

Dick problem once again.

Ignoring him—it—I pull on my tee and sweatshirt, sit down to tie my boots.

"So," he says as I get to work on my second lace.

I flick my eyes to his. "So what?"

"So," he drawls again, "are you going to tell me why you've spent the afternoon being *extra* growly and grumpy Riggs?"

I straighten and shrug. "I'm tired."

Not a lie. But not nearly the truth either.

"*Bzzt*." He shakes his head as he yanks on his pants. "Liar, liar pants on fire." He leans around me, pointing at Lake. "*That* man is grumpy. You're the steady and even, but quiet one of our trio."

I scowl.

He points at my forehead. "And to support my case, I present growly, grumpy frown lines."

Lake snorts from next to me.

"Hilarious," I grumble.

"I know I am." Knox collapses onto the bench next to me, sweats hanging low on his waist, expression light, but his eyes are serious.

And I know he puts on the effect of everything being a joke, but the fucker doesn't miss a thing.

"Now," he orders, "spill."

I *should* talk to him. Ella's his sister and he knows her better than anyone except maybe Nova. But something stops me from actually spilling my guts, from telling him what went down.

Maybe it was the look in her eyes, the sadness that bottle of vodka did nothing to hide.

Maybe it's fucking cowardice because divulging what went down means admitting to the shit that happened to me because who wouldn't want to have wild, drunken sex with the woman they've claimed as their own?

A man who worried that she might wake up in the morning and regret what happened.

Like I had all those years ago.

I clench my teeth together so tightly that pain shoots through my jaw.

A man who is weak, useless—

My phone buzzes and I yank it out of my pocket, nearly tearing the material in order to get a view of the screen.

So, imagine my disappointment when I see that it's not Ella calling.

It's my dad.

"And yeah," Lake mutters from next to me, "*that's* a normal reaction to a phone call."

I grit my teeth together again, ignoring the pain this time. "Fuck you."

"Fuck you right back," he says, shoving his feet into his boots.

A hand on my shoulder, clenching tight enough to leave bruises.

I look up at Knox.

"What'd you do?"

I *should* have done more. Shouldn't have slept. Should've blown off practice and tracked her down.

"I need to go," I mutter.

He doesn't release me, just squeezes tighter. "Riggs," he warns. "What did you do to my sister?"

"I didn't hurt her. I didn't do shit," I snap. "She was drinking when I came home last night, wouldn't talk about what's bothering her—" I sigh and admit, "I'm worried about her. She was drunk and wouldn't talk, so I put her to bed, intending to hash it out this morning, but she skipped out before we could talk about it." I rub a finger over the throb in my temple. "She cleared her schedule at the salon, wasn't at any of her normal spots and has avoided my calls and texts the last couple of days and Nova said—"

"What did Nova say?" Lake asked, rigid possession in his question.

"You don't know?"

He just lifts a brow.

"Nova said that she's worried too, but that it's Ella's story to tell."

A nod. "That's what Nova told me too."

"Fuck." I shove my phone in my pocket when it starts ringing again, my dad's fucking unrelenting. "I—"

Raucous laughter echoes through the room.

Christ.

Fucking idiots.

Knox's grip tightens further.

I rip his hand free. "I told you I didn't hurt—"

"Reading that loud and clear." He tilts his head to the door. "Let's go. I know where she is."

CHAPTER TWENTY-SEVEN

Ella

My head is pounding, but I force myself to hold still, to not reach for the bottle of aspirin in my purse.

I deserve the hurt.

I deserve the punishment.

I deserve—

"Enough," I whisper, forcing myself to focus on the lake, on the waves lapping against the shore and the sky changing colors in the distance. On the clouds drifting in, threatening to dump even more snow.

Good.

Bury me.

Give me frostbite.

Make me go numb so I don't have to feel what I'm feeling now.

God, Kit. And Riggs. And—

My dad.

Another tear escapes the confines of my lashes, drips down my cheek, the hot trail it leaves behind cooling almost instantly in the growing cold of evening.

I've cried too many tears today, and yet they show no sign of abating, of stopping.

Maybe I'll dehydrate one drop at a time, turn into a withered husk of a woman destined to become dust on this snow and sand-covered beach.

Not dramatic at all.

I dash my hand across my cheeks and exhale.

At some point, I'm going to have to woman up and walk back to my car.

But this is not that moment.

I bring my knees up to my chest, curl my arms around them, and I study the sky, watching as the first couple of stars begin to appear overhead. I want to get lost in the vastness of space, in the fact that it's so big when my life is so small.

But right now…all of this seems—

Huge. Awful and giant and overpowering and—

Huge.

I shake my head, eyes leaking again, distraction of the stars not enough to pull me out of my misery.

Especially when I hear footsteps crunching on the ground nearby.

Not wanting anyone to see me like this, I burrow deeper into my blanket, push myself further into my alcove, hoping the shadows will hide me.

But I know that's a false hope the moment I see him.

Knox unerringly heads for my spot, dropping down beside me and tossing a blanket around my shoulders. "How long have you been out here, kid?"

"Not long enough for you to locate and replace my Barbie Dream House you ruined," I quip.

Jokes.

Distraction.

Hide from the real problems at hand.

My brother just sighs, slings his arm around me, and I don't realize I'm shivering until he starts rubbing his hands up and down my arms. "I thought it was your EMT Barbie ambulance that I ruined."

Despite the knot in my stomach, I giggle. "Nope. It was my A-frame Dream House with a doorbell and elevator that you ruined."

"In fairness, Mr. Hoppyness loved his time in the Dream House."

"That he did," I admit. "At least before he chewed that hole in the floor and the whole thing collapsed."

Knox laughs, but only for a moment. Because then he's freezing, head cocked as though listening. Then he cups my jaw, tilts my head up, stares deep into my eyes. "Don't hate me," he murmurs.

I frown, then hear what he must have already clocked.

The crunching of more footsteps.

My gaze slides from my brother's, drifts over his shoulder, and—

I sigh and slump against him. "You've really done it now."

A hand on the back of my head, holding me tightly against him. "I already ordered your replacement A-frame Barbie Dream House, complete with a doorbell and elevator to make it up to you."

"*This* requires more payment than that."

"I know," he murmurs, kissing the top of my head. "It's why I got the ambulance too."

I want to laugh.

But I'm too sad, too guilty, too panicked—

"Ells."

My eyes go back to his.

"Dad doesn't fucking know what he's missing out on with you."

I shake my head. "You don't know what I did—"

"No," he agrees, "but I know *you*."

My heart squeezes.

"And you're beautiful." He touches my chest. "In here, kiddo."

"I messed up."

A kiss to my forehead. "And you'll fix it." Then he's extracting himself from around me, pushing up to his feet, and clapping…

Riggs on the shoulder.

"Be gentle on her," my brother murmurs.

I wince.

Because Riggs's face…

It's impenetrable and cold.

Already leaving me.

Maybe already gone.

He nods at Knox and my brother walks away and…

Then it's just Riggs and me.

"I'm sorry," I say before he can speak, goddamned eyes leaking all over the place again. "I'm so, so sorry. I—*I*—"

He drops down behind me, gathers me close, tucking the blanket around the front of me, warming my back with his chest. "Breathe, *chérie*. Just lean against me and breathe."

I *should* pull away. I'm a horrible jerk who doesn't deserve him being nice to me.

But I can't break out of his hold, can't make myself move away from the warm chest and the strong arms and the gentle words.

And Riggs doesn't make me.

He just holds me close, keeps me warm, and we sit like that, in a quiet embrace, as the sky turns into a beautiful mosaic of blues and oranges and pinks, as it begins to darken, as clouds from the west, from the Pacific, crawl their way up the Sierra Nevada to cling to our basin.

A dusting of snow is ahead.

But right now we're safe in the cool kiss of winter.

I keep waiting for him to speak, to press, to demand.

But…that's not Riggs.

This quiet, patient man is content to sit here in the cold with me, to watch the sky darken, to feel the temperature drop, to witness the stars overhead turning into beautiful, untouchable crystals in the sky.

"We used to do this, you know?" I find myself saying.

Silence for a long moment, and then Riggs tightens his arms around me. "Who's *we, chérie*?" he asks gently.

"My mom and dad and I," I whisper.

His draws me closer, wraps me even tighter in the warmth of him. "Tell me."

I close my eyes, remembering. "Knox was busy a lot with hockey, always traveling, always at the rink for games or practice, but sometimes my parents would wake me up when it was dark outside and we would climb onto the roof. My dad would wrap me in a big blanket and my mom would show me all of the constellations, telling me the stories behind them and —" I sigh. "My dad would always bring a thermos of hot chocolate with lots of marshmallows and a Snickers bar because that was my favorite." My eyes burn again. "We ate pretty healthy as a family. There weren't really any bad foods or things we couldn't have, but at night? After I'd brushed my teeth and we had dinner and dessert and Knox was in bed? That candy bar and cup of cocoa seemed like the most decadent of treats."

I haven't been able to eat one since.

Riggs smooths a hand over my head, gently running his fingers through my hair, but he doesn't say anything, doesn't interrupt, just lets me talk.

"When my mom was pregnant, we skipped the roof, but we'd still bundle up on the back porch and look at the stars and catch up on all of the things that were going on with me." I close my eyes. "It was my special time, and I didn't get a lot of that."

"*Chérie,*" he murmurs, brushing his lips over my jaw. "I'm sorry you didn't get that."

"I don't resent Knox," I say quickly, "and he would be the first to admit that him being so good at hockey meant that sometimes *my* stuff was a second thought."

"Baby," he murmurs.

"It wasn't his fault," I add. "When he was home, he was the best big brother ever and…after—" Tears blur my vision. "Well, he was there for me. He's always been there for me. And truly, I didn't need them as much. I've always liked being on my own, free to do my own thing—"

I pause as something occurs to me.

Another kiss to my jaw. "What?"

"I was just…I guess I was just wondering if I've always been independent and free because that's my personality…or if it's because of who I *had* to be. Because I only had those small moments of acknowledgment. Because I was alone so much." My nails bite into my palms. "Like maybe because my parents couldn't be what I needed the rest of the time, I had to…I don't know, figure out a way to be okay with the parts they *could* give me."

My heart is thudding at the realization, but I recognize something else, recognize that *he's* gone statue still.

I turn in his arms. "What, honey?"

An exhale that teases across my lips and then he touches my cheek. "I—" A shake of his head. "It's just that I know *exactly* what you're saying."

"Honey," I whisper. "I'm sorry that your dad wasn't—"

"I know you are." He turns my head so he can press his lips to mine. "You're pretty fucking smart, you know that, right?"

Finally, a glimmer of something that's not self-loathing or pity or worry or guilt curls through my stomach.

Seizing it, I blow on my knuckles, buff them on my shoulder, desperate to make him smile. "Yeah," I say lightly, "I *do* know that."

A chuckle. "Adler ego?"

I settle my forehead against his. "*Ella* ego."

His mouth curves.

But the lightness in my belly disappears the next instant.

Because he wasn't smiling last night.

Because I fucked up, and now he's here despite all the shit I pulled and—

Shame burns through me.

I drop my gaze to my lap.

His hand captures my chin, and he lifts my head, holding my eyes as he brushes his lips over mine.

"All right, *chérie*," he says and there's no teasing in his tone.

"I need you to tell me about it, baby. About *all* of it."

CHAPTER TWENTY-EIGHT

Riggs

I HATE that she's so obviously been crying.

I hate that we're sitting here in the cold when she's shivering.

I hate what happened last night and that I don't know how to fix the hurt in her eyes, can't take away the fragility in the way that she holds herself.

And I hate that I have to push this.

But…I need to.

We can't have another night like last night.

We can't move forward if she's going to shut me down and push me away and…use my trauma against me.

God, I hate how pathetic that sounds.

But—

I had to figure out a way to be okay with the parts they could give me.

I don't want to be like her parents, don't want to give her half of myself, don't want to hide—fuck, that's clear enough considering all I told her. And…if I ignore last night, she's treated me with care.

And if I don't…well, her face tells me enough. As much as I hate how things went down, it doesn't take a genius to see that she's ravaged by what she did last night.

"*Chérie*," I say, cupping her jaw. "I trusted *you*, baby. Trusted you with my deepest darkest secrets and now I need you to let me in, to talk to me, to trust *me*."

Silence for long enough that I'm almost certain she's going to bolt, but then she exhales and goes limp against me. "But I hurt you. I ruined things and—"

"We're going to work through that."

"How?"

"Because I hurt you first and you forgave me."

Her eyes slam closed and a tear slides down her cheek. "I'm scared," she whispers. "Because I like you too much. Because I'm falling for you and when you leave—"

My hands convulse, but she's still talking.

"When you leave me like he did, I don't know how I'll go on."

"Leave you like who?"

Silence for long enough to hear the whistle of the wind and the waves on the shore.

"Like my dad left me. I—" Her eyes close and then she exhales. "When my mom died, we were devastated because we didn't just lose her, but we lost our brother too, and we lost our dad, our family, every bit of stability that Knox and I had. The difference is he had hockey and he could escape there. I had Nova, but things weren't great for her either. We…*I* didn't want her to have to deal with my stuff too."

"So you held it close to your chest?"

"I was a teenager. I was hurting, but I was okay. I was surviving. I was finding a way to make our family whole again." She shudders. "And then my dad brought Anne home."

"Who's Anne?" I ask gently.

"My dad's new wife." A beat. "She can barely look at me,

not now and certainly not then. And neither can my dad." Ella's eyes come to mine. "Everyone says I look like my mom. I think…" She swallows hard. "I think that's why he left. Because I remind him too much of her. He has a new family now—two kids. Sophia's in kindergarten and Luke's in preschool. And—" A tear slips down her cheek. "I saw them outside Mack's."

The sandwich shop.

I still.

More tears are flowing. "They're fucking cute—his kids— and they were so good and polite with giving Steve belly rubs, and…my dad doesn't remember my birthday, didn't know I lived up here, didn't even know that Knox plays for the Sierra. It's like he slammed the door on the past and forgot about us." She's sobbing now, her body vibrating against mine, tears pouring down her cheeks, soaking into the collar of her jacket. "If *he* can do that, if the person who's supposed to love me unequivocally, love me more than anyone else on the planet can just leave me and make a new life, how in the hell is anyone supposed to love me enough to *stay?*"

And now we've come to it.

"*Chérie,*" I say and then stop.

Because how the fuck can I possibly assure her that I'm different?

That I love her enough to stick when her dad didn't?

That I won't just leave her behind and—

"You know why I like to play matchmaker?" she asks.

I shake my head as I use my sleeves to dry her tears. "No, *chérie.* I don't know."

"Because happy endings may not be for me," she whispers, "but I can make sure that the people I care about have them."

The wrench in my heart is intense enough that my lungs freeze, that I can't breathe, can't speak, can't move.

Then I manage to unstick.

I crush her against me, bury my face in her hair. "Christ, baby, I'm so sorry."

Pathetic and meaningless words that can't change anything.

"He's…" She drops her head more heavily against my shoulder. "There's nothing I can do to change it. I tried so hard. I really did," she adds in a rush, lifting her gaze to meet mine. Her eyes are earnest, as though desperate for me to believe her.

I've only known her a short time.

But I *know* what she's saying is true.

"So, I started drinking. Way before I was twenty-one. At first it was to see if he'd protest, if he'd snap out of it and become a parent again. But—" She dashes her hands over her cheeks. "He didn't seem to notice. And then I thought I could be like him, could use it to bond with him. If we sat on the porch next to each other, drinks in hand, he'd have to see me then." Her breath fogs in the cold, shuddering out of her. "Well, he didn't," she whispers. "And pretty soon, I was using it to numb my feelings. If I drank I could be fun, could forget, could be the Ella that everyone likes."

My heart convulses again. "*Chérie.*"

"But it's *never* enough," she admits. "It's a crutch. It's—" She drops her head again. "No, it's worse. It's a problem because it's hurting the people I—"

I brush back her hair from her face, tangle my fingers in the strands.

"It's hurting the people I care about. And it's hurting *you.*"

"I'm okay," I say. "And, *chérie*, this isn't normal. You had a shock and things went wrong—"

Her head pops up. "I *hurt* you."

I smile at her. "I'm a big, tough hockey player. I can take a blow and keep going, especially if it means that we're here now, doing this."

"Holding a crying woman in the cold?" She's going for light but fails miserably.

I tuck a strand of hair behind her ear. "I'm holding the woman I've loved from the first time I saw her smile as she trusts me with another precious piece of herself."

Her inhalation is so sharp it sounds fake.

And then she's crying again, burying her face in my throat.

But that's okay.

This is another type of trust, another gift from her to me.

My body is warm and my arms are strong.

I have tissues in my pocket and nowhere more important to be.

And…

I love her.

That's enough for now.

CHAPTER TWENTY-NINE

Ella

"Come on, *chérie*," Riggs says a minute, an hour, an eternity later.

He shifts and scoops me up in his arms, keeping the blanket around me as he starts carrying me down the beach.

"I can walk," I rasp, my throat so raw the words are barely distinguishable.

"I know you can," he murmurs, but he doesn't put me down, just continues holding me as he tromps through the sand and snow, making his way to the parking lot.

The closer one that was full when I parked earlier in the day.

"My car—"

"Knox took it home," he tells me, gaze coming down to my shocked one for a moment before focusing back on the path, carefully climbing the stairs that will take us to the lot. "My car's here, baby."

I see it now, the medium-sized SUV parked just a couple of spots away.

He approaches it without breaking pace, pulling the handle once to unlock the door, and then again to open it. "It's cold in here," he murmurs as he settles me on my seat, buckles me in, and then covers me with the blanket. "But it'll warm up fast, I promise."

I nod, even though I'm not feeling the cold, not really, not with the gentle way he held and carried me, the careful way he'd set me on the seat and buckled me in.

Fingers on my cheek, my jaw. "I'm here," he says softly.

My lungs inflate in a rush, hearing the rest of what he's left unsaid—that he loves me and that he's not going anywhere.

I want to believe that…but how can I?

"There's time yet," he murmurs, cupping my jaw, kissing my forehead. "We have a *lifetime* ahead of us for me to prove it to you."

I want that, perhaps more than I want my next breath.

And that has panic sinking its claws into my belly.

I shove it down, cover his hand when he begins to pull away from me, needing him to know that I really mean it when I say, "I'm so sorry about last night. And I promise you that will never happen again."

His big hand shifts, dipping into the strands of my hair, and he just holds me against him for a long moment. "Thank you for saying that, *chérie*," he rumbles.

One more moment being held by this man.

And then he's pulling back, rounding the hood, sitting in the driver's seat.

A press of a button and the engine turns on. Another and the heat is blasting. And then we're driving out of the parking lot, snowflakes hitting the windshield in tiny, fluffy flurries as we wind our way through the quiet roads and up into the hills surrounding the lake.

Not driving to my place.

But to his.

My pulse picks up as we pull into his driveway, pausing for a moment as the garage door rolls up. The snowfall is increasing, icy confetti swirling all around the outside of his SUV.

"Stay there," he orders quietly once we're inside, turning off the engine, popping open his door and coming around to tug mine wide.

The soft *shush* of the snow landing on the concrete behind us makes it seem like we're the only two people on the planet. "Let's go inside where it's warm, *chérie*," he says as he reaches over and unbuckles my seat belt, lifts me from the warm leather and into his arms.

He hits the button to close the garage and then pushes into the house, pausing only to stomp his boots on the thick rug just inside the door.

And suddenly... I'm fighting back a sudden surge of nerves.

I've been to Riggs's house before.

But this feels like something big.

Like he really isn't going to hold last night against me.

And I don't know if it's that or the long hours of the day closing in on me. I don't know if it's the stress of my dad and all the feelings that churned up. I don't know if it's the guilt for how I acted with Kit, the awful shit I said to everyone, or the drunken disrespect I so carelessly tossed at the man I've fallen for...

I just know that I'm suddenly exhausted.

I don't protest as he sets me on the edge of his mattress and disappears—hell, I hardly see his bedroom at all. White walls, one of which has a huge TV mounted on it, a couple of doors dotting the others.

And a big ass bed.

Normally, I'd bounce on the mattress, make a joke about checking the durability of the springs.

But…I just don't have it in me.

Especially when Riggs reappears and gently tugs the blanket from around me. It lands soundlessly on a chair tucked into the corner next to a floor lamp and small bookcase.

A tiny reading nook, I realize.

"Here, baby," he murmurs and I tear my gaze from the cozy space, from the small insight into what this man does in this room, to see him holding up a T-shirt.

He kneels in front of me, tugs off one boot and then the other, tossing them against the wall. The next moment, he's lifting me from the mattress enough to shimmy my pants down, sending them in the same direction as my shoes.

I shiver and he moves a little faster, unzipping my coat and pushing it down my arms, tugging my sweater and thermal I'm wearing beneath it free.

"This comfy to sleep in?"

A slow blink at his gorgeous eyes before I process where his fingers are brushing.

My bra.

Mutely, I shake my head, and a second later, he's opening the clasp, sliding the material off my torso, down my arms.

The cold barely hits me before he's covering me in a tee that smells like him.

Spice and man and *Riggs.*

I inhale and then again when he lifts me and tucks me beneath the covers. The cool bite of the sheets makes me shiver again, but not for long because he's crawling in behind me the next heartbeat, pulling the blankets over us, drawing me flush against his chest, and wrapping his warm, strong body around mine.

My eyelids droop again.

"Sleep, *chérie,*" he orders softly.

I shouldn't.

I need to keep apologizing.

I need to make it up to him.

I need to find a way to—

"*Sleep*, baby," he says, rubbing a hand lightly up and down my arm.

I need to—

But then I lose my battle with sleep.

And darkness pulls me under.

CHAPTER THIRTY

Riggs

"RIGGS," she moans softly.

I want to know every detail of what has her calling out my name in her dreams, what has her eyes moving beneath her eyelids, her lips parting on unsteady breaths, her ass pushing back and undulating against my cock.

"Riggs," she moans again.

Christ.

I tighten my arms around her curvy body, bury my face in her hair and inhale deeply. I don't know what magical shampoo she uses, but her hair always smells incredible.

And thankfully, holding her close seems to have calmed her.

She's motionless in my arms, her breathing evened out, slow and steady and calm.

I hold her while trying to plan what my next steps should be.

We have a game tonight and she likely has clients, but I can't just wake up and go on with my life like the last few days haven't happened.

Her father—*God*, I want to hunt him down and beat him to a pulp.

Which is illegal and would take me away from the woman I love, so is likely the wrong solution to the problem I'm pondering. So, I need to plan. I need to talk to Knox, need to be here for Ella, need to…

Take her pain away.

But, as much as I want to, I can't just make it disappear like a fucking magic trick.

"Riggs."

Not a moan.

I look down, see that her eyes are open.

"Morning, *chérie*."

Her lids slide closed, but not before I see another glimmer of guilt and pain and fear.

And I know I'm not going to get any further right now with this.

It'll just take time.

I smooth back her hair. "Think I can tempt you into making me some of those muffins from the other day?"

She went stiff when I first started speaking but then softens, her mouth tipping up. "One night at your house and you're already trying to get me in the kitchen?"

"Damn right," I murmur, lightly swatting her ass.

"Rude."

"I'll show you *rude*," I say, nudging her to her back, rolling on top of her.

She parts her legs, letting me in, allowing me to settle my pelvis against hers. Smooth skin, hot flesh, lapis eyes deepening to a deep Tahoe blue. "You can show me rude and naked and hard," she murmurs, running a hand down my chest—

And then freezing, guilt creeping back into her eyes.

Damn.

I take her hand, bring it back to my chest. "You've got to stop, baby."

An exhale, eyes sliding closed. "I can't. I keep thinking about what I did and what I said to Kit and—"

"What happened with Kit?"

She shakes her head, expression one of complete and utter misery. "You'll hate me as much as he does."

"Baby," I say, shifting us so she's cradled against my chest. "Tell me."

"I can't," she whispers.

"Kit is your friend. He cares about you. He knows that you're not perfect," I say softly. "You apologize. You accept that he might be upset for a while, but you're not the first person in the world to make a mistake and you love him, *chérie*. He'll come around."

She groans, drops her head against my shoulder. "I'm supposed to be the person who fixes everyone else's lives."

"Sucks to be the one needing the fixing, huh?"

Her head pops up, nose wrinkled adorably. "What do you know about needing to be fixed, Mr. Perfect? You're emotionally adjusted," she answers before I can remind her of my own heavy baggage and the memories that crop up at the worst possible times. "You don't fly off half-cocked and say and do terrible things. You don't—"

"I didn't push you away?" I counter, tilting her head up so that she has to look at me. "I didn't hurt you?"

"It's different."

"It's the *same, chérie*. We're human. We fuck up. We apologize, do our best to make it right, and then we move on."

"You make it sound easy."

I laugh. "It's fucking hard, baby. But my dad's lived his life in this cycle—hurting the people he cares, feeling guilty, then doing the whole damned thing again. The difference is that he never gets to the making it right part. He just skips right over that and moves on." I shake my head.

"Knox says your dad is an asshole."

Amusement bubbles up in my chest. "He is." I sigh. "But

then he has these moments where he's awesome, where he's my dad again—though they've come less and less frequently over the last few years."

He's completing his metamorphosis into grumpy old man.

"Ever since our fight, I haven't been able to bring myself to pick up the phone," I tell her. "Even before that, it was hard. I never knew if I was going to get the asshole or the dad I knew growing up."

"Honey," she whispers.

"It used to derail me—" I pause, laugh, but it's not one of amusement. "Hell, who am I kidding? It *still* derails me. Mostly because I think that I'm prepared for it, but I never am."

I see it then.

The softening, knowing that she knows I understand the whirlwind of emotions our shitty parents can churn up in us. "Riggs," she murmurs.

"I know."

All that she's feeling.

All that's in her heart.

"No," she says. "You don't. I..."

But she falters and I can't bring myself to leave her to struggle. "You'll make me muffins?" I ask hopefully.

She smiles, and it's another gift, another piece to hold close and safe. Her hand lifts to my cheek, fingers stroking through the strands of my beard to press against my skin. "Yeah, honey," she murmurs. "I'll make you muffins."

"Yes!" I fist-pump then wrap my arms around her and draw her to me, settling my forehead against hers. "Now," I order. "No more apologies. No more being hesitant to touch me."

A flare of emotion in those Tahoe blue eyes.

But...

She nods, relaxes against me, free hand lifting to rest above my heart.

We stay like that for a long moment.

And then she shifts enough to press her lips to mine.

And…

I fall in love with her again. With her courage and strength. With her big heart and emotions that are intense enough to take my breath away.

But mostly, I know that I've fallen in love with this imperfectly perfect woman.

And I'm never letting her go.

CHAPTER THIRTY-ONE

Ella

"WELL," I say on a sigh after surveying the contents of Riggs's pantry, "it's hard to make muffins without flour or sugar." I shift in front of his big, strong body, soaking in the feel of his strength caressing along the tips of my breasts, the fronts of my thighs before shifting to rest against my back as I peer into the fridge. "And butter," I add. "Or eggs."

"Sorry, *chérie*." He reaches past me and shuts the door, moving us to the side and pinning me against the counter, one hand on either side of my hips. I'm surrounded by him and it's fucking beautiful. "I was going to go grocery shopping when I got back from the road trip," he says. "But..."

He didn't get to that because I was being a giant jerk to everyone I care about and then hiding out.

Right.

Fun times.

"Enough," he mutters, but before I have the chance to ask him enough of what, he turns, sweeping me up into his arms and setting me on the kitchen counter. His lips seal over mine, tongue thrusting into my mouth, and then he's kissing me like I'm the source of his oxygen, his life, his future.

Only when he releases me, allows me to gasp in air, do I realize I've plastered myself against him, that my legs are around his waist and he's come over the top of me, pressing me back into granite.

Cold beneath me.

Hot on top of me.

Hard between my legs.

He smiles and it contains no little amount of wicked. "I think I have a better idea."

"Better than hot, straight-out-the-oven delicious apple cinnamon muffins?"

"Those taste good." He drops to his knees, presses a kiss to a bruise at the top of my thigh then rucks my T-shirt up to my waist. "But you'll taste better."

He pushes my legs wide, reaches for the gusset of my underwear—

And the doorbell rings.

"Ignore it," he says, slipping his finger under the elastic, brushing it over the slick heat of my pussy.

I shiver, propping my elbows under me, and the sight of him, mussed from sleep, burning need in his eyes, and positioned between my thighs is enough to nearly send me tipping into orgasm.

"Fuck yes," he rasps, clearly feeling the flood of my desire the sight of him there creates. He leans in and trails his tongue over me, licking from bottom to top in one sure stroke.

"God!" I cry when he sucks my clit without warning, making my hips buck and my elbows slip out from beneath me.

"Look at me, *chérie*," he murmurs, and I manage to lift up enough to see him smiling wolfishly at me, his beard coated with the evidence of my need for him. He presses a finger inside me, the blunt intrusion not nearly enough, especially when he leans in again and licks me, suckling at my clit, fucking me with his fingers.

I'm already hovering on the edge of completion, so close I can almost taste it, and when he slips another finger inside me, I moan loudly.

"This fucking cunt," he growls, nipping at my clit, sucking hard at a spot on my labia that is excruciatingly pleasurable. "I just want to spend the entirety of my life fucking it." He sucks again, shoves another finger in, and I start to shake. "With my fingers." A thrust of his hand. "With my tongue." He flicks it against that sensitive bundle of nerves. "With my cock."

"Riggs!" I moan, needing more, needing him inside me.

"I want to be in you too, *chérie*," he murmurs against me. "But I haven't gotten my fill of this pretty pink cunt yet."

"Oh fuck," I say as the peak of my orgasm hits, pleasure exploding through me. "Oh fuck, oh fuck, oh—"

"For fuck's sake!"

I freeze, body quivering, thighs around Riggs's head, underwear askew and his fingers and tongue fucking me.

I freeze not because of the mind-blowing orgasm he just laid on me, nor the pleasure still shivering through my body…

But because the voice isn't his.

And I know the moment that Riggs recognizes the same thing.

He launches to his feet, spinning around, his big body blocking me from view of whoever has come into the kitchen —not from the front door, but…

From the hallway that Riggs carried me through last night. The one that leads to the mudroom and…to the garage.

"What the actual fuck?" he snaps.

"Don't you dare talk to me like that, son."

My eyes go wide, so fucking wide I'm sort of surprised they aren't popping right out of my head.

Son?

As in…*son?*

"Jesus fucking Christ," Riggs snaps. "Turn around and I'll talk to you in a second."

"I said, don't you dare talk to me like—"

Riggs moves so fast that I gasp again, my eyes going wider as he shoves the man—his father?—out of the kitchen and down the hall. I catch a glimpse of a bulky form and a shock of white hair before they disappear from sight.

Voices lift, but I finally snap out of it enough to adjust my underwear, to hop down from the counter.

There I falter—should I go and intervene in the conversation…well, argument that's growing louder in the hallway? Or should I go put some clothes on?

I glance down at my bare legs, figure that pants should probably be my first priority, and hurry up the stairs.

Riggs's bedroom is a lesson in sunshine and warm masculine energy, but I don't have time to soak in all the details I missed last night and earlier this morning before he coaxed me out of bed and into the kitchen. I rush over to the dresser, yank out a pair of his sweats and tug them on, having to get creative with the tie around the waist in order to ensure they won't fall down.

Socks are next and just before I'm about to head back downstairs, I catch a glimpse of myself in the mirror on the far wall.

Rat's nest hair and smudged makeup and…nipples beading against the fabric of Riggs's T-shirt.

"Shit," I mutter, hurrying to the bathroom and doing my best to wipe off yesterday's makeup and tame my sex hair.

The nipples…

Well, I snag a sweatshirt from Riggs's closet, tugging it over my head and yanking it down to cover me.

I've gone from half naked to swimming in fabric.

Not the ideal way to meet my prospective father-in-law.

CHAPTER THIRTY-TWO

Riggs

It takes everything in me to not continue squeezing, to not choke the remaining years from my father.

"What the fuck are you doing here?" I grit out, forcing my hand to open, to release my hold on him.

My dad—my fucking dad who just barged into my kitchen while I was eating out my woman—shrugs like it's no big deal. "I rang the doorbell."

"And did I fucking answer it?" I snap. "Stay there," I order, turning my back on him and rounding the edge of the wall that leads into the kitchen. Ella's not sitting on the counter any longer, not a woman in the bliss of an orgasm, body equal parts tense and not as she shatters around me.

The space is empty.

A good thing considering that my dad is right behind me, not listening—which isn't a fucking surprise. The man listens about as well as a toddler intent on a different colored plate.

Which is to say, not at all.

I grind my teeth together and turn to face him, arms

crossed, mind and heart braced for whatever bullshit he's going to dish out.

"Help yourself," I mutter when he marches by me and opens the fridge, adding when he pulls out a beer, "It's nine in the fucking morning."

He slams the door shut. "It's like a fucking wasteland in there."

"We were planning on going to the grocery store."

His brows flick up, mouth curving into a smirk. "That didn't look like you were making a grocery list, son."

I hear a giggle, turn to see Ella clamp a hand over her mouth. She's put on my old college sweatshirt and a pair of sweats that dwarf her petite frame. "Sorry," she says, the word slightly muffled before she manages to peel her hand free and shakes herself. "Sorry," she says again. "I—" A helpless shrug. "I don't really know what the correct social response is for this situation."

Christ, she's funny.

And beautiful.

I move over to her, wrapping my arm around her waist and drawing her into my side. "I'm sorry, *chérie*," I say for her ears only. "I—"

"I liked your other outfit better."

Ella stiffens in my arms, but I only notice because I lose a bit of her softness, because her hand on my back clenches into a fist. "So did Riggs," she says mildly and I fucking *love* her for the mild warning that creeps into her next words. "*Before* you interrupted."

This is the Ella I first fell in love with.

The bright and fiery woman who fights for the people she cares about.

And right now, she's decided that person is me.

Aside from a few of my teammates, it's been years since I've had that. Years certainly since this cranky old fucker in front of me decided to stop acting like a real father. And the women I dated were just as bad, only out for what they wanted, what they needed. Even the coaching and training staff see me more as a commodity to be used to its full potential rather than a real person to be looked after.

And I get it.

That's the job. That's why I get paid the millions.

But still…it unlocks something inside me to have Ella on my side.

My dad just chuckles at her gentle rebuke, taking a long glug from the bottle of beer and leaning back against the counter. "So you're the reason that my son hasn't been taking my calls?"

"No," I say quietly. "I didn't want to talk to you."

She sucks in a breath.

Clink.

The bottle hits the counter, and my dad straightens. "You play better when I give you my pep talks."

"No," I say, not sure why I'm bothering to argue. He won't listen. He won't change. "I don't."

Ella exhales, hand sliding down to the back of my pants, fingers tucking into the waistband. "Why don't we all go get some breakfast and catch—"

"My son is a stubborn prick," my dad says instead of acknowledging her—or me, for that matter. "I suspect if you haven't learned that already, you'll learn it soon enough."

Ella's fingers tighten around the material. "Your *son* is an amazing and kind man who deserves the best this world has to offer."

My heart rolls over in my chest.

This woman.

I draw her around to my side, kiss the top of her head, then capture her chin between thumb and forefinger. "I fucking *love* you."

Her eyes go glassy, body softening against mine.

I see her love in those watery depths, even if she doesn't give voice to it.

I wouldn't want her to, not right now, not here with a grumpy audience.

But I don't stop her when she lifts her hand to my cheek, softly strokes her fingers through my beard, and rises on tiptoe to press her lips to mine.

My dad clears his throat before she pulls away, and I want to plant my fist in his face for interrupting, want to make him hurt like he's hurt me so often, make him feel something that isn't anger or bitterness.

And...I want my old dad back.

The one who's so rarely seen nowadays.

Ella sighs softly, shakes her head slightly.

Then she's dropping back onto her heels, turning to face my dad, her side resting a little more heavily against mine as she asks, "Who's up for apple fritters?"

CHAPTER THIRTY-THREE

Ella

"You sure you'll be okay?" I ask, body swaying forward to press against the strength of his.

He brushes his fingers over my cheek, ignoring his father practically vibrating with impatience behind me. "I'll be fine, *chérie.*"

We had apple fritters. We listened to his dad complain about the early flight and the cold air and the snow still on the ground. Oh, and the table was sticky, there wasn't enough glaze on his fritter (not possible, I practically get a cavity every time I eat one), and the sun peeking out from behind the clouds is too bright.

"I'm not sure I've seen a glimpse of the good side of your dad yet," I whisper as he turns to glare at a kid who's accidentally bumped into him.

Riggs sighs. "I'm not sure either." He leans in, brushes his lips over my forehead. "But every time I think he's gone permanently, my old dad makes a reappearance."

I resist the urge to narrow my eyes at Todd Ashford,

grumpy old man who I've yet to see anything positive from. Instead, I focus on what's important.

On Riggs.

"I can free up some time," I tell him. "Can have lunch with you and—"

His palm flattens against my cheek, tipping my head up, and he kisses me lightly. "I'm going to eat early, *chérie*, and then get a nap in before puck drop. He"—a tilt of his head over my shoulder toward Sir Grumps a lot—"can't argue with my game prep, so it'll give me a buffer before I head to the rink."

My heart squeezes at the pinched look on Riggs's face. "And then I'll swoop in with my charm, escort the old man to the game, and maybe we'll get a glimpse of something that *isn't* grumpy."

Riggs smiles and it's so fucking beautiful, it takes my breath away. "Don't hold your breath, baby. You can take the old, grumpy man to the ice rink, but you can't take the grumpy out of the old man."

I snort then exhale, dropping my forehead to his shoulder. "I don't like leaving you with him."

Fingers in my hair, lacing through the strands, pressing me lightly to him before he tugs lightly.

I lift my head.

"My Ella," he whispers. "I love you so much."

How this man, who I thought—in the months before I really knew him—was taciturn and closed down can raze me with just a few words, I don't know.

There's part of me that's still worried he might leave, might one day look at me like I'm unworthy, but...

I'm addicted.

I know that softness in front of me, have had the soft glow of it shined in my direction, and I won't be able to let it go.

Not until I'm forced to.

"Hey, Ella!"

I freeze, turn to see Donna, my first appointment of the day, coming up the walk in front of the salon. She stops next to us and looks Riggs up and down. "There's that hot hockey player again."

Riggs's cheeks go pink.

"How's the haircut?" she asks and I don't miss her eyes going wide, likely seeing the bald patch I'm responsible for.

"Fantastic," he says before I can come up with an excuse.

And Christ, I *like* this man.

My heart flutters, fear warring with those big feelings, but I step in, shore up my Adler spine, and save my man from further prodding. "What'd you bake up today?" I ask, nodding at the tin in her hands.

"Zucchini bread." She lifts the container. "Want a piece?" she asks Riggs, pulling off the lid and offering him a slice.

He takes the piece she all but thrusts at him and shoves it into his mouth whole. "Delicious," he says around the massive bite.

I grin at him then decide to put him out of his misery, lifting on tiptoe and kissing him lightly. "I'll see you later, honey," I murmur before I take Donna's arm and start drawing her toward the salon. "Bye, Todd-o-Rama," I call sweetly as we walk by Riggs's dad.

Realizing I know the grumpy old man, Donna starts to stop, to make another offering of zucchini bread, but I save us all the hassle by snagging a piece, thrusting it into his hands and ordering, "Enjoy."

Something I doubt is actually possible.

He grunts in reply but I don't delay, just toss him a jaunty wave and lead Donna up the stairs to the salon.

"Um," she says as we walk. "Who was that?"

"Riggs's dad."

"His *dad*?" Donna asks, brows shooting up. "That's a big step for my Ella who never sees a guy more than once."

There those nerves go again, twisting and twining and making my knees quiver. "Riggs is different," I tell her—and myself. Because I don't want him to be another guy—because he isn't. And because I'm not going to lie to myself and pretend otherwise. Yeah, I'm shaking in my boots because I care far more than I should, but…

The feelings are there.

I'm not going to be able to shut them off.

What else can I do but ride that Adler courage and see this through to the end?

"Yeah, sweetie," Donna says, resting her head against my shoulder for a second and sighing. "I had *different* once too." A beat. "Hold tight to him, okay?"

My heart squeezes and I don't like the sad in her voice. I want to see her giddy, want to see her smile again. So, I ask, "How was your date with George?"

Now it's Donna's turn for her cheeks to go pink.

"*Pooh,*" I tease lightly. "*I* may have a hot hockey player, but you have a hot silver fox."

She swats at me and we're both laughing as we walk into the salon, but my laughter stoppers up in the back of my throat when I see Kit standing at the front desk, holding court in his domain…

And doing it while looking like shit.

Pale skin. Dark circles. Puffy eyes.

I freeze, barely hearing Donna as she continues talking.

My eyes are on my friend. On another person I hurt because I'm so fucked up inside that I—

A pat on my hand draws my attention from Kit. "I'm going to pass these out," Donna says softly, holding up the tin and disappearing further into the salon, though not before leaving a slice on top of a napkin on Kit's desk. Voices lift and exclamations about the deliciousness of her yummy baked goods reach my ears, but I just stand there like a lump, struggling with what to say, how to make it right.

Then I know there's not anything that will make this easier.

So…I start with what I owe him most.

"I'm so sorry."

His shoulders hitch up around his ears, and I wait there in front of the desk, my feet all but glued to the floor, hoping that he'll lift his head and look at me.

He doesn't, not for a long moment, not for long enough that the guilt starts tearing through my insides again.

Then he does, his eyes finally coming to mine.

Cold and unyielding and everything I deserve.

"I'm so sorry," I say again. "I—" I shake my head. "Some bad stuff went down, my head wasn't right, and I took it out on you." I take a step forward, reach out to take his hand, freezing, my heart wrenching when he jerks out of reach. "I'm sorry. I know it's not enough and you're not under any obligation to forgive me—"

He snorts, looks at the computer, unceremoniously dismissing me.

And…I don't blame him.

"—but you're my friend and I was a jerk and I *am* really, truly sorry."

I wait for him to say something, to look at me again.

Instead, he just keeps his focus on the computer screen and I hear clicking as he starts typing.

Right.

I've apologized. I know I can't push this further.

"I'll see you later," I murmur and then I go to my station and give Donna the best blowout she's ever had.

After that it's a blur of one client after another, my schedule doubly packed because I've slotted in several clients that I rescheduled from yesterday, but when I finally get a break and head to the front of the salon, running through the possibilities of what I can say or do or how many apple fritters I can buy him to smooth things over…

Kit's gone.

CHAPTER THIRTY-FOUR

Riggs

"Got a live one on the hook," my dad mutters as we walk back to my car.

It's sunny and beautiful for the moment, but I can already see the clouds thickening as they climb over the Sierras to the west. Soon enough the sky will darken and the gorgeous day will be ruined. Already, there's a chill in the air.

And if that's not a fucking allegory to the shitstorm of my morning so far, then I don't know what is.

"I love her," I say without preamble.

My dad's brows shoot up, but I just keep walking, bleeping the locks and climbing in the driver's seat of my SUV.

His door opens after a second and then he's sitting next to me. "Son," he begins.

"Don't," I mutter, jabbing at the button to start the ignition. "I put up with your shit because you're my dad, but if you say anything about Ella, I'm going to send you fucking packing."

He huffs, crosses his arms. "I'm just saying, I don't think you need the distraction."

"Sometimes having something to focus on besides hockey evens out the ups and downs."

"Professional athletes can't afford to have ups and downs." He slants a look in my direction and I see the familiar scowl on his face out of the corner of my eye—the one that precedes a lecture. "Especially, ones who are overpaid like you. If you want to see the full life of your contract—"

"I need to pull my weight," I say. "I fucking know."

"I'm just saying—"

"You know what makes me play like shit, Dad?" I ask, whipping my head in his direction, matching his scowl with one of my own. "You *really* want to know?"

He rolls his eyes, turns his stare out the window.

"Being kicked when I'm down," I growl. "Hearing ninety-nine negative things to every vaguely positive statement. To never have my own dad on my side, never taking my back, never reminding me that life—including hockey—has good days and bad days."

"You're out of line, son."

"No," I say, "you're just used to me *toeing* the line." But seeing Ella's face last night, hearing the shit her dad pulled and how deeply it hurt her, feeling that same wound pulse inside me has loosened my tongue. "I'm not going to do it anymore. I'm not going to listen to you shit on me or take your phone calls or reply to the asshole texts. It doesn't help me with hockey and it sure as shit is not good for my mental health."

Silence for long enough that my anger banks slightly, that a blip of hope flickers to life in my belly.

Maybe this time he'll listen.

Maybe this time it will be different.

Maybe this time he'll actually hear me.

"You're not seriously going to start talking about this mental health woo-woo bullshit now, are you?"

I grind my teeth together, bite back a reply—because what

good will it do?—and grip the steering wheel tightly as I navigate out of downtown proper and start winding my way up to my house.

"Now," my dad goes on, like I'm not anything more than a robot to program, a virtual player in a video game to tweak and modify and mold to be exactly what he wants. "With this new system Coach is running, you need to be quicker on the breakout—"

I roll my eyes.

Always the fucking breakout.

"Then clean up your play through the neutral zone," he says. "You're not connecting your passes like you should."

I flick my gaze at the clock, weigh the likelihood of driving off the highway and putting us both out of our misery in the cold Tahoe water.

Unfortunately, that won't keep Tahoe blue, will it?

Thinking about the often-sported bumper sticker in this area steadies me enough to ignore his droning.

Mostly because the water I'm getting glimpses of as I drive by reminds me of the blue of Ella's eyes.

"…and if you do that, then you'll play better…"

I don't reply.

But, of course, he can't take a hint.

"Did you hear me?" he asks.

"I hear you," I say. "But I'm not discussing this."

"Son, I've watched you play for more than twenty years. I know what you need—"

I flick my gaze at him. "Do you really think so?"

Because I've told him *exactly* what I need—or *don't* need, anyway.

"I sure as shit do," he says. "You need to work harder. You need to spend more time in the gym and focus your game play on the breakout and in the neutral zone. You need to feed the puck to Lake because he's the team's leading scorer—"

"And I'm right behind him, you realize that, right?"

Despite what my dad thinks, my last few seasons have been the best of my career—it's why I got the pay bump, why I'm on the top line, why I'm the second leading scorer on the team, and why the Sierra are at the top of the Pacific division (even though we're in a neck-to-neck fight with the Eagles to keep that spot).

"Lake is the man with the finishing skills," he says, "and add in Knox to clean up the traffic in front, and those two are going to keep the team moving up in the rankings."

But not me.

Apparently, *I* have nothing to do with that.

I turn into my neighborhood, the truth settling heavy on my heart.

Apparently, my dad isn't going to hear me. Not now. Not *ever*.

"I'm going to drop you off and then I'm going out."

Another scowl. "Where?"

I shrug. "I've got pregame shit to do."

He opens his mouth then clamps it closed, not pushing me for once.

Sort of.

Because the next question out of his mouth shows off exactly how much gall the old bastard has.

"Are you still getting the ticket for me later?"

I take a right onto my street.

I should tell him to fuck off.

Should flip a U-turn and drop his ass at the airport—or hell, on the side of the road—and never look back.

But…

God, I'm a fucking pussy.

This is the person who raised me, who took me to practice, who made sure I was clothed and housed and safe.

This is my *dad*, for better or worse.

So, yeah, I *should* turn my back on the old bastard.

But I find…I can't.

I don't stop. I just keep going, pull into the driveway, park in the garage, then sigh as I hit the button to unlock the passenger side door. "It'll be in your account."

He gets out, slams the metal panel shut behind him.

(All without a thank you, a goodbye, or a see you later).

I watch as he strolls into my house like he owns the fucking place then reverse out and hit the button to close the garage door.

And then, head pounding, I drive to Ella's.

I won't bug her at work, especially since I know she has a full day, but I'm not above taking a nap in sheets that smell like her—or eating some of the muffins she has on her counter when I wake up.

They're a few days old, but they're still fucking delicious.

In fact, they're so delicious that I steal one for the drive to the rink as my pregame snack.

CHAPTER THIRTY-FIVE

Ella

"Fourteen dollars for a beer is an absolute crime," Todd grumbles as we make our way down the long flight of concrete stairs.

"Our seats are in row ten," I say, ignoring his grumbling.

Riggs got us club-level seats, which means that fourteen-dollar beer could have been directly delivered to our seats (and I bet Riggs already covered the cost for the night...even though his dad doesn't deserve the courtesy).

"Row *ten*," he sniffs.

I roll my eyes. "It's my favorite place to sit."

He pauses mid-step, glances over at me, eyes and tone sharp when he asks, "Why?"

"It's high enough up to be able to see all of the ice, but still close enough to hear and keep track of the small plays."

He starts walking again. "Like what?"

I shrug, keep my pace beside him. "Digging the puck out along the boards, finishing checks, who's screening who in front of the net." I shrug. "All of the things that make a game a game, aside from scoring, of course." I nod at the row, start making our way over to our seats. "Which you can see well from here also."

Todd follows me across the row, sitting down in the seat next to me with a grunt. "Maybe," he says, eyes on the ice. The overhead lights are slowly brightening as the maintenance crew finishes setting the nets, getting the rink ready for warm-ups.

"It's dark in here," he grumbles.

"It'll be bright soon enough."

A grunt as he takes a sip of his beer. "Ugh."

I lift an eyebrow.

"All foam," he mutters.

I roll my eyes, settle in and enjoy *my* fourteen-dollar beer. That's not all foam.

He sighs.

"What?" I ask, amused as I wonder what his next complaint will be.

"Just wondering if Riggs is going to pull his weight tonight."

That sends my brows shooting up almost to my hairline. "Excuse me?" I ask setting my beer in the cupholder and shifting in my seat to stare at Todd.

"Lake and Knox are producing. They're top forwards in the league." He shakes his head and takes a sip of the beer, apparently tasty enough now that he's complaining about something else. "I keep telling Riggs that he needs to step up. He needs to work as hard as your brother does."

"Have you watched *any* of the games this season?"

Todd scowls. "Of course I have."

"And did you miss the part where Riggs is the second leading scorer on the team?" I flick my eyebrows up again. "Even higher than my hardworking brother?"

"I—"

"You do realize the hours Riggs puts in right? The extra time and workouts?"

"It's not enough," Todd snaps. "He's not a good outlet on the breakout and his passes are shit and—"

I sigh. "And you like to point out everything that goes wrong instead of any of the good things. You like to tear him down instead of zeroing in on the parts that will build him up, will build on each other and make him play better."

"This isn't a kids' sports team where everyone gets a participation trophy."

"No," I agree. "It's just what your son has chosen to make of his life, and I don't discount that likely he's made it this far because you helped him a lot along the way. But here's the thing, Todd-o-Rama, your brand of *help*"—I hold his eyes—"it's not something that Riggs is going to keep around forever. He's tired and sad and *hurt*, and sooner or later you're going to cut too deep, create a wound that won't be able to heal"—my dad's face flashes through my mind—"and when that happens, you'll lose him forever."

"Excuse—"

"You have a chance to do better." I lean back in my seat, lift my beer toward him in salute. "So make sure you don't squander it."

He opens his mouth. Closes it.

Then scowls again. "What are you?" he mutters. "A fucking fortune cookie?"

"Nope," I tell him cheerfully, "just a woman with a dad who's not in my life." I sip my beer, the cool liquid soothing the burn that truth elicits.

"Why isn't—"

"Ella!"

I crane my neck to the left and see Evie waving at me, her shock of red hair so bright it's almost fluorescent.

Saved by the child.

"I'll be right back, Todd-o-Rama."

"Who's that?"

"Evie," I wave back and push to my feet. "She's the daughter of the Sierra's trainer, Ivy."

Ivy is…well, I've only met her a handful of times in person since she's a single mom who's busy with her job and her kiddo, but she's…scary.

And coming from me?

That's fucking *scary*.

Evie, on the other hand, is a bright spot of sweet exuberance.

"A woman as a trainer," Todd sniffs. "The world nowadays doesn't make any sense. Now, even though you're far too outspoken, at least you do something that befits the female race."

I freeze, rage skating down my spine.

But when I look at him, I see it in his eyes.

He's fucking with me.

I pat his arm. "Nice try, Todd-o-Rama," I say. "But you know as well as I do that men can make excellent hairstylists too."

He grins, and shaking my head I leave him, I cross the rest of the way through the row and make my way down to Evie. "Hey, good lookin'," I say, smoothing a hand over her hair and immediately getting to work with the part. "The same as usual?" I ask.

Wide brown eyes, so much like her mom's, come to mine. "Can you do two braids today?"

"Sure thing, Evie girl," I say, pulling a couple of hair ties out of my pocket (because what kind of hairstylist would I be without extra hair ties on hand at all times). I make quick work of her hair, plaiting it into two pigtails and securing the ends, and then because I'm me and I knew that Evie would be here tonight, I reach into my jacket and extract the bows I ordered for her.

Navy, forest green, and Tahoe blue, they're accented with plenty of sparkles.

"Whoa," she whispers.

"They're epic, right?"

She grins. "Totally epic! Can I have glitter too?"

"What's the world without glitter?"

"Boring!" she declared, making me laugh.

"Exactly," I tell her, spraying a bit in her hair before capping the container.

"Can you do mine next?" a little boy with shoulder-length locks asks.

"If your grown-up says it's okay."

"Dad?" he calls. "Can I get my hair braided?"

The handsome man sporting a Sierra jersey a row back smiles. "If it's okay with the nice lady."

"Two or one braid?" I ask.

"Two!"

"Done." I set to work, corralling the kiddo's hair into two sleek braids. "I don't have any bows though."

"That's okay," he says, wiggling with excitement as I finish the second one.

"Glitter?"

An eager nod.

Sparkles placed, we fist-bump and then he's running off to show his dad.

"Braids? Me?" a girl who's maybe four and adorable in her tiny Sierra jersey asks.

I find the grown-up who belongs to her and she nods, and then I'm the braid master—pigtails for the little girl in front of me and then shifting course to wrangle tiny ones into a boy's short hair before I secure his sister's longer locks into a single plait that hangs down her back.

I've just run out of hair ties—oh the humanity—when I hear—

Tap. Tap. Tap.

I look up, see that the guys have come out onto the ice. Knox is running through his usual routine near the bench,

Lake is stretching while the ladies drool on, and Riggs—my heart flutters, absolutely fucking *flutters* in my chest—is right in front of me.

He holds up a puck, and the flutters go again.

But I shake my head and point to the kids around me.

His mouth twitches, but he bends and grabs a different puck, tossing it up and over the boards, and then repeating the same until the kids all around us have them.

"You're going to run out," I mouth.

He just winks, holds one last puck up, and mouths, "Yours."

I inhale, look around as though that will calm the nerves, and when it doesn't, I embrace the inevitable and hold out my hands for the puck.

He tosses it over the glass, and it lands unerringly in my palms with a quiet *smack*.

I pretend like I'm going to shove it in my pocket—

Tap. Tap. Tap.

Lips twitching, I meet his gaze through the glass, watch as he mimes looking down at an invisible puck in his gloved hand.

Mischief brewing, I glance down at the puck in my hand then back up and shrug.

He rolls his eyes, repeats the movement.

I hold up my hand, show him the puck in my palm.

I've positioned it with the Sierra logo facing up, hiding whatever spicy message my man has no doubt written on it.

Another *tap, tap, tap.*

He flips over the invisible puck in his hand.

"I think Mr. Riggs wants you to turn the puck over," Evie whispers—or tries to, anyway, because whispering in kids her age always ends up sounding like shouting.

"You may be right, Evie girl," I tease lightly.

Tap. Tap. TAP.

I widen my eyes at Riggs, but he just mimes flipping the puck over again.

And so, rolling *my* eyes, I mirror his actions, flipping the real puck over in my hand, greedily devouring the words on the black, vulcanized rubber, pulse picking up, knees almost giving way.

Because Riggs Ashford—*my* Riggs Ashford, had written *that?*

CHAPTER THIRTY-SIX

Riggs

"You the reason Ella's got a smile on her face today?" Knox asks.

I snag my water bottle, take a small sip so my stomach won't be overloaded and make me feel like shit out on the ice.

Nothing like trying to hockey with a bunch of liquid sloshing around in there.

"Would there be *another* reason?" I say when I drop it back into the holder, trying to get a glimpse of her across the rink, to make sure my dad isn't…

Well, that he's not being my dad.

"I can handle the old man," she told me when I checked in with her before the game, making sure she didn't want to bail on coming tonight.

I think that Ella can do anything.

But I don't want the *thing* she's doing to be enduring my dad being an asshole.

And he's likely to be in an even worse mood considering that I pushed back earlier.

"Riggs—"

I pull my stare away, glance to Knox.

"She can handle your dad," he says quietly.

And seriously, the fucker has far too high of an emotional IQ for his own good—pushing me to take that first step with Ella, snagging my phone and keeping me distracted when my dad is on a rampage, knowing exactly what was wrong with Ella yesterday and how to go about fixing it.

Knowing that I'm worried *today*.

She's here. She's smiling.

But...she still has pain buried deep inside, pain that's eating at her more and more by the day.

I need to find a way to help her set that aside.

I flick my brows up in question. "What makes you say that with such confidence?"

"She can handle assholes like the best of them." He shrugs then slides down the bench when the next line hops on the ice. "She'll smile and the bullshit they dish out will slide right down her back." A rueful laugh. "But it's the silence she can't stand. The walls she can't breach. The problems she can't fix. The failure that eats at her from the inside." He sighs. "And worst of all is standing in a room unseen by the people you love."

"You talking about her?" I ask as the whistle goes and we stand up, prepare to take our shift. "Or you?"

Riggs freezes in the open door, one foot poised above the ice.

Then he shakes his head, eyes flicking behind us, drifting down the hall that leads to the locker room like he's doing some searching of his own.

I have a feeling I know precisely who he's looking for.

And whose walls he has made absolutely no progress in breaching.

"We grew up in the same house, asshole," he says and skates away before I can ask what he means—or ask after a certain redhead who's extremely good at *not* seeing him.

I follow to the face-off circle, line up to the side and slightly behind the dot, ready to pass it back to our D when Lake wins the draw like he always does.

The whistle blows.

The ref drops the puck.

Lake wins it.

I go to make the drop pass, but I see the flash of white out of the corner of my eye. Not the blue and green with a touch of white jerseys we wear on home ice, but a full arm of white, the winger on the other team closing with explosive speed and ready to pick off the pass.

Yeah, our goalie won't appreciate a breakaway this late in the game, with us up a goal and the win within sight.

I halt my movement in a flash, flick the puck back to Lake, who's strong as shit, annoying as fuck to play against, and always ready to receive a pass.

He corrals the puck, wins the battle with the other center, skating to the corner to free up some space for us to make a play.

You're welcome, Willie, I think to our goalie, shoving off the defenseman guarding me and cutting hard to the net, watching Lake as he skates behind the goal, tracking Knox when he moves in and hangs close enough to split the coverage on us.

I grunt when I take a crosscheck to the back, do some shoving of my own in return, biting back a curse when the stick makes contact beneath my shoulder pads. Assholes always miss the parts that are actually protected.

But while I'm battling to keep position, to be an option, to screen the goalie—and to do all three of those things properly, I see our D cutting in.

Lake clocks him too.

I know that in our flash of eye contact as he skates out from behind the net, and then I'm moving before I even consciously think about it—breaking the hold the bastard defending me has on my stick, returning the crosscheck he gave me earlier, and then digging in and skating by the fucker, reaching my spot on this play we've practiced at least a hundred times…

Just as Lake saucers the pass to me.

I catch it out of mid-air, drag it to the far side of the ice as I deke around the defenseman who's followed me.

Not trying anything fancy, just buying time, gathering focus, leaving space to find—

Now.

Knox open.

They expected the pass to go back to our D.

It's the obvious play.

But they forgot about the man with the dangerous hands who's nearly impossible to corral.

I whip the puck to him, knowing Knox can handle a hard pass, knowing that it'll have to *be* hard in order to make it to him at all.

But I don't stand there and watch like a lump when the puck flies off my stick.

I *move.*

Sprinting toward the net, not stopping until I'm in the mix, until I'm fighting for position, until I'm contributing to the chaos the goalie and defense has to keep track of.

Knox fires off a shot.

The goalie makes the first save, kicking it out to the corner, but Lake is there already.

He corrals it, whips back to the net.

The goalie slides hard in that direction, making a herculean fucking save in my opinion.

It pops off his pads…

And drops right out to my feet.

I kick it up to my stick, get a slash to my legs for my trouble, a shove to my back, but I fight through the pain radiating up my arms, along my spine, and hold my ground.

I'm close to the goalie.

I don't have a ton of space and he's good—he's going to be covering the ice, and he's able to maneuver, to move his pads to guard against the eighteen inches above that.

And he's fucking good with his stick.

I just…need to be better with mine.

Hockey players and their sticks.

Ella's voice rushes through my brain in a flash and I'm smiling when I flick my wrists, sending the puck up in the air.

Above those pads.

Above his glove.

Straight into the top of the net.

I'm still smiling when the red light goes and the buzzer sounds and…

The crowd roars.

I'm still smiling when my eyes flick to the side, when I see my dad in his seat, face expressionless.

But most importantly, I'm still smiling when I shift my gaze to see Ella on her feet, cheering like a fiend.

Because…

It's *Ella* who's become the most important person in my life.

And I'm not going to stop until she knows it.

Hell, even *then* I'm going to keep going.

Because she is *mine*.

CHAPTER THIRTY-SEVEN

Ella

"FUCK, RIGGS," I moan into the pillow I grabbed, trying to not scream so loud that Todd will hear me.

It's five in the morning, my hot hockey player has the day off, and I've been woken up without my eight alarms.

It's fucking glorious.

He nips at my thigh and I jump. "Pay attention, *chérie*."

"Is this where you're going to do what you promised on that puck?"

I feel rather than see his smile, and the flick of his tongue that follows has my hips bucking, seeking the purchase of his talented mouth, the friction of his thick, bushy beard that I know will send me over the edge.

But I don't get there.

Instead, I find myself maneuvered in a flash, his big, strong body suddenly beneath me, my thighs straddling his waist, his thick cock nestled in the slick folds of my pussy.

"Get those tits up here," he orders, bucking his hips, sending me toppling forward, having to brace myself on the headboard…

And positioning my breasts—

"Oh God!" I moan.

—in the perfect position for him to suck my nipples into his mouth, to roll his tongue over them, to nip and kiss and lick—

To drive me fucking insane, all while the tip of his cock is almost inside me.

"Fuck. Fuck. Fuck," I moan.

He sits up, sending his cock deeper inside me. "Ride me like I promised you would, *cherie*. Take me deep and fuck me hard. I want you to feel me for the rest of the day, to remember this every time you sit down." He grips my hips, pulls, and—

"Riggs!"

I'm suddenly full of him.

Full and stretched to the limit, his cock so much deeper, so much *bigger* in this angle.

"Ride me good, *cherie*."

And then his mouth is too busy sucking my nipples to continue speaking. But he groans against me, the sound vibrating through my flesh.

And I...*move*.

His hips buck, and he's grinding his cock up into me as I'm stroking down.

It's fucking glorious.

It's fucking perfect.

It's fucking incredible.

It's *fucking*—

He smacks me hard on the ass, sting flaring through my cheek, the blip of pain exactly what I need.

Pleasure and pain.

Hard and deep.

"Oh, God, Riggs!" I cry out, far too loud, but unable to stop myself.

But it's fucking *there*.

My orgasm blasts through me.

My body goes limp and it takes everything in me to keep moving, to not fuck up his own release—

But, like always, Riggs takes care of it, flipping us, thrusting into me, each stroke sending another starburst of pleasure through me.

Once. Twice. Three times—

"Fuck, I love you," he groans as every muscle in his body goes taut, his beautiful brown eyes locked onto mine, the love he has for me—for *me*—shining out like the brightest rays of the sun.

But even with all that…

I still find that I can't give him the words back.

———

"ARE you sure you have to go in to work today?" he murmurs a while later, lips on my throat, teeth nipping at my earlobe.

My mouth tips up as I finish pouring the muffin batter into the tins then lean back against his hard chest, press a kiss to the side of his neck, inhaling deeply.

Yummy.

He used beard oil this morning, something I had the pleasure of witnessing after he carried my limp body into his bathroom and we showered together.

Well, really, *I* sat there like a well-pleasured lump of a human while he soaped me up, gently washed my hair, dried me off, then scooped me up and plunked me on the counter.

Where I got to see him groom that glorious beard.

Yum.

I inhale the scent of cinnamon and orange then kiss his throat again before dropping back onto my heels.

"Yup," I say. "I have to go in to work. I have a full day of clients and I've been flaky enough lately."

He scowls, but not at me, at his dad barking into his phone

in the other room, yelling about some perceived inconvenience.

"…and then the doctor said…"

"You know what he told me last night after you scored?"

"In my bedroom?" he murmurs, pulling me flush against him.

I swat his arm, but don't resist being wrapped up in him. "No," I tell him, spinning in his arms, needing to see his face. "After your goal in the game last night."

He rolls his eyes. "It doesn't matter, *chérie*," he says. "I think I've finally got to the point where I don't really care."

I touch his cheek. "I respect that," I tell him gently. "Really, I do. But he…he was proud. He cheered and clapped."

"I saw him sitting like a grumpy old man statue next to you, baby." He covers my hand with his own then peels it from his cheek and presses a kiss to my palm. "You don't have to sugarcoat it for me."

"I'm not. He didn't cheer for long, but when the crowd quieted, he told me that was a heads-up play with a good finish."

His eyes widen.

"I'm not saying that you need to have him in your life—hell, based on what I've experienced and the shit Knox has told me he's pulled over the years, you're well within your rights to tell him to fuck off forever." I sigh. "But I…I guess, if there's a part of you that's unresolved, that's searching for…something that's missing or you had once or—" I shrug, throat tight.

"Ella," he whispers.

"I'm just saying it might be worth trying to hash it out," I push out. "Set some boundaries, find something together that doesn't tear you apart."

Because I hate the idea that he has the same wound in his heart that I do.

And if there's some way to repair it…

"I love you," he whispers.

I close my eyes, the words washing over me in a warm rush of emotion. "Riggs," I whisper.

I want to give voice to the feelings in my heart—I'm almost desperate to do it. But...I can't. Not yet. Not when I've made so many mistakes.

Not when I have so much to make up for.

He cups my jaw, and when I peel open my eyes, I see his face has softened. "I'm here," he murmurs.

I swallow hard. "I know."

He strokes a finger over my jaw. "So, a full day today?" he asks. "Or do you have time for lunch with your boyfriend and his grumpy dad?"

"Such a tempting offer," I tease, tapping my finger against my lips and letting him shift our conversation to something lighter. "How ever could I turn that down?"

"I can think of a hundred reasons." He grins.

"Hmm," I say, slipping out of the circle of his arms and sliding the muffin pan into the preheated oven. "But you *were* very skilled with that beard of yours when it was between my legs this morning." I tap my bottom lip again. "That might have bought you lunch?"

One half of his mouth hitches up and he starts to speak, to presumably give me some more of those dirty words I love so fucking much, but he's cut off by stomping.

We turn as one to see Todd marching into the room, brows yanked together, steam all but coming out of his ears.

"All good, Todd-o-Rama?" I ask, turning for the coffeepot and filling three mugs.

His scowl deepens as he tosses his cell on the table. "Sure isn't, Ells," he grumbles, coming toward me.

I lift my brows and pass over a mug. "Want to talk about all those big feelings you're having right now?"

His mouth kicks up, but he doesn't bite, just takes a long

sip and exhales before lifting the mug in my direction in a quiet salute. "You make good coffee, kid."

"Actually," I say. "Riggs made the coffee." I lift my brows higher. "Because he's good at a lot of things." A beat. "Like hockey. And cooking." And fucking me senseless with his tongue. "And making coffee."

He snorts. "That's not all he's good at, if what I heard this morning is any indication."

This man...he's just freaking impossible.

"Dad," Riggs warns.

"Sorry," Todd mutters and I freeze with a rebuttal on the tip of my tongue. "I'm a surly old bastard," he mutters. "And I don't know when to quit." He sinks down into a chair and takes another sip of coffee. "And I'm a *particular* asshole in the mornings."

My eyes jerk to Riggs's.

He looks just as shocked as I am.

And that's *before* Todd sets his mug aside and says quietly, "You played good last night, son."

CHAPTER THIRTY-EIGHT

Riggs

I GRIN when I walk off the ice the next day and see Ella leaning back against the wall, her mouth tipped up and eyes staring me up and down.

"What's it about guys in hockey helmets?" she says, rising on tiptoe and brushing her lips over mine. "Ups the hot factor by a hundred."

"I thought you had to work."

"I had a cancellation and thought I'd peep in on my boyfriend," she says, dropping back onto her heels and glancing around. "Plus, I wanted to make sure you were good."

Because my dad is here.

Ever since that moment in the kitchen, when my dad stepped outside the asshole and said something halfway decent, things have been…weird.

I keep bracing, ready for the asshole to lash out.

Instead, he's been…almost affable.

And I don't really know what to do with that.

I slip off my gloves, tossing them to our equipment guy

who needs to finish up his duties without waiting for me to flirt with my girlfriend, but when I turn back to Ella and touch her cheek, she wrinkles her nose.

"Whew," she murmurs, "I forgot about the glove funk. Ugh." She pretends to gag. "It's bringing back memories of being trapped in the car with Knox and his stinky ass gear."

"*Chérie*, I had them on for an hour."

The wrinkles in her nose grow. "And that's more than long enough."

I tug a lock of her hair. "Always got something to say, don't you?"

"Yup." But she's smiling. "Now," she says. "Are you really okay?"

"I'm sweaty and exhausted and Knox is going to kick my ass in the weight room after this in a way I'm so not looking forward to—"

She opens her mouth.

"But—" I cup her jaw. "But I'm *fine*. My dad has been…" I shrug. "Fine."

"Super convincing." But there's something in her tone, a clue as to why she's here. "Fine. Fine. Everything's fine."

I tug that strand of hair again. "Well, I'm not going to lie and tell you that my dad and I spent the morning painting each other's nails."

She giggles.

"But considering how rough things have been the last couple of years…I'll take fine."

"That's fair."

I study her closely. Yeah, she's here because she wants to look after me, but also…there's sadness clinging in her eyes.

"How'd it go with Kit?"

She winces. "The same. I try to talk to him and he ignores me." She lifts a shoulder, allows it to drop just as quickly in a delicate, one-shouldered shrug. "I don't blame him. I just…"

Dammit.

I draw her close, hockey funk be damned.

"You just want to fix it."

Like she's trying to fix my relationship with my dad. Like she fixed Donna's loneliness and set up Nova with Lake.

Because she can't fix what happened to her.

"I know I'm overstepping."

God, I love this woman.

"*Chérie*," I murmur, stroking a hand down her back.

"You give good hugs," she whispers, "even while dressed like a marshmallow."

"Hey now," I tease, letting her change the subject. "This is protective equipment. Hell, some might even say it's *armor*."

She lifts her head from my chest and smiles lasciviously. "And you're my dirty-mouthed knight in said armor who will save me with orgasms?"

"With orgasms *and* apple fritters."

Her laughter—it's the best feeling in the fucking world.

But it doesn't last long, the sad creeping back in.

I lean down, the distance further than normal because of my skates, and press my forehead to hers. "Want to play hooky and go hang out at your spot? I'll blow off Knox and the old man. You reschedule your afternoon appointments." I wink. "Then we'll make some trouble."

I want the worry that's been eating at her about Kit, about me, to disappear.

But I also get it's not that simple, so I'll do what I can to distract her.

And the smile she gives me in response to my teasing words…

Well, I've accomplished that for a bit.

"I have a full highlight with my client, Cassie," she says. "She's getting married this weekend, so I can't blow her off."

I tap her on the nose. "Then we'll make trouble later."

Her smile grows. "That sounds like a plan. Well…I should go." She glances over my shoulder and I watch as her expression changes. Mischief to protective. "Want me to take the old man with me?" she asks, voice lifting enough to be heard by my dad who's coming up behind her. "I can touch up those grays, give him a fresh new cut to attract the ladies. Maybe then he won't be so grumpy."

My dad's laughter reaches my ears a second later, rough and a little rusty from disuse. "I don't think there's much that can help this mug," he says, scrubbing a hand over his face. "But if you want to dull your scissors on this mop"—he fusses with his hair—"then I won't stop you."

Shock has me rocking back on my heels.

Ella slips her hand into mine and squeezes, getting it in a millisecond, understanding exactly how fucking monumental this shit is.

Laughter? Self-deprecation? Offering himself up as Ella's haircut sacrificial lamb?

Obviously, she wouldn't fuck up his hair—especially since she's retired her clippers—but…

That my dad is going along with it? That he's putting himself in a vulnerable position and—

I don't know this person.

Or maybe…I thought he didn't exist any longer.

"Ella!"

Heart pounding, I manage to pull it together as Evie runs down the hall. She's a spitting image of her mom, Ivy, aside from the brightness of her hair and the sweetness of her personality.

Ivy's hard, all barbed wired and crocodile-filled moats.

Evie is…sunshine on a cool spring morning.

Ella intercepts her with a hug, and they start talking about bows.

"She reminds me of your mother," my dad says quietly.

"Evie?" I ask. *Her* mom is our head trainer and the lead ass-kicker of the Sierra's player development department.

A.K.A. the director of high performance.

Which basically means that she gets us all in fighting shape...and then kicks our asses all over again, just for good measure.

"No," my dad says. "Ella."

My throat closes up.

This is fucking uncharted territory. We don't do this. Don't talk about my mom, don't discuss what she was like, don't mention the faint memories I hold tight to that are the only part of her I still have aside from the much-worn teddy bear in my closet at the house.

"Your mom was like Ella—she wouldn't put up with my shit. She'd dig in her heels, would call me on it, and do it all with a smile." He shakes his head wryly. "And before I knew it, I was doing exactly what she wanted all along just because I wanted to keep that smile on her face. She was special, your mom." A breath. "So fucking special and when I lost that...I didn't handle it well."

"Dad."

"I fucked up with you."

My heart lurches in my chest.

Remorseful eyes lock onto mine. "I fucked up in a lot of ways, too many to fucking count. I didn't see that before...or was too fucking lost in my own misery to understand. Not until Ella made me see—" Breaking off, his gaze goes back down the hall, and I see Ivy's joined Evie and Ella as he sighs. "Do what you need to do here, son. I'll look after your woman until you get home."

And then, like he hasn't just pulled the biggest personality change of all time, he just...

Strolls away from me.

He corrals Ella with a gruff, "You can't be late for your client. She's got a wedding to get prepared for, right?"

Man's got ears like an elephant.

I shake my head.

"You're absolutely right, Todd-o-Rama," she says before

tossing me a wicked grin. "How do you feel about becoming Patches 2.0?"

Laughter in my throat.

My woman waves as the group breaks up—Ivy turning for the weight room and Evie skipping off down the hall to hang out in her mom's office like usual. The girl's hair is in a complicated-looking bun-braid combo that I have no idea how Ella managed to create in such a short time.

My woman can work miracles.

Creating gorgeous pieces of art.

Taming grumpy old men.

I wave back and then she and my dad are heading the other direction, disappearing down the corridor that will lead out to the parking lot.

I watch them go.

Then turn for the locker room to get changed.

But I don't miss Knox coming through the door before I get there, same as I don't miss him heading directly for the weight room…

Where Ivy is.

Hmm.

And then I wonder what kind of miracles my woman can work there too.

CHAPTER THIRTY-NINE

Ella

I PARK in my usual spot and grab my purse from the back before popping open the door and getting out.

Todd follows me and I try not to look at him suspiciously.

He's been *nice.*

Easy-going.

I don't trust it.

I also…well, I also want this to be some sort of permanent change.

For Riggs's sake.

"I can recommend a good coffee shop nearby," I tell him as he starts following me to the salon. "Unless you really want that haircut. If so, I'll get my client started and give you your trim while they're processing."

A pause. "What's processing?"

"Processing the chemicals I'll put in her hair," I explain as I start up the stairs. "In this case, the products that are going to lighten certain parts."

He walks next to me, quiet for a moment, as though processing—*heh*—that.

But as I reach for the handle of the door to the salon, he nods decisively, some unspoken decision reached. "I'll stay."

Color me—no pun intended—surprised.

"Okay then." I start to pull the wooden and glass panel open, but he beats me to it, holding it wide so I can enter before him. I study him closely. "Why are you being so nice?"

"You don't have to sound so suspicious about it," he grumbles, but his mouth is curved up.

"Look, Todd-o-Rama," I say, pausing on the threshold and holding his stare. "I don't know you all that well, but if you're going to go full Dr. Jekyll-Mr. Hyde on me, I'm going to demand some explanations. Especially when it affects the man I…care about."

He scowls, pulls the door a little wider, gestures me inside. "There's a chill in the air."

I just flick up my brows.

He sighs, and it's a disgruntled, frustrated sound.

Good.

He can be annoyed with me instead of Riggs.

"Well?" I press.

His scowl deepens. "Maybe I thought about what you said at the game," he eventually says.

"And…?" I coax.

He sounds like he's cutting glass when he says, "And…I think you may be right."

"Of course I am," I say calmly, even though I'm fist-pumping inside. I turn and walk into the salon, allowing some of the victorious feeling in my heart to creep into my smile.

Until I see that Kit's here.

Standing at his desk, his eyes on me, his expression careful.

"Afternoon," I say softly.

"Afternoon."

My eyes slide closed, relief filling my insides with helium, and I have to force my gait to stay steady, to not rush over to him and kiss his adorable cheeks.

Because it's the first thing he's said to me since that day.

One word and it feels like he stood up on the counter and recited a monologue about our friendship to the whole salon.

But…that's all he says.

"Kit," I begin, moving closer.

He steps back, expression immediately closing down.

Dammit.

I exhale quietly. "I'm here if you feel ready to talk at any point." My words are quiet, but I know by the stiff way his shoulders hitch up that he can hear them. "And please know that I won't push you. I get that I fucked up and you're allowed to be mad." A beat. "You're allowed to hate me."

His throat works and he looks down at his keyboard, dismissing me.

I want to press, to fix this, to make it all go away…

But I can't.

I've apologized and now I have to give him time.

So, I force myself to keep walking.

"You can sit there, Todd-o-Rama," I say, nodding to the empty seat next to my station. It belongs to a stylist I know isn't working today. "I just need to drop my stuff in the back," I tell him, turning away. "Can I grab you any coffee or water? A snack?"

"What happened?" he asks.

I pause and glance over my shoulder. "Well, we met up at the rink and then drove in my car here, and now"—I force a smile—"I'm going to squeeze giving you a kickass haircut into my already busy schedule."

"Okay, smart ass," he grumbles, but his eyes are dancing. "Also, you're talking up this haircut so much, it had better be the best one I've ever had, and not that shit you pulled with my son. I'm not into bald patches."

"Oh, the cut will be amazing." I spin around, plunk my hands on my hips, and narrow my eyes threateningly. "So long as you hold still," I warn. "Very, very still."

He snorts.

"So, coffee?" I ask. "Or water—"

"I *meant*, what happened with the boy at the front desk?"

"First," I say, "Kit is a grown man."

Todd rolls his eyes. "He's got to be all of twenty."

"Twenty-*three*," I correct. "But that's an adult."

"A baby."

I roll my eyes. "Okay, I'll bring you a coffee."

He catches my arm as I start to walk away. "What happened with Kit, the grown man of twenty-three?"

"Why?" I ask quietly.

"Because it's upset you."

"Why does that bother you?" My tone is snarky. "You don't know me, and clearly, you don't give a damn when you upset your own son. Why should you stick your nose into my business?"

His fingers tighten, tone sharpening. "Because my son loves you and I fucked up with him for long enough that I want to do something helpful for a change, okay?"

Of all the things Todd could have said…

This is the one that tugs at my heartstrings.

He messed up. He wants to fix it.

"Dammit," I grumble. "I don't *want* to like you."

"I don't even like me on a good day," he mutters.

I snort.

He releases my arm. "Tell me."

"I fucked up," I admit for some reason. "I said some things that are unforgivable and—" I sigh. "I just… fucked up. I'm trying to fix it, but it takes time." My throat is tight. "Especially when I'm the one in the wrong."

His expression sobers. "Yeah," he agrees. "It'll take time."

And I know he's reminding himself of the same.

"Right," I say, needing to change the subject. "Black coffee?"

He nods. "Yeah, thanks, sweetheart."

That settles…well, it settles in a father-sized hole deep in my soul. It shouldn't be a balm. The endearment shouldn't even register. Like I said, I don't know Todd, not really, and he's a grumpy bastard.

But…

It settles deep anyway.

Because my dad would have never bothered to ask.

I shake myself and head into the back, stowing my purse and making the cup of coffee. As I'm passing it over, I greet Cassie, who walks in. It only takes a moment to get her situated in her cape, to come up with a game plan for her hair, and then I'm mixing up some lightener, grabbing my foils, and giving the bride-to-be the best balayage the world has ever seen.

And in between working my magic with Cassie, I give a grumpy old man the best damned *haircut* the world has ever seen.

With nigh a bald spot in sight.

I can't fix my dad.

I can't erase what happened with Kit.

But I *can* spread a little happiness one strand of hair at a time.

———

"YOU SURE YOU don't want another?" Nova asks as she plunks down next to me on the couch. "Did I mix the proportions wrong?"

I lift my gaze from the copper mug in my hand to my best friend's. "No, it's perfect. I just…" I push the cup away. "I think I've been a little too familiar with your honey-rosemary mules lately, is all."

Her green eyes gentle. "Ella," she whispers.

"It's fine," I say, even though it's anything but. "*I'm* fine." I nod toward the menfolk, Lake, Leo, Knox, Bear, and Todd, who's still grumpy, but has managed to turn off the asshole, especially because Evie's joined in on the *Rummikub* action of game night. "Things are getting intense over there."

"Yes," Nova agrees.

But she doesn't say anything else, just sits there, stare pinning me in place, and I know…

I owe her more.

I tilt my head toward the door that leads out to the deck. It's cold and breezy out there, but the sky is mostly clear, no more snow slated in the forecast for the next few days.

Thank God. I'm so damned tired of snow.

"Let me grab us a blanket," she whispers, squeezing my hand. "Meet you out there?"

"Yeah."

Riggs's eyes come to mine when I stand, but I just shake my head slightly, letting him know I'm fine.

He lifts a brow in response and I know he might stay in that round of *Rummikub*, but he's going to be keeping an eye on me.

And I don't miss that Lake has a similar nonverbal conversation with Nova.

Heart warming, I step out onto the deck, stare up at the stars twinkling like tiny diamonds overhead.

Orion. Big Dipper. Little Dipper. Venus and—

"That used to be what I wanted to feel," I tell Nova as she comes to stand next to me, nodding up at the constellations. "So distant, so cold, so untouchable."

A long blip of silence before she hands me half the blanket and we cuddle up under it. "You're far from cold, Ella."

"I wish I was." I huff out a laugh and plunk my head onto her shoulder, but I'm not amused, not really. "I feel so much, *too* much. Sometimes it hurts so bad that I just want to feel nothing."

"Honey," she whispers.

"He broke me," I say, not willing to hide from this any

longer. "My dad—I didn't know how to be an unloved daughter, a discarded piece of trash. I thought...I thought if I just pretended, it would all be okay."

"Pretended what?"

"To be the best version of me—funny, loud, fixing every problem, ignoring that my own heart was hurting so I could help everyone else. So I could be happy for them. So I didn't *have* to be happy with my own life." I swallow hard. "And... pretending I was fine, that I was great when I wasn't—" My voice hitches and I break off.

"I didn't know," she whispers, her eyes glassy with tears.

I touch her cheek. "I became an expert in hiding it."

"I don't think so."

Surprised, I rock back on my heels.

Her mouth curves, just slightly. "I wasn't *here* to call you on that." She sighs. "And who am I to talk now that I am? I spent years running from my problems—hiding from them in the Arctic, burying them in the desert in Asia, leaving them in the clouds thirty-thousand feet overhead while I flew as far as I could from my pain. I didn't know anything about myself, about my feelings, about what I really wanted —" She crouches a little to meet my eyes. "Not until you helped me."

"Novs."

"You're my best friend and...I wasn't here for you like I should have." Watery green eyes on mine. "I'm sorry."

I laugh and it's broken. "You have nothing to apologize for."

"I should have been here. Should have done more."

"Now you sound like me," I tell her, swiping at a tear sliding down her cheek. "Can we try to stop fixing everyone else and just enjoy the fact that we're here, we're together, and we both have hot hockey players in our beds?"

"With big sticks?" she teases.

I laugh and it's still uneven, but at least it's laced with real humor now. Because I've teased her about Lake and his *stick* far too often.

She touches my cheek. "But you're happy now? Here? With me and Knox? With Riggs?"

"Happier than I ever thought possible." I close my eyes. "He knows more about me than anyone—more than maybe even you and Knox."

Her arm tightens around my shoulders. "Good."

"And you know that I liked him from the beginning—I thought it was just going to be sex—"

"A common problem with hot hockey players and their sticks," she quips.

"But he…understands in a way I never thought would be possible. And he's patient and sweet and…he sees me. *Me*—not me with vodka being the life of the party, not me trying to fix the world, not the hurt little girl, but all of them and none of them and…he just sees *me*."

"Isn't that the best feeling in the world?"

I nod. "It really is."

She smiles. "I'm glad you have it."

"Me too."

We fall silent, listening to the wind in the trees, the rustle of the needles, the crunch of the snow.

"On a serious note?" she asks a few moments later. "Should I stop with the mules?"

"I—" I exhale, heart squeezing because, God, I love my best friend. "I'm not abstaining exactly. But…I came *unglued*, Novs. From a five-minute interaction with my dad. I had all of these feelings I thought were long gone—but really were just there, right beneath the surface, ready to explode out and ruin everything."

She hugs me closer.

"And all I wanted was to not *care*—to forget what happened with my mom, with him after. To forget what he so clearly thinks of me now and how cold his eyes were that day."

"Honey," Nova says. "God, I'm sorry—"

"It's infuriating," I whisper. "He's not my dad and hasn't been for a long time. But seeing him like that with his replacement family and—" My eyes sting, but I don't let the tears fall. I'm done with crying over a man who can't be bothered to love me as he should.

"And," she says, "it tore open all of those old wounds, let the feelings free."

I nod. "I couldn't cope, so I avoided you. I knew you'd see. And I didn't tell Knox or Riggs. I just…" I sigh up at the sky. "I tried to find some reality where I felt like them—cold, unaffected, distant. But it didn't work, anyway, and because of that, I hurt Riggs and I hurt Kit, and…I hurt you too."

"I'm fine—" she begins.

"I was a jerk. And then I drank enough to turn into the worst version of myself. *And* I pulled a disappearing act." I shake my head. "Something I gave you a hard time about, if you remember."

Her smile is wry. "Oh, I *remember*." Then she touches my jaw, expression softening. "Just like I remember how you got my head out of my ass with Lake and now I have more than I ever thought was possible."

"I'm glad you have that."

"And now you do too."

I swallow hard. "*If* I don't fuck it up."

"I kind of think, considering all you've told me, that you and Riggs are going to be good, honey."

I want that to be true, and my heart is full, knowing Nova believes in me. But…

"Think of this as just another problem to solve with your patented Ella magic," she says. "You've already begun figuring out all the moving parts, studying which pin to push, how to put the pieces together so everything fits right. It's just that the problem is inside your head and heart for a change instead of someone else's."

My lungs inflate on a sharp breath. "Novs—"

"And, all of that aside, I've known you for long enough to *know* you, honey. You may fuck up every once in a while—like the rest of us mere mortals—but you don't make the same mistake twice."

"Except for wanting my dad to be different," I say quietly.

Now her smile is sad, so fucking sad. "That's not a mistake, Ells. That's called being human."

I scowl. "Well, I don't like it."

Now she grins and all those ragged parts inside me smooth out. "Every once in a while you have to come down out of the clouds."

I groan and shove her lightly. "Rude."

"Woof!"

We turn to see an indignant Steve standing on the other side of the door, slobbering all over the glass panel.

"Watch out," she teases, "my protector has teeth."

"Which one?" I ask lightly.

A smirk. "I don't think you want to hear about all the ways Lake uses his teeth."

"Oh, I definitely do," I say, looping my arm through hers and guiding her back inside, bending down and giving the goodest boy there ever was his requisite scratches (and getting Steve's obligatory snorts and sniffs and sneezes in return). "Because then I can tell you *all* about the ways Riggs uses his tongue."

She looks at me, mouth agape, eyes dancing. "You're the best kind of menace, you know that?"

I buff my knuckles on my shoulder. "Damn right, I am."

CHAPTER FORTY

Riggs

"Your dad is going to stay here tonight," Nova tells me as she deals the next hand of *UNO*.

I freeze, my beer halfway to my mouth, and stare at her.

Then Lake.

Then my dad.

What the actual fuck?

I push my chair back, stand, and meet my dad's eyes. I tilt my head to the door. "Outside," I growl.

"The deck's sure getting a lot of use tonight," Lake quips.

Nova smacks him on the chest but I ignore both of them as I march to the door, push it open, shaking my head at Ella when she starts to push up out of her chair, as if to follow.

My dad lumbers out in front of me, looking completely at ease despite my friend's woman just declaring that they're having a sleepover.

What's next? Face masks and manicures?

I shut the door firmly. Okay, maybe it edges into a slam.

But...what the actual fuck is going on right now?

I lean back against the railing, cross my arms, and lift my brows, silently asking that question.

My dad answers without preamble. "She needs help lugging her gear up for a shoot." A shrug. "Lake has a meeting with a prospective sponsor and I'd like to learn more about photography."

"Like you want to learn about cosmetology?"

He's gone into the salon at least once a day since Ella cut his hair almost a week ago. Hell, last night at dinner, he was discussing the merits of something called 40-volume over 20-volume.

Jesus.

I need to do more Googling.

My dad crosses his arm. "I like to learn new things, son." A beat. "You know that."

I inhale. I *do* know that. It's what he did when I was a kid—dive into hockey, learn all of the small parts, help me put them together into something that means I'm now playing the sport professionally. Then moving on to the next subject that interests him—car engines and geocaching, painting and rowing.

He's always taking a new class in something.

But that's at home.

That's not *here*, not in my town, with my friends...my *family*.

"None of that explains why you're still here at all."

He lifts an eyebrow. "Doesn't it?"

"No," I mutter.

He sighs, mirroring me and leaning back against the railing. "I don't know how to go back."

I frown.

"I just know that these women are important to you"—he nods to the window, through which the game of *UNO* has gone on in typically rowdy fashion—"I know that Knox and Lake are too, and I know...that if I keep going like I have, that I *won't* be."

"And what?" I ask, thinking back on what he told me at the rink, that Ella's like my mom, that Ella made him realize he fucked up. "And now you've just decided to turn over a new leaf?"

I sound bitter and I hate it.

"Yes."

Laughing, I shake my head and stare up at the sky, at the stars, at the faint gray streaks of the clouds crawling in over the mountain. "It's just that simple?"

"I know you don't believe me," he says. "I know it's going to take time—"

That his words echo what I told Ella about her situation with Kit, about us moving forward together doesn't escape me.

"—but I don't know what else to do aside from telling you again that I fucked up, that I'm sorry I was so damned hard on you and pushed you away and took out the gaping hole in my heart on you." He exhales. "You didn't—*don't*—deserve that and I'm sorry I ever made you think that you did."

I don't know what to say, what to think.

"So, I'll help the people that are important to you," he says, nodding at the table full of friends who've become family. "And I'll help *you* if you'll let me. But mostly, I've decided that I'll be here, like this, without the asshole bullshit, and I'll stay here until you're ready for us to do something different."

"And then what?"

He pushes off the railing, claps a hand on my shoulder.

"And then *I'll* be different."

———

"ARE YOU OKAY?" Ella asks a couple hours later as we drive home.

My dad is staying in Lake's guest room.

Something my teammate just shrugged at when I tried to

apologize and give him an out. "Nova," he said by way of explanation and then proceeded to start washing dishes.

Millionaire Lake Jordan, captain of the Sierra, face of many a brand—from watches to underwear—washes dishes.

The TikTokers would enjoy that snippet of his life.

Blackmail material, I suppose.

"I'm still stinging from Evie kicking our ass in *Phase 10*," I tell Ella, not wanting heavy, not after our various conversations on the deck and my woman not drinking.

I know it's because of me…and I know it also has *nothing* to do with me.

"The student has surpassed the master," she says quietly.

I glance over at her, mouth quirking, knowing she sees right through me. "Are *you* okay?" I can't help but ask, despite my pledge of lightness.

She reaches across the console, squeezes my thigh. "I'm as okay as you are, I think. My head is in a constant state of flux. Things are great and yet all twisted up and…" She sighs and I glance over at her again. "And I have you," she says, reaching an invisible hand into my chest and grabbing on to my heart, "so it can't be *all* bad."

I brake hard, pull onto the shoulder.

"Um—"

But I don't give her a chance to finish that statement because I'm throwing my SUV into park, shoving my seat back, and unbuckling her seat belt.

"Riggs—*eek!*"

I tug and a second later, she's in my lap.

A moment after that, my lips are on hers, my tongue is in her mouth, and my hands are on those gorgeous curves.

"What—" she begins when I give her a second to breathe.

"I'm going to finish what we started all those weeks ago—"

Her eyes go wide as I yank at the zipper of her coat, dragging it down, pushing it off her shoulders. I grip the edge of her sweater, tug it up so that I can get at her tits.

"Fuck, I love these things," I mutter, burying my face between her breasts, then turning my head and dragging my beard over the sensitive flesh. She gasps as I suck her nipple deep, flicking my tongue over the sensitive peak.

Nails in my hair, hips grinding down against me.

But I don't stop suckling her breasts.

The horn goes as I reach for the button on her jeans and flick it open. "Push them down, *cherie,*" I say, working the zipper, our hands tangling as she does as I ordered, getting her jeans down her hips, past her knees, low enough that she can straddle my waist and get to work on my own jeans.

"*Fuck,*" I growl when she all but tears open my pants and grips my cock.

"I want to suck it," she demands, stroking hard.

"No room, *cherie,*" I say, even though I would love to push my dick past those plump lips, would love to fuck her mouth until I come.

That'll have to be later.

Right now I need to be inside her.

"Climb on, baby. Climb on and ride me."

Thankfully, she doesn't delay, just shifts up, notches me at her entrance, and…sits right on my cock.

"Fuck," I growl again, the slick, taut heat of her surrounding me, driving me crazy. I grab her hip, dragging her down as I stroke up into her, using my mouth on her breasts, her throat, fucking her with my tongue to the same rhythm of my dick.

Fast and hard and deep.

Rapidly launching us toward the edge.

Already, I hear it in her voice, in the way her moans are hitching.

And I *feel* it.

"Your tight little cunt loves this, doesn't it, *cherie*?" I rasp, nipping at her earlobe, feeling that pussy flutter around me.

"Loves thinking about someone driving by and catching us, thinking they might see you coming on my cock."

She bucks, but I don't let her stop, just keep yanking her down as I thrust up.

Until I feel it—

"Riggs!"

I don't even try to hold back…

I just let my orgasm come.

"Fuck, Ella," I groan. "Fucking *hell*."

We move together in nothing that approaches gracefulness, but I don't give a fuck, not balls deep, not as her orgasm peaks and begins to ebb, as she collapses against me, the aftershocks of her pleasure milking my cock again and again and *again*.

Not as I hold her close and headlights flash behind us.

I get one glimpse of Knox's concerned face through the steamed-up back window before I see he understands what's happening.

He spins on his heel, and a minute later those headlights disappear.

Probably scarred for life.

But I don't give a fuck.

I go back to holding my woman.

CHAPTER FORTY-ONE

Ella

"Are we going to talk about the sparks between Knox and Ivy tonight?" I ask when I can breathe again.

My pants are up and Riggs has deposited me back onto my seat.

"You mean the attraction that nearly sets the room on fire anytime they're together?" he asks, leaning over to buckle my seat belt. "Or the fact that Ivy can't stand him?"

I find the energy to grin. "Both."

He straightens his clothes, cleaning up with the stack of napkins he retrieved from the glove box and used on me first. "Both," he agrees, jabbing at the button to turn on the engine again, sending warm air into the rapidly cooling interior of the SUV. "I think Knox might need a taste of his own medicine." He glances over at me, waggles his brows. "You ready to pull out those matchmaking skills?"

I wink. "I was *born* ready."

"Damn right, you were." A tilt of his head. "Your house or mine?"

"Yours," I tell him. "You need to pack for your road trip."

Because while he's been home this week and I've gotten to enjoy spending this time with him—even with the side of grumpy old man (who I'm starting to like despite myself)—the team has more games to play. A series of important ones that will likely determine where they'll end up for the playoffs.

"I know your wardrobe options are limited at my house," he says. "And you have a full day tomorrow. I can just get up a little early and go home to pack."

"Honey, you're going to get up earlier than five?"

He shrugs. "I'm used to sleeping all sorts of weird hours."

"But you shouldn't have to just so I can pick out a cute outfit."

He smiles then snags my hand and places it on his thigh, pressing it down lightly so that I keep it there.

That—well, *all* of it—this conversation, the way he's inviting me to touch him—it all hits…

Hard, maybe, but also soft.

It's a mental shock to realize how far we've come from the night in this car not all that long ago, but it's also…right? *Perfect.* Everything I never thought I wanted.

I love him so much.

This is so fucking great.

And…we might not work out.

He might leave.

I might fuck up in a way that can't be fixed and—

No, dammit. I won't let that happen. I *won't*. I fucking—

"Ella?"

I blink, realize that he's looking at me, that although he shifted from park to drive, he hasn't taken his foot off the brake, hasn't maneuvered onto the road.

Damn. I'm messing up, even right now.

"I'll just steal that flannel I've been eyeing of yours," I say lightly. "With these leggings"—I nod down—"and my boots, I'll be full-on lumbergirl chic."

But he doesn't bite, doesn't smile, and he doesn't look

away. He just holds my gaze, his seeing far too much, I realize, when he cups my jaw, leans over to brush his lips over my forehead. "I'm here, *chérie*," he says softly. "Just know that I'm here."

I clench his thigh. It's tense beneath my palm, and holding on to the strength of him, inhaling the scent of him, helps me shove down the panic eating away at my insides.

I nod. "I know."

He closes his eyes for one brief second, features softening, relief in his eyes, and then brushes his thumb over my cheek, nods once. "Good, baby."

Then he drives us back to my place.

Because, of course he does.

And when I wake up to my eight alarms in the morning, it's to find his flannel at the end of the bed, and a note on the pillow next to mine, the one that smells like Riggs.

Turns out he can write sweet nothings too.

I'll be thinking of you every moment, chérie. How can I not? My heart is half-empty when you're not with me.

———

"APPLE FRITTER?"

I hear a few days later and freeze, mid-wrap of the cord around my blow dryer handle—shh, don't tell Donna, who I just lectured on not ever doing that this morning—then turn to see that Kit is standing there with a white, grease-stained bag.

My heart starts slamming against my rib cage.

His eyes slide from mine then come back. "I was…" A shrug. "Well, I had an extra and I thought it'd been a while since you had one."

That's not true.

I devoured two before I came into the salon this morning because I bought my usual extra for Kit before I remembered we aren't talking—or weren't, anyway—and they've sat in my stomach like lead all *freaking* day.

Now, though, with the offering up for grabs, my stomach rumbles.

He grins, shakes his head, and passes it over, slumping into the seat next to my station. "That last one was tough, huh?"

I'm here well beyond when the appointment should have finished, so late that I figured everyone else had gone home.

Everyone except for Kit, I guess.

I slump into my own chair and rub at my throbbing temples. "Yeah," I admit. My client didn't like what I did and it was a I-want-more-blond-but-now-it's-too-light, more-brown-but-now-it's-too-dark situation.

I should have known better than to change from Priscilla's usual color.

Now I've wasted hours and a shit-ton of product trying to return her hair to normal…and I've only managed to get us to a point where neither of us is happy. Not to mention, her hair needs a break, or it might be ruined permanently, so I can't take any further steps to fix the color.

She sure as shit wouldn't be happy with me—or she'd be even more *un*happy—if her hair broke off.

Already, she was going to have to baby those damaged strands, give them some tender loving care and wait a while before we begin again—*if* she even comes back.

I sigh. "I should have known better."

"You tried to warn her," Kit says, pulling another bag from somewhere and munching away on his own fritter. "And you were more than accommodating." He takes a huge bite, his next words slightly muffled. "Plus, that first color was fire, at least until she bitched about it being too light." He swallows and rolls his eyes. "She wanted more blond and you gave it to her."

I had—a gorgeous blond that was bright but not icy. I

thought it made her eyes pop and didn't wash her out and was exactly what she wanted.

Apparently, the joke was on me.

"Well," he says when I just wrinkle my nose and start in on my own fritter, "*I* thought she looked good."

"Thanks, honey."

"I'm your biggest champion," he says, "you know that."

And suddenly, the fritter tastes like saw dust, the bite in my belly like lead all over again. "And I wasn't yours," I say softly.

Quiet falls between us.

Then he sets the bag on the counter and swivels in his chair, turning mine so he can take my hand. "You said something out of pocket, Ells." A squeeze. "You had a bad day and messed up and...ultimately, you were right." His throat bobs. "Patton was cheating on me."

"What?" I gasp, leaning forward and taking his other hand in mine, holding them both tightly. "I'm so sorry," I tell him. "What happened?"

He sighs. "I found the dating apps on his phone again, but this time I didn't let him brush me off. I made him show me and...there were messages and dates of hookups that coincided with when he went out of town for work and—"

A tear slips down his cheek.

"Shit, honey, I'm so sorry."

"You warned me to break up with him. You knew he wasn't a good guy."

"Patton sent off my asshole detector, for sure. But I'm no genius," I blurt when his face falls. "I hurt you and Nova and I...almost screwed up things with Riggs when we were barely getting started." I nibble at the corner of my mouth. "And... I'm still fucking terrified almost every day that he'll wake up and see reason like my dad did."

Kit frowns. "Like your dad?"

My pulse speeds, but...I know there's no point in hiding it.

Not anymore.

Not if I want to be different, want to do better.

"You up for the long, painful as shit story?" I ask him. "Or the Cliff's Notes version?"

"Ells," he warns.

I squeeze his hands again. "You know he's not in my life" —Kit nods—"but you don't know what went into that because…" I sigh. "I don't talk about it. I don't like to think about it, but…it's also something that drives every decision I've made, including the shit I pulled on you."

His face gentles. "Tell me."

And so, I do.

I find the courage and I give him everything.

I tell him about my mom and the brother I never got to meet. About what my dad did afterward. About his new family and how he reacted to me at lunch with Nova.

And by the end, we're both crying.

"I was too scared to have anything meaningful before Riggs. I thought it was because I didn't want to be tied down, but really, it was fear. Fear that he'll leave like my dad did. So, I numbed myself when the wants got too hard to ignore, threw up walls when the men got too close—" I exhale in a shudder. "And…I needed someone like Riggs to make me see beyond that."

"A stubborn, quiet hockey hottie who sees right through the bullshit and goes after what he wants," Kit says.

My throat has gone tight but I manage to nod, to rasp out, "Yup."

He grins then sobers, passing me the box of tissues he stole from my station. "I'm sorry that happened to you."

I take one, wipe my eyes then pass it back so he can do the same. "I'm the one who's—"

"—going to stop apologizing to me," Kit says more firmly than I've ever heard him speak. "Just like you're going to stop holding everything so close to your chest and keep opening up to your friends."

I crumple up the tissue. "I'm so done with tears."

"So, we'll make some happy memories instead." A pause. "Together." His mouth twitches. "And with your hockey hottie."

I snort, but, *God*, he's the best.

"You drive a hard bargain, Kit Monohan," I mock-grumble.

"Well, you've spent the last few weeks finding yourself." He tosses the box of tissues back onto my station. "I think I've spent them accepting what I want." He exhales, eyes coming to mine. "I want someone to love me for me."

"Kit—"

"And I want you to help me with that."

My heart rolls over in my chest.

"Will you help me with that?"

I lace my fingers together, stretch them out in front of me. "Oh, honey, I thought you'd never ask."

"Good." He picks up my fritter and hands it to me. "Now stop planning my happily ever after and eat," he orders.

"So bossy all of a sudden."

His mouth quirks. "You better watch out," he says. "Because I intend to come to my full power now that I've lost the dead weight known as Patton."

"Damn right, you do."

I pop the rest of the fritter in my mouth and stand, Kit following suit. "Speaking of that. Do you want to use those newfound powers for good?"

"You mean this *isn't* my villain creation story?"

I grin, but when I explain my plan to give Knox a taste of his own medicine, his eyes light up so brightly that I know he's on my side even before he declares, "I'm in."

I reach over and hug him. "I'm so glad to have you back in my life."

"Because I'm awesome." He buffs his knuckles on his shoulder.

"You really are."

He nods to the door. "Dinner?"

"How about you join the girls and me at Nova's place?"

"Watching hot hockey guys?"

I nod. "Do we do anything else?"

A wink. "Not if I can help it."

"I'll meet you at Nova's," he says. "I want to change and my clothes are at my new apartment."

I wrinkle my nose. "I hate this for you."

"Why?" he asks. "You finally helped me find my wings so I can fly." He grins. "Plus, I need to make a pit stop to pick up those special dog treats. I'm determined to get Steve to love me the mostest."

I narrow my eyes at him. "That's not even a word."

A shrug. "You're just worried you might lose your top dog spot."

"Puns." I sniff. "You're hilarious."

"Yup." He hugs me tight. "I love you."

My heart rolls over in my chest and I hug him back. "Thank you for forgiving me."

"Always."

Then he presses a kiss to my cheek and strides out the door.

And…

I've finally started to breathe again.

I can do this.

I really think I can.

CHAPTER FORTY-TWO

Riggs

"Push, Patches," Ivy says as I squat. The bar resting on my shoulders isn't loaded with the maximum amount of weight I can lift, but it's heavy enough and add in the fact that Ivy is relentless, and I've lost count of the reps. "Engage your core, push through your whole foot, and get that fucking bar in the air," she snaps.

"You are the fucking worst," I grunt as, legs shaking, quads on fucking fire, I straighten.

"Yup," she says cheerfully. "Now, give me three more."

Christ.

But I grit my teeth and manage to push through the trio of reps, each harder than the last, and I can't lie, I'm relieved when she helps me rerack the bar.

"Stretch," she orders, nodding toward Lake, Leo, Storm, and Bear, all of who've been equally tortured and are "stretching" on the mat behind me.

And by *stretching* I mean they've become prone piles of men who've lost all will to live.

I join them, flopping down and making a half-hearted attempt at a figure four.

Thankfully, Ivy has turned her attention to other matters—

Or *matter*, singular.

Knox is working on some sort of combination squat—his back leg in a resistance band that's been hung from a chin-up bar, a dumbbell in both hands as he curls his leg behind him and descends, slowly enough that I can see almost every muscle in his body working.

How do I see this?

Because he's shirtless and wearing the smallest pair of gym shorts I've ever seen.

Why—one might ask—would a hockey player have crammed himself into those tiny shorts?

Let's just say that Ella is devious and determined on her own, but put Kit, Ella, *and* me together?

We're spreading happily-ever-afters like fucking glitter bombs, bitches.

Or those were Ella's words, anyway.

My part in this was to make sure Lake made the bet…and to make sure that Knox was the one to lose it.

Storm, considering he spent half the night putting his hotel room back together last time Knox pulled a prank, was only too happy to assist—both in getting Knox to join in *and* ensuring the sneaky bastard lost.

And now I present…short shorts.

Which seem to be doing the trick—Ivy has been avoiding Knox like the plague, even though she's normally riding his ass to push harder—and now he's the only one left to work with her one-on-one.

"Your knee is in the wrong position," she snaps, reaching forward as though to correct it then drawing back, probably because Knox is still squatting and her leaning in means that she's nearly received a faceful of Knox's junk.

"My knee is in the correct position if I want to target the abductor," he says, locking gazes with the petite redhead.

Or horns, one might say.

Because you don't question Ivy—not if you want to be able to walk the next day.

"Excuse me?" I can practically see the steam coming out of her ears.

"I said what I said." Knox grunts as he does another rep.

"If I wanted you to target the abductor," she grits out, "I would give you a list of exercises for that. We're working quads, glutes, and hammies right now—"

"Those muscles are strong enough." A nod down at his legs on display.

Ivy's color begins to rise.

"I need to work on…"

I rotate my head, see that Lake's registered the same thing I have.

Imminent death.

Or hate fucking.

He nudges Storm and Leo while I knock my foot against Bear's. There are hand signals and raised brows, nods to the door and mouthed admonishments as we peel ourselves up from the floor and creep out of the room.

Because I don't want to be in Ivy's crosshairs when she's done with Knox.

Because I want those short shorts to have the opportunity to work their magic.

And…because I'm ready to go home to Ella.

I start down the hall but stop when I see my dad standing a few feet away, reclining back against the wall.

Scowling.

And just that quickly, all the amusement I soaked up from riding on Ella's matchmaking coattails disappears.

Because—

Here my dad goes again.

I can tell just from his expression that I'm about to get a verbal reaming.

So much for him changing.

Something twists in my gut.

It doesn't matter. I don't need him.

He pushes off the wall, scowl deepening as he takes in the lot of us hobbling in his direction, but he doesn't say anything as the guys peel off, Lake pausing with raised brows, silently asking if I want him to stay. I wave him on. I need to handle this shit on my own, need to prove to my dad once and for all that I'm not going put up with him treating me like garbage—

"Can you believe this shit?" he asks, shoving his phone in my face.

I blink at the screen, trying to process the images in the quick flash he gave me, but it's there and gone so quickly that I don't.

"Some asshole is talking about Nova's pictures online"—Nova was recently featured online in a national magazine—"and he says they're *uninspired and juvenile*." My dad makes a sound of disgust and pockets his phone. "I was with her when she took some of these. The woman finds art in the smallest details." He scoffs and starts walking for the exit. "Certainly much better than an idiot pecking away at his keyboard."

He's complaining about a negative review Nova received.

What the actual fuck?

I'm unable to comprehend that for a moment, not when I was so primed for a fight, ready to yell and scream and stand up for myself.

But he's standing up for my friend, my family.

He's not giving me a hard time—in fact, he *hasn't* since the game he and Ella attended, since that conversation with my woman. Yeah, he's given me a few tough critiques, but none have been laced with any of the meanness from before, and I can't disagree that they've been helpful.

It's…

Like having my old dad back.

My throat goes tight.

That hope in my belly grows.

I've missed him.

"Gah," he snaps, voice echoing down the hall before he marches back, tosses up his hands. "And then there's that *woman* at the salon. It was bad enough she fired Ella after that terrible appointment, but the gall of her trying to switch to another stylist! Like anyone could have done better." He shakes his head and starts off down the hall again. "I'm glad that Kit banned her from coming back. She'll regret it. She damned well will. I've seen her work. I know…"

Maybe I do.

Maybe I really do have him back.

Just thinking that is like removing a thorn from the bottom of my foot, like in one instant, the small stab of pain that has been jabbing at me for years is gone.

I can walk without thinking about it.

I can be pain-free.

"Come on, son!" my dad calls. "I know what will cure those sore muscles. A dip in the lake and apple fritters."

Shaking myself, I hurry after him as fast as my sore legs can carry me. "Absolutely fucking *not* on the dip in the snowmelt-fed lake—"

He looks at me, mouth opening, argument in his eyes.

"—but hell yes on the apple fritters."

My dad slows, eyes on mine, expression unreadable for several long moments.

Then he chuckles and shakes his head. "I'll take that. Come on," he adds, walking forward again. "I want to get a hot one, and Freida says they don't bake any more after three o'clock."

I don't ask how he's on a first name basis with Ella's favorite baker. I just…

Embrace this.

That my dad is here and he cares and he's fulfilling the promise he made to me.

Showing me. Following through. And…

He's finally back.

He still needs to get his own place, though.

I'm tired as shit of running into him in my kitchen wearing only his tighty-whities.

CHAPTER FORTY-THREE

Ella

"WHAT'D you think of the game last night, Todd-o-Rama?" I ask as I run the comb through his hair.

We sat in the stands while the Sierra trounced the Grizzlies —that's right, bitches, payback is sweet, and while I heard *all* about the fourteen-dollar beer, he didn't have one negative thing to say about Riggs or the guys.

He was positively sunny.

I grin when he scowls today, the grumpy exterior thin and plastic, barely holding. "I'm going to find a way to smuggle my own beer inside. I won't be paying fifteen bucks for luke-warm swill that's mostly foam."

"I thought it was *fourteen* dollars."

He narrows his eyes at me but doesn't take the obvious bait I laid out. "When are you moving into my son's place?" he asks.

"When you stop showing up in his kitchen in your under-wear," I say without missing a beat.

That has him waggling his brows. "I'll have you know that I'm in very good shape for my age."

"And *I'll* have *you* know that I only have eyes for *one* man, and he might share the same last name as you, but he's *not* you." I clip a few errant strands then dust off his shoulders with the brush.

"Ageist."

Now, I'm laughing as I unclip his cape and sweep it from around him. "I am glad that Riggs comes from good stock." I wink. "Just have to make sure he keeps up all the hard work and doesn't go soft in his old age."

"Exactly." He reaches for his wallet.

"Todd-o-Rama," I warn, "what did I tell you about that?"

He pulls out a couple of twenties, sets them on the counter. "I'm not going to stop paying you, sweetheart." A quick kiss to my cheek. "Want me to wait while you clean up?"

"No," I tell him. "Kit's going to swing back by and we're hitting up Target for some decorating supplies for his new place." I glance at my watch. "He should be here in ten."

"I'll wait."

I shoo him toward the door. "Go, old man. Terrorize some young children, yell at the clerk at the grocery store, get all huffy when someone points out you're going the wrong way down the stairs—"

He stills for a moment.

And then something wonderful happens.

He laughs—full out and loud. It's Riggs's laugh but different, something that's also solely Todd's.

It's beautiful.

"There's only one way to go down the stairs." He leans in and I accept his quick hug. "And I'll take up the beer issue with Riggs. I think the kid might have some pull."

I grin. "You do that, Todd-o-Rama."

He smirks, reaches for the door handle, then nearly topples forward when the glass and wooden panel is yanked open.

"Easy, asshole," he mutters catching it before it collides with the wall.

I open my mouth, about to warn him off from yelling at potential clients, but my words stick in my throat.

And my knees go weak…

As my father crosses the threshold and walks right into the salon.

The cape falls from my hands, lands on the floor in a wrinkled puddle of black material.

I distantly process Todd stepping outside, the door closing behind him with a quiet *snick*.

And then I'm alone.

"Daniela."

I close my eyes for a long moment, long enough that the name echoes through my head over and over again.

Daniela. Daniela. Daniela. Daniel—

"Actually," I manage to say, bending and picking up the puddled cape, "I prefer Ella."

He doesn't say anything so I wad up the material and carry it to the back, hoping that if I take long enough to put it in the laundry bin, to pack up my stuff, that he'll be gone when I come out.

Unfortunately, that's not to be.

He's standing awkwardly next to my chair when I step out from behind the curtain, staring at the set of drawers.

At first, I think he's trying to look at the stuff I have pinned there—a photograph of Nova and me, a little drawing from an elementary-aged girl who loved my haircut, a sticker that says *Other Dogs Drool but Pugs Rule*.

But then he says, "Your last name isn't Adler."

And I realize he's looking at my cosmetology license, which has to be displayed where customers can see it.

I still, tightening my hands on my purse.

He lifts his head, eyes coming to mine. "You're a Jacobson."

"I haven't been a Jacobson since the day Mom died," I say quietly. "You made sure of that."

He rocks back like I've hit him. "I—"

"Even after all these years"—my voice is still quiet—"after all this time, you don't even know that we changed our name? That Knox doesn't play as Knox Jacobson, but Knox Adler?"

Fury like no other balls tightly in my stomach.

Todd was certainly no gem, especially over the last few years, and I hate how he treated Riggs. But also…he's trying to do better.

No. He's *doing* better.

What's my dad's excuse?

Except, the kernel in my belly, the hope that's begun to bloom because he's here, because he's put in effort to seek me out…

Maybe this will be that defining moment too?

Maybe he can change like Todd has.

"You treated Anne abhorrently," he says, not acknowledging my questions and cruelly quashing that ember of hope beneath his boot. "Both of you."

"Nova has nothing to do with this—"

"You *and* Knox," he says, slamming his palm on the top of my station, rattling the contents of the drawers, nearly sending my curling iron to the floor.

"Knox wasn't there," I say, thinking about the interrupted lunch, my spiraling, and all that had changed afterward.

"Not then!" he shouts. "Before."

I stumble back a step, backing into the corner of Kit's desk and wincing.

"I think you need to leave."

Gasping, I whirl and see that Todd's standing just inside the door, arms crossed, fury deepening the lines of his expression.

"This isn't your business," my dad says, taking a step toward Todd but stopping, likely because Todd is about twenty pounds heavier and six inches taller.

"It's my business if you're harassing her," Todd snaps.

"It sure as—"

"This is my dad," I interrupt quietly.

That has Todd's mouth dropping open, but only for a second because then he's clamping his teeth together, face hardening. But he doesn't engage further, just looks at me. "Let's go, Ella girl."

"Her *name* is Daniela."

I close my eyes for a moment, exhale quietly. "Why are you here, Dad?"

"Anne and I have a house here."

I brace, ready for that blow to tear through me, but…

Somehow it doesn't.

In fact, I'm not sure that I feel *any* of this.

I'm just numb…

All the way to my very core.

CHAPTER FORTY-FOUR

Riggs

My PHONE RINGS right as I'm about to leave the locker room and join Knox on the ice.

We're going to fine-tune some skills—tipping specific shots in front of the net, feeding passes through traffic, practicing some dekes we've been working on.

Just…getting those ten thousand hours in.

Something my dad knows I'm doing.

Which is why my nape prickles when I see his ringtone come through.

I put my phone Do Not Disturb while I got ready for practice.

Which means that only repeated calls will get through.

Frowning, I reach for my cell, but Knox comes out of nowhere and stops me, snagging my phone and scowling at the screen. "There are ten texts on the screen and two missed calls," he says. "Something you need to tell me?"

My stomach twists.

Because this was Grumpy Todd's previous modus

operandum—wear me down until I'm forced to give in and listen to him.

Shit.

"I have to answer it," I say when the call ends and then immediately starts up again, adding when Knox doesn't release me, "I have to know either way."

He sighs, but releases me, swiping a finger across the screen and answering the call on speaker.

Fucking Adlers, pushy and nosy and ready to do battle for those they consider family.

"Hello?" my dad snaps, sending my gut twisting further. "Riggs, are you fucking there?"

"Yeah, Dad," I rasp. "I'm here—"

"Shut up and listen to me." His words are a rapid clip of fury.

Fury that has Knox reaching for my phone, as though to hang up.

But before his finger hits the button, my dad keeps talking.

"There's an asshole here with Ella at the salon and I don't like the look he put on her face when he walked in. You know how she is with me, all strong and tough, but she needs you, son," he says. "I can see that clear as fucking day."

"Dad—"

"I need to get back in there," my dad says. "Get your ass here."

"Dad!"

But he's already hung up.

Knox and I look at each other.

Then we all but tear our skates off.

I grab my keys, and with Knox on my heels, we sprint from the rink.

———

MY TIRES SQUEAL as I pull into the salon's parking lot, turn off my car, and jump out, not giving a fuck that I'm running across the cold pavement with no shoes on, nor that it's soaking into my socks, my feet.

I take the stairs two at a time and burst into the salon—

"So, you're here because I upset your wife," I hear before the door slams into the exterior wall behind me.

Ella jerks, whips around, her gaze coming to mine as some other man rotates to face me, his scowl deep and his expression disapproving.

"Riggs?" she asks, like she can't believe I'm standing here.

Or maybe because I'm standing in the salon fully geared up minus the helmet, skates, and gloves.

Knox bumps into me from behind, and I realize I'm just standing in the open door, so I move forward, crossing the room, positioning myself between my woman and whoever the fuck the man is.

Though…I have a sneaking suspicion exactly who the asshole putting that look on Ella's face is.

"Who's this?" the man sneers.

"No one you need to know, Dad," Ella replies coolly.

I clench my hands into fists because…suspicion confirmed.

"—and everything in the world to me."

"Excuse me?"

She lifts her chin toward the door, completely composed. Together. Or is she…numb?

Fuck.

I can't have her numb.

I need her alive and bright and beautiful, that gorgeous soul of hers shining out, her heart—battered and bruised and somehow still kind enough to love those around her to distraction—safe to continue caring.

Because if she allows the numb to take over…

"You should go, Dad," she says, still speaking in that completely neutral tone. It's devoid of everything that makes

Ella, *Ella* and I fucking hate it. "Tahoe's big enough that you should be able to visit without bumping into Knox and me, and if we happen to cross paths, then I'll make sure to be… polite to Anne."

I frown.

"Daniela—" he begins.

"Ella," I correct, once again drawing her dad's focus.

He narrows his eyes. "Excuse me?"

"You're not excused," I say. "You have a lot of nerve showing up here with that fucking attitude. This is your *daughter*. The little girl who needed you when her mom died—"

"She was a teenager—"

"And she was still your little girl," I snap. "You should have protected her. Should have been there for her when her whole world fell apart." Ella rocks next to me, and I draw her back against my body, feeling that she's trembling against me. Thank fuck. *Thank fuck* she's not as composed as she appears to be. Thank fuck she's not lost in herself, shutting everyone out. Thank fuck she's not shutting *me* out. I glare at the prick. "And you sure as shit shouldn't have gone off and built a new life without her and Knox. I've experienced some shit parenting in my day"—my dad jerks but doesn't comment or otherwise react—"but at least I always knew that I was loved."

Ella's hand finds mine and she squeezes tightly. "Riggs," she murmurs.

I look down into those beautiful blue eyes of hers.

"I've got this."

I settle my forehead against hers for a heartbeat. "I know you do." But when I start to lift, she slides her hands in my hair and holds me in place. "I love you."

Every cell in my body shifts and realigns, becomes different. *More.*

Because I know exactly how big this is.

It's the most precious gift of all.

"*Chérie*," I rasp.

"You're here," she says. "I see you. And I love you." Then as those words are wrapping around my soul, she turns to her dad. "It's time for you to go."

"Daniela—" he begins.

"Ella," my dad and I correct together.

The fucker just opens his mouth and I can tell by the coldness in his eyes that what he's going to say next will be unforgivable and will probably end up with me getting assault charges.

Before he gets that far, Knox steps in. "Let's go talk outside, Dad—"

"No."

But it's not from their dad.

The word is from Ella.

She steps in front of me, takes Knox's hand. "He's not our dad." Then to the man who fathered her. "What you did was inexcusable. But what you continue to do means that I won't ever have a relationship with you. Not today. Not in a year. Not fucking *ever*."

For a long moment, no one moves.

But then *my* dad, who I thought was a lost cause, who I thought couldn't change, but who has, I realize. Who's nothing like the asshole who's spent years hurting Ella and Knox.

Instead, he's become someone I want in my life again.

And he steps up again, moving to Ella's dad.

"It's time for you to leave."

And maybe it's old, grumpy man camaraderie or maybe we've all just said it enough times that it finally sinks through the asshole's thick, dumb skull.

Ella's dad turns on his heel and stomps out of the salon.

The door slams behind him hard enough to rattle the glass.

Knox follows him, and so does my dad, nodding to me before he steps out as though to say, *You watch that one. I'll watch this one.*

He's different. Better. *Changed.*

The door closes softly behind my dad.

Ella steps away from me, pushing her hair out of her face and exhaling.

"*Chérie.*"

But she only spares me a quick look before heading for her station. "I'll just grab my stuff and get you back to the rink. I know you and Knox were looking forward to the extra time—"

"Ella."

She glances at her watch, winces. "Or not," she says. "I think by the time you get back, the slot will be over and—"

"*Ella.*"

She stops, brows drawn together. "What?"

"Are you okay?"

Her frown deepens. "Um, yes?"

"Baby," I say, taking a step toward her then stopping, completely thrown. "Last time you saw your dad, you were inconsolable for days, and that was just from a short conversation. This was…" I trail off, waving my hand, unable to know what the fuck to say.

A shit show? Yup.

Fucked up? Also that.

"I…" She exhales. "He doesn't hurt me anymore."

"Doesn't hurt?" I ask. "Or you've shoved it all down so deeply that you no longer feel anything?"

Her eyes soften, and she crosses over to me, placing her palm on my chest and mine over her heart. "I feel you," she murmurs. "I feel you *here*. Just like I felt you and Knox storming in here, and your dad coming back in—"

"He called me."

Her smile is gentle, so fucking sweet that my heart squeezes. "I figured."

"And you're…really okay?"

Her palm flattens and she steps closer. "I feel what's in here and…" She sighs. "Honey, I don't think I ever grieved the loss of what Knox and I had. Not until you held me on that beach, not until you spoke of your own hurts, not until *your* dad realized he'd gone so wrong and tried to change." She shakes her head, laughs humorlessly. "He actually wanted *me* to apologize to her for being rude to his wife. Like what? And then he tells me that he wants me to be okay with being left behind because *he* was hurting? What the fuck?" Her exhale is clipped. "Knox didn't leave me. Nova didn't either. And… you're so deeply sewn into my soul that I know you'll always be part of me."

"*Chérie.*"

"So…I'm done." She presses her lips together then releases them. "Because he's gone—the dad I had and…that's okay. It's a pain that maybe won't ever go away, but it has nothing to do with the man who was just in here. That's *not* my dad, and he won't ever be."

"Christ, baby," I rasp, eyes burning. "I don't want you to have to bury your pain or pretend—"

She cups my jaw. "Don't you see? Don't you understand the gift you've given me? I don't *have* to bury it or pretend to be okay because *you're here*. Because you'll hold me and wipe away my tears. Because you love me. *Me.*"

Fuck. *Fuck.* I'm going to cry.

I hug her tightly, burying my face in her throat. "I'm here."

"I know."

Love and relief tangle in me as I blink back my tears, as I hold the woman I love close and know that neither of us are perfect, that we're still healing, but that she believes in me, in us, and so…

We'll be okay.

Eventually, she runs her hand through my beard and whispers, "You're sporting hockey funk."

Surprising me.

Always.

I can't wait for a lifetime more of them.

Grinning, I lift my head and tug a lock of her hair. "I'll remember to change and shower next time before I ride to the rescue."

"Good." She slips from my arms and I get to take in the beauty as her special brand of mischief takes over, as my *Ella* shines through, as she...

Surprises me once again.

Because she walks to her station, pulls open a drawer, and unearths her...

Clippers.

"Should I touch up that haircut of yours, Patches?"

EPILOGUE

Ella, Three Months Later

"*Chérie.*"

Sleep is a heavy, comfortable blanket.

I grunt and yank my pillow over my head.

Too early.

Five has come far too early.

"*Chérie.*"

"Too early," I rasp, giving voice to my thoughts. "Too damned early."

"It is early, baby, but you need to wake up anyway." His words are gentle and paired with him sliding the blankets down my body, tugging me from the last vestiges of sleep with the cool air hitting my naked skin.

Frowning, I manage to peel open my eyes and see…

"What the hell?"

It's dark outside.

It's nowhere near morning.

"It's three—"

The rest of my complaint is cut off when Riggs tugs a

sweatshirt over my head, lifts my leg one at a time and tugs thick socks over them.

It's firmly springtime in the Sierras, but the middle of the freaking night is still chilly.

Sweats come next and then my thick, fuzzy boots.

My heavy, puffy jacket.

I don't know how he found all this. My stuff's in boxes all around the room because I just moved in today, but I don't have a chance to ask because Riggs is sweeping me up in his arms and carrying me from the room. "What—"

"Hush, *chérie,*" he whispers. "Unless you want to wake the old man."

Because Todd's still here.

Though, he's moving out next month when he closes on his house…three blocks away.

So, less tighty-whities…but just as frequent visits to the salon.

Lips twitching, I don't make a peep until Riggs carries me through the back door, and then it's to gasp.

Because—

"What did you do?"

"Up you go, *chérie,*" he murmurs, nudging me toward the ladder propped against the side of the house.

I can see the twinkling lights from the deck, but it's not until I reach the final step and climb over onto the roof that I see the cushions, the blankets, and…the thermos.

"Keep moving, baby."

Somehow I manage to make my way to one of the cushions. "What did you do?"

He settles next to me, cups my cheek. "I'm here."

"I love you," I whisper.

"I know." A grin as he reaches for the thermos, as he pours me a cup of…

Hot chocolate. Of course it's hot chocolate.

And then hands me a Snickers bar.

My chest hitches.

"I see you," he whispers.

"I haven't had one," I say, unwrapping the candy. "Not since the last time we—" I shake my head, eyes stinging.

"Is it too much now?"

I stop, consider that. *Really* consider it. Because this man gives me the space to. Because this man makes sure I'm *safe* to take that time.

"No," I eventually say, breaking the candy bar in half and passing him one piece. "It's...perfect."

Because he's here.

Because I don't have to be anyone but myself with him.

Smiling gently, he brushes his thumb over my bottom lip. Then he hands me a cup of hot chocolate positively overflowing with mini marshmallows, and asks—

"Will you tell me about her?"

Overhead, the stars glimmer, all those constellations she once taught me beautiful and sparkling and...not cold at all, I realize.

They blaze with memories.

With love.

With my *mom.*

And suddenly, more than anything, I *want* to tell him.

So, I recline back against the cushions, nibble on my candy bar, drink my hot chocolate with loads and loads of marshmallows, and...

I tell the man I love all about my mom.

———

Knox

"You never learn, do you?"

I straighten with a grunt, my legs on fire—

Hell, my entire body is on fire.

But I don't stop moving.

I *can't* stop.

If I stop, the voices get too loud and—

The dumbbells are ripped out of my hands and I growl, "What the fuck?"

Ivy drops them onto the rack and whirls around to face me. "The workout ended two hours ago."

God, she's beautiful.

Even when she glowers at me.

I shrug, move to the bike, I'll just do more cardio.

I sit down, start to clip in, and—

She yanks the plug out of the wall. "It's *enough*," she grits out.

Fucking women.

I stand up, avoid the weights, because she'll probably just take those away too—or try to, anyway—and make my way to the pull-up bar, jumping with a grunt (and significant burning in my quads).

Ignoring that, I start driving.

One. Two. Three—

A hand on my leg, yanking down, nearly succeeding in dislodging me.

"Get a fucking clue, lioness," I say, shaking her off and continuing.

"Ugh!" She tosses up her hands, shakes her head. "Fine. You want to fuck up your body by pushing it too hard? Whatever. But just remember that your team needs you for the playoffs, so if you injure yourself like an idiot because you don't know when to quit that's on *you*."

Rant complete, she marches away, giving me a glimpse of those seriously toned legs, that lush ass.

Fucking sexy as shit.

And she hates me, no matter how hard—or not—I work.

Ignoring the bolt of lust as I always do—or as I've done

since she made it very clear she wasn't interested, I keep going.

Four. Five. Six—

She's reached the door now, but…paused.

Seven. Eight. Nine—

No, not paused. She's jiggling the handle and…

Ten.

I jump down, swipe my arm over my forehead and move over to her. "What's the matter?"

She jerks away from me when I get close then scowls up at me. "The door's locked."

"It's *never* locked."

"You think I don't know how to turn a handle, along with knowing nothing about how to do my job?"

I wince. "I didn't say that."

"Maybe not in so many words," she mutters.

And…that's hurt in her eyes.

Fuck.

"Ivy."

She steps back, mask firmly in place. "Never mind." She nods at the knob. "Aren't you going to mansplain how to open a door for me?"

"Lioness—"

She waves a hand at the door. "Nope. Let's see it, hotshot."

Sighing, knowing I won't get any further, certainly not now that I've pissed her off, I reach for the knob.

It turns beneath my fingers and I look over to see the fury on her face when she realizes that she really *was* struggling to open a door—

But that's quickly replaced with dismay.

Because the knob comes off in my hand.

Gaping, I stare at the door, at the empty spot where the handle had once been.

"What the fuck?" she breathes.

Then pushes by me to shove at the door.

It doesn't budge.

She scrabbles at the metal pieces of the lock, trying to get them to engage—

They don't move either.

Slowly, she turns to face me, horror on her face.

Because…

We're trapped.

————

THANK YOU FOR READING! I hope you enjoyed Ella and Rigg's story as much as I loved writing their happy ending! Know and Ivy will get their chance in THE BIG SKATE. **I've sworn off love…until her. The only problem? She can't stand me.**

CLICK HERE TO READ THE BIG SKATE NOW>

————

AND IF YOU loved CAUGHT FROM BEHIND and need more Sierra hockey boys, check out SNOWED, featuring Leo and Jolie. **Leo West saves me from the floor of the bar. But he also saves me from the boring loneliness of my life. The only question is if he's going to let me save him right back.**

CLICK HERE TO READ SNOWED NOW>

————

PLUS, you'll love finding out what happens to the Eagles hockey crew in BROKEN LACES, book 1 of my new series, the Eagles Hockey series. **This team of misfits and bad boys are going to puck you in the best possible way.**

————

I so appreciate your help in spreading the word about my books, including sharing with friends! Please leave a review on your favorite book site!

You can also join my Facebook group, the Fabinators, for exclusive giveaways and sneak peeks of future books.

If you'd like to receive emails from me for new releases and monthly giveaway sign up for my newsletter at https://www. elisefaber.com/newsletter

SIERRA HOCKEY

Over the Line
Caught from Behind
The Big Skate
On the Fly

ALSO BY ELISE FABER

Gold Hockey (all stand alone)

Blocked

Backhand

Boarding

Benched

Breakaway

Breakout

Checked

Coasting

Centered

Charging

Caged

Crashed

A Gold Christmas

Cycled

Caught

Cap

Covered

Crushed

Changed

Scored

Breakers Hockey (all stand alone)

Broken

Boldly

Breathless

Ballsy

Bewitched

Blowout

Breathe

Blazed

Sierra Hockey Series

Over the Line

Caught from Behind

The Big Skate

On the Fly

Rush Hockey Trilogy #1

Big Puck Energy

Filthy Puckboy

So Pucking Over It

Rush Hockey Trilogy #2

Love, Pucks, and Other Stories

All's Fair in Pucks and War

No Pucks Lost Between Us

Rush Hockey Trilogy #3

Puck and Make Up

Blinded By Pucks

Match Made in Pucks

Eagles Hockey Series (all stand alone)

Broken Laces

Knotted Laces

Lace 'em Up

Sinful Bosses (all stand alone)

Ruthless Billionaire

Billionaire's Club **(all stand alone)**

Bad Night Stand

Bad Breakup

Bad Husband

Bad Hookup

Bad Divorce

Bad Fiancé

Bad Boyfriend

Bad Blind Date

Bad Wedding

Bad Engagement

Bad Bridesmaid

Bad Swipe

Bad Girlfriend

Bad Best Friend

Bad Rebound

Bad Romance

Bad Business

Bad Billionaire's Quickies

Love, Action, Camera **(all stand alone)**

Dotted Line

Action Shot

Close-Up

End Scene

Meet Cute

Love After Midnight **(all stand alone)**

Rum And Notes

Virgin Daiquiri

On The Rocks

Sex On The Seats

Life Sucks Series

Train Wreck

Hot Mess

Dumpster Fire

Clusterf*@k

FUBAR

Perfect Storm

Free Fall

Lost Cause

Roosevelt Ranch Series **(all stand alone, series complete)**

Disaster at Roosevelt Ranch

Heartbreak at Roosevelt Ranch

Collision at Roosevelt Ranch

Regret at Roosevelt Ranch

Desire at Roosevelt Ranch

Phoenix Series **(read in order)**

Phoenix Rising

Dark Phoenix

Phoenix Freed

Phoenix: LexTal Chronicles **(rereleasing soon, stand alone, Phoenix world)**

From Ashes

In Flames

To Smoke

KTS Series (all stand alone, series complete)

Riding The Edge

Crossing The Line

Leveling The Field

Scorching The Earth

Cocky Heroes World

Tattooed Troublemaker

ABOUT THE AUTHOR

USA Today bestselling author, Elise Faber, loves chocolate, Star Wars, Harry Potter, and hockey (the order depending on the day and how well her team — the Sharks! — are playing). She and her husband also play as much hockey as they can squeeze into their schedules, so much so that their typical date night is spent on the ice. Elise is the mom to two exuberant boys and lives in Northern California. Connect with her in her Facebook group, the Fabinators or find more information about her books at www.elisefaber.com.

facebook.com/elisefaberauthor

amazon.com/author/elisefaber

bookbub.com/profile/elise-faber

instagram.com/elisefaber

tiktok.com/@elisefaberauthor

goodreads.com/elisefaber

www.ingramcontent.com/pod-product-compliance
Lightning Source LLC
Chambersburg PA
CBHW070619100726

47907CB00007B/1797